CORRUPTED

BOOK TWO OF THE TERRIAN TRILOGY

by Jenny Benjamin

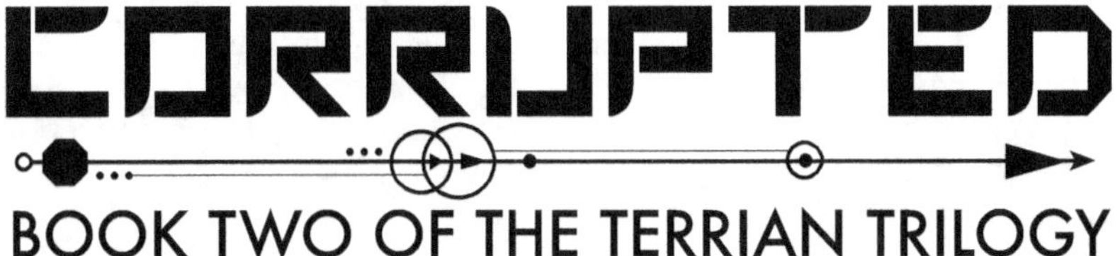

CORRUPTED

BOOK TWO OF THE TERRIAN TRILOGY

novel

Jenny Benjamin

ANANKE PRESS

Enhanced: Book one of the Terrian Trilogy
Published by Ananke Press
Copyright © 2022 by Jenny Benjamin
All rights reserved

Interior and cover design by Ananke Press

ISBN: 979-8-9865259-0-7 (paperback)

Ananke Press
178 Columbus Avenue, #230137, New York, NY 10023
anankepress.com
info@anankepress.com

CONTENTS

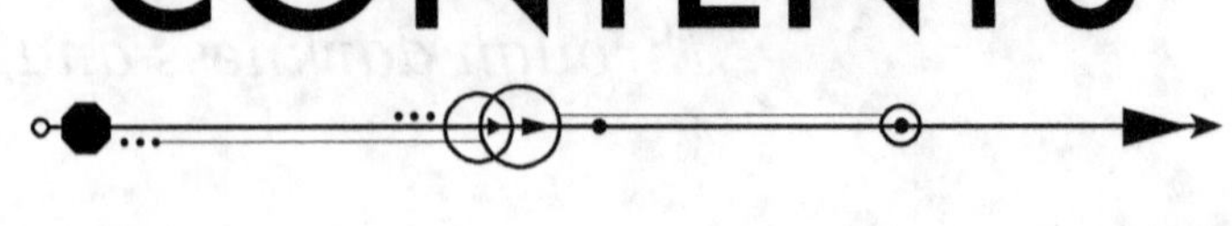

Midway on our life's journey, I found myself
In dark woods, the right road lost. To tell
About those woods is hard — so tangled and rough

And savage that thinking of it now, I feel
The old fear stirring: death is hardly more bitter,
And yet, to treat the good I found there as well

I'll tell what I saw, though how I came to enter
I cannot well say, being so full of sleep
Whatever moment it was I began to blunder

Off the true path.

The Inferno, Canto I, Dante Alighieri, Robert Pinsky, translator

Fall 2012

Ten days. The ship's instruments displayed the time that Jesse and the rest of the Triumvirate had been sailing through soundless, limitless black. They followed the blood-red liquid wake of the Belite-Gelfs who had Jesse's girlfriend, Sofia, suspended in a bubble. Jesse could not see her, but every time he shut his eyes, rage burned in his chest, hot like a furnace. He remembered the Gelf leader Nosh laughing and saying, "She's a sweet one, Jesse. Won't be so sweet after Gelf initiation."

Had it really been only ten days or had time collapsed? Jesse spent his time reading documentation on the Terrians that was stored on the ship's computer. The Keepers, the Terrians who had planted the power source and the ship for the Triumvirate, had kept things pretty current. But there was no way to link to Earth's satellites to know what was going on there. Nor would Jesse do that if he could. Jesse and his friends had learned that the Terrians could find them when they used any form of communication, or when they left any cyber trail. They were cut off. The thought sent a quick chill down Jesse's back.

Jesse stretched and focused harder on the writing. He now understood the Terrian groups, for the most part, and he knew he hated them all. Well, not Eruk and Palk, the banished ones. But then again, Jesse only thought of them in terms of how they could help him save Sofia.

He pushed away from the blinking screen; the rows of Terrian writing were slashes and loopy curved letters he now read like it was human English. It was his shift to pilot the ship, but once they figured out how to follow the Gelfs while cloaked, "piloting" meant staying awake, monitoring the controls, and making sure they stayed on course.

Kate and Hayden were asleep in one of the thousands of compartments in the ship. They each had selected one on the same level, even the same hallway. Jesse chose one in the farthest corner, three doors down from Kate and right across from Hayden. Were they asleep? The Earth clock told them it was night on Earth, and they dimmed and brightened the ship's rooms to mirror a twenty-four-hour cycle, but it was hard to sleep without the rise and fall of the sun.

Night didn't matter in space. Dark and more dark, but the luminous bands of stars, colorful nebula, and sudden streaks of light did distract Jesse from his quest at times. The only other balm was the Earth's books he had found in the data base. Most were religious or philosophical texts. Jesse didn't look at the Bible; he had had enough of that during Sunday school. But he poured over Lao Tzu's *Tao Te Ching*. A few moments of peace with it were all he allowed himself. Then he was back to soaking up more Terrian information and imagining different ways to kill Nosh, that pink faced Gelf leader.

Jesse could smell Kate behind him even before she sat in her metallic navigating chair right next to him.

He saw some lines from the *Tao Te Ching* in his mind as he breathed in.

The Tao is like a well:
used but never used up.
It is like the eternal void:
filled with infinite possibilities.

It is hidden but always present.
I don't know who gave birth to it.
It is older than God.

How did Kate manage to smell so good, like wildflowers and fresh air, even now? After their five days of hiking to Chicago, finding the power source, and fighting the gelatinous Terrians in their enhanced forms, she still seemed to have sprung from moist dirt after a long spring rain. Jesse inhaled deeply again and sighed.

No more Kate, he thought.

"Hey," she said. She wore a pair of form-fitting white stretch pants and a long white sweater. They found all kinds of clothes in the storage compartments. They were all monochromatic outfits: The pants were made from a sleek stretchy material and the warm pullovers were woolly but not itchy.

"Hi," he answered and looked back at the text on the screen. He was reading about the history of the Gelf rebellion.

"Learn anything else while I slept?"

"Yeah, loads," he said. "Terria is one screwed up planet. These aliens play gods to humans, and they're more messed up than we are on Earth. On Terria and as gods on Earth, Shaaris have been in control for the last two thousand years or so. They pushed for helping the monotheistic religions along on Earth. Belites agreed, reluctantly. Actually, that's about the time that the two factions formed, with the hair and skin color to signify the group. After fifty years or so, a Shaari leader was appointed to oversee religious emissary relations with Earth. Things were all right then for generations, but the Shaaris were the ones to appoint the leader, or Doma-Terra. Hundreds of years go by and with each passing generation, Shaaris have more power and the Belites have less. And then, about five hundred years ago, this dude, named Umon, was appointed Doma-Terra. Under this guy Umon, things got pretty out of control. He went all military, took total control of the planet's Liquid Light, and started to ghettoize Terrians who believed in the Ancients' ways. Soon that morphed into adding specific groups to the ghettos, enemies of the Shaari State."

"Like who?" Kate's eyes were bright. They looked like blue crystals.

"What?"

"Who were the enemies of the Shaari State?"

"Oh, I read one account of a woman who was a Shaari emissary, one who went to Earth and blended with the human population to get a pulse on changes within Islam. She fell in love with this Arab dude and got pregnant. Well, she was snatched up and put in a ghetto. The Shaaris killed the baby with these injections. She wrote her story secretly in the ghetto and snuck it out to the Keepers who are basically a secret group made to uphold the Ancients' ways, even if that only meant archiving injustices for, well, I guess for us to find, here, on the ship. I still don't know who the Keepers are, but I think we need to find them."

"And Eruk and Palk."

"Yeah, them. Gays were considered enemies of the state, too."

The main cabin, a sleek room the size of his kitchen at home, was silent, save for the occasional whir or beep of the controls.

"The Shaaris are evil," Kate said finally. "Pure evil."

"From what I've read, all these groups have gotten corrupted over the years. The Shaaris may have set it in motion, but the way I see it, they're all our enemies. After the Shaaris got the Liquid Light, they made the Belites basically servants in their society, or they banished them to the Outlands. But now the Belites have their own army and leader, not sure when that happened, or how. The Shaaris made the ghettos, and then right around the time of our World War II, the Gelfs formed, totally rogue and dangerous. But the Shaaris made it so much worse. The Shaaris made these horrible prisons for the Gelfs. I don't want to go into it."

Jesse couldn't look at Kate any longer. He didn't want to tell her about the rapists and killers in those prisons. Instead, he explained how all the Shaaris had voted whether they should exterminate the Gelfs but ended up voting against it because it mirrored Earth's brutality too much. Yeah right, Terrians were worse. So, they penned the Gelfs up and made them into the worst kind of criminal group.

"The Gelfs broke out though and started this total underground movement. The Keepers say the Gelf headquarters is somewhere underground. Literally in the bowels of Terria. But no one knows where. They recruit Belites, Shaaris, anyone who wants to tear down the Shaari system. Gelfs wouldn't care if Earth is destroyed, as long as they bring down the Shaaris."

"What about the regular Belites? Do they just want to take over, you know, become the new Shaaris?" Kate asked.

"Yeah. Pretty much. At least as far as I've read. I've been focusing on the Gelfs because I want to obliterate them after we get Sofia."

Sofia's name out loud had the same effect it had had for the past ten days: An uncomfortable silence filled the cabin. Jesse grew hot and then pained, like a cramp in his gut came out of nowhere. Kate usually turned red and twisted her hair with her fingers.

The two didn't say anything for several minutes. Jesse couldn't stand it much longer, so he stood up and paced behind the chairs. He watched his socked feet slide along the silver, slippery floor.

After several minutes of pacing and rubbing his closely shaved head until the back of his scalp felt raw, he sat back down to read. Kate stood and went to get another cylinder of water. The Keepers had stocked the ship with enormous water tanks. They found oddly shaped containers and utensils they assumed were for eating and drinking; many were slender glass cylinders they filled and re-filled with water. Something about space made them all thirsty.

"The thing that I don't get," Kate said while glancing over the controls, "is why bring their war to Earth? Why not simply fight their fights on Terria, then whoever wins can figure out the whole gods-for-humans thing?"

"I know. I need to find that answer, I really do. There's something I'm missing. At first I thought it was about controlling the rogue Gelfs who are corrupting humans and trying to use them as marks for destruction. But that didn't explain why the Shaaris and Belites were obviously fighting in Earth's atmosphere, like we saw."

"But that may have only been to get control of the right Triumvirate – us. It happened to be us because we got the power source."

"Yeah, I know. But I feel like there's something more," Jesse said. He felt restless again. He wanted to take off running, feel wind on his face, breathe normal air. There was nowhere to run, and the air, though pure, was stale and artificial.

"Jesse," Kate said. Her voice was lower, huskier. His groin stirred with the sound of it, and then the look on her face made him feel like collapsing with desire: parted lips and wide eyes, but the rest unreadable, mysterious.

Stop. He had to stop. Sofia could be beaten by the Gelfs, or mutilated, or raped. He was doing it again: imagining strangling Nosh with his bare hands, watching his baby face fly apart.

"Jesse," she said again.

"Sorry. Yeah?"

"I haven't known what to say to you, you know, about us," she said. There went her finger again, twisting the same lock of hair.

"Kate, I don't know what to say. I mean, our emotions for each other have obviously enhanced our alien abilities, but I don't think I can, you know, kiss you anymore. You know, because of Sofia."

"No, of course not. I wouldn't think of it," she said. She was filling her water cylinder again. Her back was to Jesse, so he could make out the perfect curve of her backside beneath her sweater.

"You wouldn't?" he asked.

"Well, I think of it." She smiled, one of her first smiles in a long time. "I just feel like you do, not exactly, but guilty and sick, like my actions somehow caused Sofia's capture."

Jesse didn't know if he was annoyed by this or not. Mostly, it made him feel even worse because now he had to worry about how she felt too.

"That's crazy. Just your Catholic guilt stuff. No, I did this. I need to get her back."

Kate's face flushed red. "Right." She busied herself with controls and screens that hadn't changed in days.

He instantly regretted what he'd said. He wanted to grab her and kiss her, but then again that too would make him feel worse. Did he want Sofia back? He wanted her safe. So if that meant having her back, then yes, he wanted her back. And he was going to do whatever it took to get her.

Dear Triumvirate,

You know now that you are the chosen three to attain the power source, and the purpose of that quest was to lead you here, this ship. We, the Keepers of the Ancients' ways, have nurtured and protected their wishes for thousands of years. At first, this sacred keeping of texts and information was easy, our paths smooth as stones worn by a river, but over time, as our species grew more corrupt, our duties became more covert. The very idea of a ship being built unknown to the leaders in government on Terria shows exactly how secretive our mission became. Each member of our society takes a vow to protect the location of the power source and the knowledge of this ship, for one day, the Ancients predicted it would be instrumental in aiding you, our Triumvirate. The information gathered here is eclectic and vast, and you must keep in mind that though certain key points of Terrian topography, history, anatomy, etc. were compulsory and updated through the ages, other tangential topics, such as selected Earth texts, were added on an individual basis. You have at your fingertips the varied intellect and interests of Terria's Keepers. We have existed since this all started, and we will keep protecting you and the information that aids you until we perish.

Keepers Data Update, Earth 21st century,
Jesse Woods, translator

Jesse smelled fresh-baked bread. Was he dreaming? He shot awake; his neck was stiff from slumping over in the command chair. Kate was next to him, her hand on the orb, which was now cradled in the control console. Her eyes were closed, her mouth in a sultry pout. Jesse stared for a moment too long because she sensed him and opened her eyes.

"Everything all right?" His voice cracked. He coughed into his sleeve and looked back at the history of plant life on Terria he had been reading before he had fallen asleep.

"Yes, everything's fine. I was talking to Eruk and Palk," she said.

"Great, do they know where the Gelfs' headquarters are underground?"

"I believe so, but I'm not sure. We aren't actually writing. It's like how the three of us can send short messages to each other. But we're working on longer telekinetic conversations. It's pretty cool, but it'll take practice."

"Maybe I can help you?"

"No," Kate blurted and blushed. "It's something I have to do. But once I get some information we can all sit down and talk about it. Then we can make a plan," she said. She spoke with the finality he had gotten used to. Kate didn't talk a lot but when she did, it mattered. If she was done with a topic, she was done. This was so different from Sofia who needed constant reassurance and conversation. Why was he doing this? Stop comparing.

Hayden slid into the room in his stocking feet. He adopted an all-blue outfit: He went with the spandex-like pants Jesse refused to wear and a thick blue sweater the color of Kate's eyes. Jesse thought the whole look was girlish, but he didn't dare joke about it because he had quickly become the group homophobe.

"I did it!" Hayden said. "I baked bread, real bread. Kind of. Bread synthetically speaking, but it smells like our bread and tastes a little like our bread, so I'm closing my eyes and imagining that it's Earth bread."

He held a platter out to Jesse and Kate. A blobby, doughy circle of "bread" was in the center of the plate.

"Looks great, Hayden," Kate said and stood. She broke off a small bite and chewed with vigor, probably more vigor than regular old bread needed. "Yeah, it's good."

"Okay, I'll try it too," Jesse said. He was more than tired of all the vacuum packaged Terrian food, but they had hundreds of storage units devoted to the stuff. All of it had a gritty texture and bland taste. This was at least soft and fragrant. He put a bite in his mouth, and the first taste was heaven, but then the piece got harder as he chewed. He had to chomp and work it from his teeth, kind of like taffy, until the one bit went down. He slammed an entire cylinder of water after that.

"What's with the texture?" Jesse asked.

"I know, I'm working on it," Hayden answered. "You know, you two could spend some time in the kitchen. I'm starting to feel taken for granted. I know you've been reading as much history as you can, Jesse, and Kate you've got the communiqués with our alien liaisons, but hey, I don't need to be the only one trying to feed us and figure out the food, clothes, living space thing. These things are necessary, you know."

Jesse laughed. Not only did Hayden look like a girl in blue, he sounded like one.

"Okay, bro, that makes it worth it. To see the Dark Lord laugh again," Hayden said and stuffed a huge piece of bread in his mouth. "I don't think you've laughed since we started this crazy chase." Hayden had to stop talking for a moment because the bread got too dense to chew and speak.

"Hasn't been much to laugh about," Jesse said.

Hayden held his hand in the air and chomped harder. He spoke through bites: "I know, but we're almost there. It's been, what? The clock on the console says it's been ten days. You two figured we'll reach Terria's atmosphere in another three days, give or take, depending on that whole Worm Hole factor. When we hit that, whoosh! Then we'll get Eruk and Palk first, and they'll help us infiltrate the Gelf headquarters. Way I see it, Sofia will be sitting here with us soon, very soon." Hayden gulped a half cylinder of water. His eyes danced between Jesse and Kate.

"Since we're all here, and I just finished my 'talk' with Eruk and Palk, maybe we should start thinking up a strategy," Kate said.

When did this happen? When had Kate and Hayden turned into the ones coming up with the plan? Jesse took a breath to curtail his anger. Wasn't he the one who led them into Chicago and the one to figure out how the power source pieces fit together? He stood and paced the floor behind the chairs again. He wanted to make up the plans; he wanted to be in control. He wanted to be the cool-headed one again, the one who could think straight under pressure. But all he seemed to be able to do was read at even faster speeds, which only fed his rage. He knew the Terrians were no gods, but he hoped their history would show a more advanced and evolved society, one where reason and observation were the basis of the society's rules, where they strove to better their minds in a kind and fair way. This was how he had pictured the Ancients. The entire planet and its factions had devolved. They were corrupted, cruel, and opportunistic. They were too much like humans.

He hadn't noticed, but Hayden was talking again.

"Okay, so from what you've determined, Eruk and Palk are in what they call the Demark Ghetto. Not good, not good, from you've told us about the terrain, Jesse."

"What?" Jesse's head felt fuzzy, but he didn't wait for an answer. "No, there are two ghettos flanking the Shaari State. The Demark Ghetto is on the southern end with jungle and desert surrounding it."

"Don't get it, bro. How do both deserts and jungles surround it? I can't picture it at all."

Hayden started doing jumping jacks. Jesse had gotten used to his manic bursts of exercise. Though the ship had five major levels, thousands of compartments for living quarters, enormous kitchens on multiple levels, and long empty rooms, for what they didn't know, Hayden couldn't seem to get enough exercise. Just like how Jesse couldn't read enough.

"Think of it like Dante Alighieri's circles of hell," Jesse said.

"Human English, please," Hayden said. He started doing martial arts moves.

"It is human English," Jesse said, trying to keep the irritation from his voice. "You know, Dante Alighieri, the medieval Italian writer. On Earth. Dante made himself a main character who journeys through Hell, Purgatory, and Paradise."

"I've heard of it," Kate said. She had that eager face again where she nodded and shook her hair out, as if the action would help her to concentrate more. Jesse wanted to take a fistful of her hair and pull it over his face. Maybe then he could rest, for at least a minute of bliss.

"Look," Hayden said, panting, "we were still on King Arthur legends in World Literature class when real hell broke loose on Earth."

"Oh yeah," Jesse said, "I forgot I read ahead." He looked for something to write with and huffed. All this high-tech stuff and the Keepers didn't stock one pen. He dug in his backpack, the one from Hallia, and pulled out the pens and paper she had supplied.

"The pens are probably in the sections of the ship we haven't looked in yet," Kate said. And there it was: the most dazzling smile Jesse had ever seen. He steadied his hand by gripping the pen.

Jesse drew a small circle in the center of the page with two larger circles around it. "Here in the middle is the ghetto. The next circle surrounding it is desert. The last circle around the desert is dense jungle. From what Kate's learned from Eruk and Palk, there are about a thousand in this one ghetto. We still don't know what guards them, and we have no real plan to get them out."

"I'll talk to them soon, and I'll ask about guards," Kate said.

"What about the Gelfs? Where will they be when we're busting out Eruk and Palk? I hate to let them out of my sight," Jesse said. That hot feeling came on again. It felt like molten lava coursed through his veins. He shoved down an image of Nosh running a finger up Sofia's leg. "Damn, I just want to get there!"

"We know, bro. We know." Hayden stopped his exercises and put a hand on Jesse's shoulder. "Let's get more intel from our gay compatriots, then we'll go from there. We need their help."

"And," Kate said, her face red, "Eruk and Palk have helped us a great deal. Remember they're looking to us to help bring about peace." She checked the console and turned in her chair. "I also don't know why you need to call them the *gay* compatriots. Why can't they just be compatriots? You put 'gay' in front of everything when it comes to Eruk and Palk."

"Well, there's a very gay reason for that," Hayden said and laughed. Jesse smirked and hid his face in shirt, pretending to wipe sweat.

Kate got redder. "All I ask is that when they are on this ship, and I know we'll get them, and Sofia, too, Jesse, I ask you don't do that anymore."

"They may not even know what gay means," Hayden said.

"They know almost everything about humanity. We've been under a microscope for thousands of years," Jesse added.

"Thanks, bro. Okay, okay – just stop looking at me like that. I'd rather be pummeled with coconuts than to have you look at me like that, Kate," Hayden said.

The cabin fell silent. Jesse went back to his reading. Kate

turned her chair to face the window, their viewfinder to the universe.

Hayden said he planned to explore more of level three: "I have our handy ship map, in case I get lost." The slender portable screen looked like a cell phone but slightly bigger. "If you don't hear from me by tomorrow, send out a search party."

"Do you have your earbud in?" Kate asked. "We need to make sure we can reach each other right away through the ship's com-link."

"Got it, Fearless Navigator. You can always send me one of your telepathic notes. Something like, Want bread, Need sleep, or You're so hot."

"Hay-den," Kate said and chuckled.

"Right, you can send longer messages. It's Jesse and me who are like chimps, only two-word phrases from us. You could shorten your messages to me, Kate, you know for those of us with lesser brains. Just say, You hot, you hot, you hot." Hayden shook his hips, cracked himself up, and left the cabin.

Kate and Jesse laughed and caught each other's eyes for a moment.

Her skin glowed too, he thought; it actually reflected the star light. He had to look away. He was getting distracted. No more laughing or joking. And definitely no more being mesmerized by Kate's hair and smile and skin. He turned to his screen and began to read. Information was his best weapon. He planned to find a Gelf weakness and tear Nosh apart.

CHAPTER THREE
HUMILIATED, GUILTY

Kate lay back as if the tile floor were a bed and brought Jesse to cover the length of her body with his own. He was out of his mind with desire for her; her taut body moved with his on the floor as they kissed. He kissed her forehead, her cheeks, her eyelids, her lips, and down her neck. Several luxurious minutes passed in this way: He pressed against her breasts and legs. Each explored the other's body with tender touches. She made small moans that spurred him on until he couldn't help himself; he let his hands move under her jacket and shirt; her breasts were firm and erect beneath her bra. Kate let out another low moan from deep in her throat. She kissed his full lips with more vigor, so Jesse ran his hand down her smooth stomach to the button on her jeans.

Jesse stirred in his sleep and moaned. He didn't want to wake up; he wanted to stay in the janitor's closet with Kate. He wanted to inhale the scent of pine cleaner forever and feel cool tile on his back because then he'd know he was with Kate, stroking her and feeling her firm body on top of his own. Jesse wasn't sure how long he went in and out of this dream that was so detailed, so vivid, he knew it was an exact memory. Everything was the same: her sweaty mass of red hair, her soft lips, the perfect slope of her lower back down to her backside. His desire was so fierce he had to jerk off while he was half in and out of sleep, and his memory/dream cooperated until he was finished.

He woke and groaned in annoyance. How could he be so weak? He had to control himself. This wouldn't get him any closer to killing Nosh. He had to stay focused, vengeful, angry. He had to shut out anything that got in his way, and the way meant the way to Sofia. He had to save her, and whacking off to fantasies of Kate wouldn't bring about the resolve he needed.

But how could he control his dreams? Not sleep? No, he knew being in space was enough of a stress to his mind; he didn't need to add a lack of sleep. His mom had taught him that; she'd seen the results of ICU psychosis at work, a state that couldn't be avoided because she had to check patients' vitals so often during their stays in ICU. She had dealt with enough crazy behavior on the floor to warn Jesse about the lifeblood that sleep was. His mother. Where was she? Was she still under Shaari protection, and now that they had disappeared would the Shaaris hurt her to get to him? His insides were churning with anger again. He had to get up and get moving.

He rolled out of the bunk of his small compartment and went to the cubicle-sized bathroom that had a toilet like one you see on airplanes, a wash basin, and a "shower," which was only a stall with buttons in it. The Keepers must not have wanted to waste water on showering, so they rigged the ship with laser showers. Jesse stepped into the shower and pressed the buttons that triggered the blue lasers to run up and down his body. The blue laser light turned yellow, the signal that he was clean. By Terrian standards he supposed he was clean, but something about the process never made him feel refreshed.

On one of the first days on the ship, Jesse had found something that looked like a razor in a storage room with some hygiene items. He wished for boxer shorts, but they hadn't found anything that could serve as underwear.

Guess the Terrians went commando all the time. So Kate didn't have underwear either, he thought. Stop. He closed his eyes and took deep breaths. He imagined his last vision of Sofia in the Gelf bubble. She had underwear on: the hot purple and black number he used to love taking off of her. He clenched his fists and bent at the waist. Not good. None of this was helping. He had to shave, get dressed, and go blow off steam. He had to get out of his cabin.

He stood naked in front of the plate-sized mirror that hung on the wall in his bathroom. He hadn't found shaving cream, but there was a cool green gel that seemed all right to use. It was labeled as a generic lotion in Terrian writing. He squirted the ooze onto his head and carefully scraped the razor-like implement along his scalp. The gel looked a lot like alien drip from injured Terrians in their enhanced forms. He imagined the gel was part of Nosh's gelatinous innards seeping out. He scraped and scraped with relish then. Surprisingly his head looked pretty smooth. No lining or designs like Fred did at his barber shop back home, but it would do. Jesse dressed in a loose-fitting pair of black pants and a black sweatshirt. He had to retire his Earth clothes. They smelled bad and were so stiff they could've stood up on their own. Hayden hadn't figured out how to launder things, and Kate and Jesse hadn't taken the time to try. It didn't seem like a huge priority because there was a limitless supply of outfits at their fingertips.

Jesse headed to level two where they had designated one of the large empty rooms as the "Training Room." It was the size of two football fields put out side by side and had a gigantic domed ceiling. The entire room was covered in sleek metallic silver very much like the floor in the main cabin, their control room, and the hallways throughout all levels of the ship. At least the ones they had explored.

Hayden had moved some exercise mats and lifting equipment he had found on the first level. He also set up a table with various weapons the Keepers had stocked in row after row of shelves on level one. Hayden was the only one who could make the light lassos do anything, but then again, he hadn't done much with them, only got them to make a faint glow like a dried-out highlighter. There were other weapons: ninja stars and metal rods that none of them had any idea how to use, besides beating someone to a bloody pulp with the rod. But that didn't even seem possible given the gelatinous nature of the Terrians when they were enhanced. Most of the time, when they took turns working out, they ran laps, did push-ups, and lifted the tube-shaped weights. Kate practiced making smokey shields with the orb. She was getting so good sometimes she didn't need to be holding it to make smoke. Hayden practiced making fire and ice from his hands, and he was gaining some success at creating rings of fire like the one he had made to lasso the chimera. Jesse liked watching those demonstrations because he imagined Nosh's head in one of Hayden's fire nooses. He hated that he couldn't make something come from his hands, except the amber glow that could heal people. He knew this was valuable, but in his present state, the one obsessed with destroying the Gelfs, he wished for ice picks or fire to shoot from his hands. Something that could kill, not heal.

Jesse was on his third lap around the room when he saw a fire ring at the entrance. Hayden started to jog with one palm in the air steering the loop two feet in front of him. Jesse sprinted to meet up with him.

"Don't even think about putting that around me," Jesse said. One time he honestly thought Hayden had considered it. So what if he had been ranting about the corruption throughout Terrian history. They needed to know this stuff too.

"Just practicing my fire, bro." Hayden moved his hand up and down, and the circle expanded and contracted. "Want to join me for a run, or you finishing up?"

"I've put a couple of laps in, but I could use the exercise."

"A lot of pent-up frustration?" Hayden said and laughed.

"What's that supposed to mean?"

"Okay, I'll be honest with you. I came down to find you to tell you to watch the com-link when you sleep. Take your earbud out and turn it off from now on. I'll send you a two-word message in our heads if we need you."

"What?" Jesse was horror-stricken. What had he heard? But worse, what had Kate heard?

"Dude, you were obviously in throes of passion with yourself just a little while ago. We couldn't help but hear it. I was checking out more of the weapons on level one. Couldn't sleep anymore, and Kate has the controls. Anyway, with her on watch in the main cabin, I can't see how she didn't hear it."

"God, no!" Jesse ran faster. "Damn. Are you sure you could, you know, tell what was happening?"

"No smacking sound, but you were moaning like a dying whale, and you mumbled her name."

"No."

"Yeah, sounded fun in a one-man-show kind of way," Hayden said. He glanced at his fire ring, stretched his hands apart, and raised them higher. The ring expanded and floated toward the dome.

"Augh," Jesse yelled and ran harder. Hayden caught up.

"Look, it's not that deep. It's good to be able to pleasure yourself—"

"Dude!"

"Right, I forgot that you're all walls up with any kind of friendly conversation," Hayden said.

Jesse's chest felt tight, and his temple pulsed in his head. Why was he losing control so much? He needed to run for miles and miles, through Earth fields and along the bike path. He needed air and real water to bath in. He needed to smell leaves, dead and wet after an autumn rain; he needed sunshine on his skin. He needed to go home and have his old life back.

"Talk to me, Jesse, it's obvious you're in an ass-hard position with Sofia kidnapped by the Gelfs, but dude, it wasn't your fault. You know that, right? It could have easily been someone close to Kate or me. Sofia was the easiest target because she missed school the day of the tornado. She slipped through Shaari protection. Not that it's still in place now that we've pissed them off. I know you hate this, but maybe if you talk about how you're feeling—"

"No."

"Okay, want to tell me in two-word phrases telepathically?" Hayden grinned. His blue-gray eyes danced like an imp's.

Jesse didn't say anything. He ran harder, and Hayden clapped his hands. The fire ring disappeared. Hayden sprinted next to Jesse.

"Let's try again," Hayden said. "We know strong emotions, say sexual tension or anger, increase our abilities."

Jesse let out a pained groan. How could he let this happen? Maybe he should talk to Hayden. Maybe it would help him gain control again. But how? He was more than uncomfortable; he almost felt sick, disoriented. Was he losing his mind?

Jesse stopped and looked at Hayden. "I'm listening."

"Good. That's a start," Hayden said. "I know you're all hell bent on getting Sofia. We all are, and we will get her back. It seems to me you're conflicted about what happens after that. We're flying by the seat of our pants in terms of the aliens-as-gods and possible-war-on-Earth stuff, but on a personal level you seem all tied up about two girls. Am I right?"

"Right," Jesse answered.

"Good, you answered." Hayden clapped him on the back, and they headed to the weights. Once they chose their weights, they lifted, staring off to the far wall. "Here we go. We won't make eye contact and I'll ask questions. The two-word answer thing isn't a bad idea. Answer in two words. You're our wordsmith. This shouldn't be too hard for you."

"Okay." Jesse felt like a child. Was he really being walked through an emotional talk like a kindergartener learns to cut and paste? After the com-link humiliation he didn't think it could get much worse.

"How do you feel right now? You know, about our audio peek into the, uh-hem, private moments in your compartment?" Hayden asked and worked his biceps.

Just answer, Jesse thought. He felt hot and itchy. Why was this so hard? His throat felt tight and dry.

"Try the two–word description, bro. Maybe that will loosen you up."

"Okay," Jesse said. After a couple of reps for his pecs he said, "Humiliated masturbator."

Out of the corner of his eye Jesse saw Hayden suppress a smirk.

"Right, but what else? How about your feelings about Sofia?"

Jesse thought for a couple of minutes and then said, "Tortured. Guilty."

"Okay, just what I expected. What about your powers? How

do you feel about your mind expanding, your abilities growing?" Hayden pressed on with a light tone, but Jesse knew he was being careful.

"Restless robot."

"Heh, good one. And Kate, how do you feel about Kate?" Hayden asked.

Jesse stood still. He was lost. How did he feel? He couldn't think of just two words to capture how he felt about her. It wasn't enough. After a while he finally spoke.

"She's right here with me, but she's so far away. Unreachable because of all this shit around us. I can't be with her until things are resolved, and they may never be, so I might never get to be with her because I feel certifiable right now, crazed with rage. I can't make sense of our connection. It's so powerful. Maybe too much, you know? Maybe that kind of connection is only meant to be used to do what we need to do to fight Terrians. I don't know." He sighed. He did feel a little better.

"Yeah, I can see that," Hayden said. The side of his mouth went up in a half smile. "I'll bet money she's been able to have a longer conversation with Eruk and Palk as a result of your jerking, moaning, mumbling her name extravaganza."

Jesse cringed. "You think?" This shouldn't excite him, but it did.

"Yeah. Look, try to chill, man. You think you need to fix everything at every moment. Why not enjoy the possibility of having two girls?"

"I don't work that way," Jesse said.

"Okay, okay."

"Jesse, Hayden." Kate's voice echoed in his earbud. "You both need to come to the main cabin right now. Two things: I know more about the ghetto and Gelfs, and we're approaching the Worm Hole."

"Okay, we'll be right there," Hayden answered and turned off the com-link. "She's into you, bro. Give it time, be cool, and enjoy whatever happens next."

Jesse sighed and jogged after Hayden. None of those things seemed possible. Everything felt just out of reach: Kate, Sofia, the end to all this. All of it was star light shining brightly before him, but untouchable and burning, burning, burning.

CHAPTER FOUR
WORM HOLE

Little is known of the Gelf compound. We suspect it is underground somewhere in the Outlands of Terria, but no faction can confirm this. Gelf power is subversive. Their technological advancements are only demonstrated in guerilla attacks; they gain intellectual capital through kidnapping scientists of promise, Belite and Shaari alike. Their military ranks are led with brute force. From what we know, they will destroy whatever gets in their way. The key objective is to take over all Liquid Light reserves and destroy Shaari control on both planets.

"Gelf Objectives," Keepers Data Update, Earth 21st Century, Jesse Woods, translator

Cool, cool darkness.

Jesse tried to stand but couldn't. He bent at the waist and clutched his chair in the main cabin. He knew Hayden and Kate were beside him in their chairs, but he couldn't see them. Everything was black, black, and more black.

Beep, beep, dip. Beep, beep, dip. Sounds came from the console; the lights flicked on and off, on and off, and then they flew. Uncontrollable, blazing speed tore at the ship, and the ship tore back. It sailed and spun into nothing.

Worm hole, worm hole, let's see where you can go.

His mind looped in sing-song terror. He was losing it. Now, for sure, his mind slipped away. It crashed and raced along with the ship.

Were they on a ship? The floor felt gooey. The walls quivered like Jell-O, like enhanced Terrians ready to smother him. Darkness, speed.

His face stretched; his shoulders sank lower to the floor. He wanted to stand up, but what was pressing in on him? Weights. Weights. He knew he could bench a lot, but this? How could he bench press backwards? It wasn't possible.

Jesse moaned and had the sensation that Kate and Hayden were screaming next to him. How could he help them? What if they were injured? Was the worm hole tearing them apart? He could put them back together if he could only move a fraction of an inch.

Not one muscle cooperated. He couldn't blink or bend a finger. His legs were lead, his muscles as heavy as uncooked potatoes in a ten-pound sack.

It went on and on: limitless, unfathomable speed and the weight of the ship pressing in. He wanted so badly to stand up and check on his friends, but the weights pressed down.

Down and down he went. Into the rabbit hole.

CHAPTER FIVE

NEW EXIT

Allah takes away men's souls upon their death, and the souls of the living during their sleep. Those that are doomed He keeps with Him and restores the others for a time ordained. Surely there are signs in this for thinking men.

The Koran: 39:39

"Where the hell are the Gelfs?" Jesse shouted. He hit the buttons to scan the Terrian outer atmosphere. As soon as they exited the Worm Hole, Kate put their ship into the full-stop, cloak mode. They could see Terria, a murky green and brown planet with shots of blue; it was very much like Earth, but smaller. It had a smaller sun that looked like an ice cream cone dollop floating in butter-yellow sunshine.

"Kate," Jesse said with more severity than he meant, "where are the Gelfs? I saw the red Liquid Light trail as soon as we shot out of the Worm Hole, and then they were gone. I don't see any sign of them in the atmosphere."

"Neither do I, Jesse," she answered, still pushing buttons and looking for a way to locate the rogue aliens.

"They poofed into thin air, red blur and then," Hayden paused, "nothing." He stood at the window and scanned the sky.

Jesse couldn't stand it anymore. They couldn't lose them now, not when they finally reached Terria. He was so close to getting Sofia back, and now, he felt that she may as well be on Earth.

"What the fuck!" Jesse yelled and punched one of the smaller screens reading the life forms in the outer atmosphere. "I. Can't. Fucking. Stand. This. Where is she? Where did they take her?"

Jesse thrashed around the room, punching the air and swearing. He kicked at the wall and his foot instantly ached. He concentrated, hard, and thought about killing Nosh, taking the whole group of red Gelfs and shooting them apart with the ship's weapons. No. He wanted to kill each one with his hands. He kicked more at the air and put his hands in front of himself, willing them to shoot something, ice, fire, anything to show his rage. Instead, his hands lit like the usually did, an amber glow radiated from his dark skin, but there was something else, a red tinge to the amber, like blood, like the Gelfs. He whooshed his hands, moving the light and heat in front of him, and aimed at his command chair. It smoldered with small sparks of black and orange fire that looked almost solid.

"Whoa, bro," Hayden shouted and instantly went to put it out with ice, but when the two elements met, pure energy shot straight up.

"Jesse, stop," Kate yelled.

"Kate, do something, my shit makes it worse," Hayden said.

The cabin air was thick with smoke. The chunky bits of fire Jesse had made oozed over his chair. He did it! He made something destructive. It was a weapon he could use against Nosh and the Gelfs. He could melt them and make them into a gel that never took a humanoid shape again.

Jesse smirked at the thought and went to touch it. This

was his power. He could fight and heal. He was the leader of this Triumvirate. His hand hovered over a fiery glob that now hissed and made a new vapor the color of the inside of a peach.

Kate was saying something to him in a loud, but firm voice. He couldn't make out what she said because he felt light, buoyant with triumph. He could make out her attitude, though. Who did she think she was, his mother?

Forget her, he thought. He focused on the fire. He reached closer, closer, ready to touch it. But then a bubble of smoke and light engulfed him.

Again, Jesse tried to touch the black fire on the chair, but he couldn't gain his balance in the bubble. What was this? Did the Shaaris find their ship? How could he have missed their approach? But this bubble was not the silky, gelatinous substance that Hallia made, or even the slippery blue one Hayden conjured in Chicago. This was smoke and a pink light; it surrounded his entire body and felt warm, even cozy, like he was wrapped in a thick, down blanket at Christmas time. And yet, the cozy feeling fell away when he realized he couldn't get out of it. Every time he tried, his hands met more smoke and light. There was no point trying to wave it away, more smoke formed, more light pierced his eyes.

"Kate, Hayden, can you hear me?" he said.

He kept yelling their names. His throat started to get tight, and a panicky sensation ran through his body.

"We hear you," Kate said. Her voice was clear and calm, but where was she?

"Are you okay? Who has us?" he asked. She had to be all right; she was talking to him, and she sounded fine, more than fine.

"Yes, are you?" Kate said.

"Yeah, I just have to find a way out of this smoke thing. Are you in one?"

"No, Jesse, I put you in this," she said.

"What? Why?"

"You were totally out of control. You nearly set the main cabin on fire. Then what would we have done?"

She did this? She had no right. He glanced at his hands, the ones he knew could heal people. Images of the people he saved on the museum campus in Chicago flashed in his mind. Then he saw the ones he wasn't able to save, the screaming woman on fire. Shame made his face flush. His hands had a singed look to them; thin cracks lined his fingernails. He thought he might lose his thumbnails all together.

"Jesse, listen to me. You have to control your rage. This behavior won't get Sofia back, and we need you to be with us, and not doing crazy stuff that could hurt the group," she said. There was that final voice again.

Jesse started to shout something back, but then he heard her say one more thing.

"I need you to be with us."

His heart rate instantly settled. How did he let himself lose it so much? What was happening to him? A ripple of fear went through his mind: What if the mind expansion he was experiencing since this all began made him a sociopath or something irredeemable? How could he ever face Kate again?

"Doc, you ready for Kate to part the smoky waters and let you out? You aren't going to shoot fire-goo at us, are you?" Hayden tried to have a jovial tone, but a layer of tension pulsed through the cabin. Despite the bubble, Jesse could feel it. He couldn't let his friends fear him, could he?

"I'm ready," he said, "and I'm sorry."

The smoke instantly evaporated and there they stood: Hayden near the window with a mass of even spikier hair and hands twitching right over where he holstered his dagger, and Kate. Her blue eyes blazed right through him. Her hands were still in front of her body, like a person praying. She moved them to her side and crossed the cabin to meet him in a few quick strides.

She took his hand quickly, and Jesse felt all the angry heat dissipate. It was replaced by a different heat, electric and tingly, like something amazing, not horrific, was about to happen.

"Thanks, I don't know what came over me," he choked out. Why did he feel like crying? He let go of Kate's hand and went to sit, but his chair was destroyed. A chunk of metal stuck out of the floor and came to a point like a stalagmite.

He had to turn this around. He had to get control again. A feeling of deep remorse washed over him, and somehow it made him think of his mother. He breathed in and smelled her perfume, a trick his mind could do at times, when the memory of her was as real as his hands. Her words on how to be sounded in his head, "Fake it 'til you make it," or "If you feel selfish, do the opposite," or "You're born, but you're not buried Jess-a-peak; you don't know what you'll put up with before you die." That certainly was true: How in the world was he supposed to put up with himself?

"Guess, I'll stand," he said and smirked a little, just a little, but it was enough to convince himself that he could tackle his anger; both Kate and Hayden let out sighs of relief.

"Or, you could perch there," Hayden said and circled what used to be Jesse's chair. "That was nuts, bro, what you made from your hands."

"Yeah, it was," Jesse said.

"It was dangerous, Jesse," Kate said and paused. "You weren't in control. All of what we do with our minds is about concentration and emotion. I think bad things will happen if we lose control."

Jesse wanted to counter her, but he bit his tongue. He had to show he wasn't losing it. He had to get back to where he was the one telling them what to do. He never realized it, but now he started to see that he asserted himself as leader because he needed that role, and deep down he believed he had to prove that he could be that person, the leader, and not the sidekick.

"Right, let's move on," Jesse said. Instead of standing next to his mutilated chair, a visible reminder of his outburst, he pointed to the screen that showed the charted areas of Terria. "It looks like we've settled on the uninhabited side of Terria. Well, not completed uninhabited, but we're opposite of the Shaari State, and closer to the Belite Outlands. Without planning it, we're on the side of the planet with the Demark Ghetto, where Eruk and Palk are."

"Kate, right before the Worm Hole ride you said you had a longer conversation with Eruk and Palk. You know more about the ghetto and the Gelfs?" The side of Hayden's mouth went up in a knowing half grin. Jesse wanted to punch him. His prediction about Kate being able to communicate better with Eruk and Palk as a result of his masturbatory activities that morning made his stomach turn. When did he become such a head case?

"Yeah, it was so cool. It was like talking through the orb – more fluid, like a real conversation, but in my head. Anyway, they're okay, and I said our first plan was to break them out and then break into Gelf headquarters to rescue Sofia. They definitely want to help with that. They used to know a Brown who was a former Gelf, but he was killed by the Shaaris soon after being put in their ghetto. So they know a possible entrance to Gelf headquarters."

"Wait a minute, what's a Brown?" Jesse asked.

"Oh right, you weren't there," Kate said and blushed. Hayden coughed and muttered something under his breath.

It felt like a hot iron was pressing on Jesse's groin. He had to get it together.

"Anyway," she continued, "you know how the skin color of any Terrian corresponds with their hair and eye color, only more subdued? Well, that's a genetic modification to signify their group – Shaari, Belite, or Gelf. When a Terrian has no group, they are ghettoized and not given genetic modification, so most have brown hair, brown eyes, and shades of brown skin. Thus, they are called the Browns. Eruk and Palk think of themselves as only Terrians who follow the way of the Ancients. When I see them in my mind's eye, they both look like average humans. One looks a little Asian by Earthly standards, but they could blend in with an Earthly human population."

"So how many guard the Browns in the Demark Ghetto?" Jesse asked.

"Usually there are at least one hundred heavily armed Shaaris with Liquid Light capabilities guarding about one thousand prisoners," Kate said. "With the war going on, the numbers are down to about eighty guards, give or take. The thing is, the real deterrent for escape, are the genetically-enhanced hybrid beasts that roam outside the ghetto."

"Great, something like a chimera, or dragon, or hybrid could mean a nasty mixture of any of the above." Hayden started slashing at the air with his dagger. "How in the hell are we supposed to get them out of there, Kate? Did our ga— uh-hem, our friends, give any clue about how we'll break them out of there?"

"Oh, yes, they started formulating a plan as soon as they were able to communicate with me through the orb. They knew we were the real Triumvirate. Eruk said it was because of our connection with him; he's a descendent of the Ancients. He sensed our authenticity."

"Kate, you're starting to sound a little new-agey," Hayden said. "Does Eruk have any sense about the outcome of our most foolish of escape plans, or should I say, our non-plan, since we have no idea how to get them out."

"Let her finish," Jesse said. He had been listening. Kate said they had a plan to break out. Once they had Eruk and Palk, then they could get Sofia.

"Right, go ahead, fair lady," Hayden said.

"They plan on committing suicide."

CHAPTER SIX
SUICIDE PLAN

Terrian atmosphere and landscapes may appear to be like Earth, but they are not exact. The air is breathable for humans, but it has an atmospheric gas that does not exist on your planet. NY32, as we name it, lightens the air quality, for lack of a better way to explain it. Though we believe humans would be able to go about normal activities on Terria, should you, the Triumvirate, make it here, we are uncertain how your abilities will manifest and how the use of your gifts will deplete your reserve bodily energies.

"Terrian Atmosphere," Keepers Data Update, Earth 21st Century, Jesse Woods, translator

"Suicide – that seems a bit counterproductive," Hayden said. He moved his hands in a wide arch, his dagger in his left hand, and Jesse knew this was a sign that he was going to talk for a while.

"Let her explain, man," Jesse cut him off. Hayden half scowled, half smirked and bowed to Kate.

"They are going to fake that they overdosed on wild berries that grow freely in the gardens in the ghetto. They actually let the Browns keep gardens because they don't want to spend the time to feed them. Eruk says the berries are poisonous if a major amount is ingested, but in small doses they have medicinal qualities. This general knowledge will help them feign suicide."

Kate continued about life for Eruk and Palk in the ghetto: the sterile rooms, the size of clothes closets on Earth, the howls of hybrids outside the walls of the stone complexes, the hot winds off the desert circle, the sudden rains blowing in from the jungle circle, and the trials and tortures to get information from some. Jesse listened, partly, but found his mind skipped from point to point. Facts about Terrian terrain, eating habits, and rituals raced in his head. He tried to focus on Kate's words, but mostly he wanted to speed up what she was saying; he wanted to interrupt her and say everything she was telling him was nothing he needed to know. He needed to know about the guards, the beasts, and how they planned on moving through the landscape undetected. He didn't really care that Eruk and Palk couldn't touch or kiss openly around the Sharri guards, that they were seen as diseased; he didn't give a shit about their feelings, but then again, how often had he gone on about Terrian history to the two of them in the past days? And for the most part, they had listened, save for Hayden's fire ring, and one time Kate had left the main cabin "to practice with the weapons," but other than that, they'd seemed interested.

"And there are no children under ten years old," Kate said.

It felt like cotton was pulled from Jesse's ear after an earache. "What? No younger kids, why?" he asked.

"Systematic sterilization. The Shaari leader, Kerr, made enforced sterilization of the Browns law about eleven Earth years ago," Kate said. Her faced went red with anger. She stood and paced. "You haven't read anything about it, Jesse?"

"No, there are big gaps in what's here. I wonder when the Keepers last updated information." His stomach churned with a queasy unease. Enforced sterilization. Ghettos. What other tortures went on behind the walls?

"Okay, so Kerr, Shaari leader, let's make a note that he's a real asshole," Hayden said. "It's not that I don't want to know all about their lives there, Kate, but we need a plan, not a history lesson."

Jesse was grateful that he wasn't the jerk who said it. Kate's eyes flashed anger and then hurt, but she regained composure and sat down. He wished he had a chair. His legs ached with a tense pulsating throb, like his heartbeat had moved to his calves.

"Right, but we do need to have a sense of them," Kate said. "They'll be joining our team."

"Yeah, I know, but I'm getting pumped to get moving," Hayden said and jogged back and forth, back and forth.

"Acting impulsively won't help," she said and shot a look at Jesse. Heat rushed to his face.

"Will you please just drop it," Jesse said. "I said I was sorry. I'll make sure nothing like that happens again. Are you satisfied?" He glared at her. Why was he lashing out at her? She even flinched at the harshness in his tone.

"Right, I shouldn't have brought it up, but you two are chomping at the bit to go in there and slash your way through the Valley of the Beasts, but I think if you actually listen and think in a kind of a meditative way, then we'll be more mentally prepared."

"Again, new-agey, Kate," Hayden said. He was still jogging, and then adding a pivot slide at the far end of the room when he wanted to turn around.

"Stop that, I hate that," she said. Now her face was really red, tomato red, Jesse thought, and his stomach actually growled thinking of his mom's spaghetti sauce.

"Okay, let's all step it back," Jesse said. He moved closer to where she sat. Her eyes went to his, jeweled pools with limitless depths. "We do want to know about them, Kate." His voice was softer; it was easy to do when he looked directly into her eyes. Her gaze bore into him like a thousand points of starlight bursting across space. Goose bumps ran from the back of his neck and down his arms. She glanced down instantly and saw his arm hair standing up. She reached out her hand and it hovered over his forearm for a fraction of a second before her fingertips came down on the hairs. The slightest brush, infinitesimal contact, and his knees buckled. She pulled her hand back like she had touched a hot oven. An unreadable smile creased her face.

"Okay, a step back," she said, her voice cracking with something, maybe laughter, joy? Did he make her feel joy? Even when he was a raging, masturbating, fire-chairing, fact-chasing asshole? The thought made his stomach turn again. He stepped back, allowing his back to hug the far wall, as if he always assumed a casual-leg-bent-at-the-knee-and-resting-on-a-spaceship wall pose when planning to enter the Valley of the Beasts.

"Wait a minute," he said. "It's actually called the Valley of the Beasts?"

"Yeah, in the desert circle you talked about, there's a huge valley surrounded by rock. Eruk said the Shaari guards will dispose of their bodies there because it's where all the garbage goes, and then carrion-eating beasts feed on it. Sometimes other hybrids will be there to attack the carrion-eating beasts."

"Sounds like one great dinner party," Hayden said. "So they play dead, go out with the trash, and then we pick them up and bring them to the ship."

"Yes, that's the plan," she said.

"Seems pretty solid," Hayden said. "We go in armed to the teeth, kill whatever gets in our way, and bring them back."

"I have a few questions, though," Jesse said. "Doesn't the complex have any kind of surveillance that could pick up on us?"

"Not that far out. The Shaaris haven't had a problem because, you have to remember, these are shunned Terrians, not one faction cares about what happens to them. If they had any family or friends from a different group, they've been deemed outcasts once they went to the ghetto. As far as I can tell, there isn't a real need for heavy surveillance because the Shaaris don't think there's anyone who will care enough to try to break in, and then they have an inordinate number of hybrids as the ultimate in security. They feed the hybrids regularly with Browns they've killed or ones who've died from illnesses, suicide, or if no one's died, they make a game of it and send some Browns into the Valley for entertainment."

There went his stomach again. It turned flip flops. If this was what the Shaaris did in the Ghettos, what did the Gelfs do to prisoners at their headquarters?

CHAPTER SEVEN

THE JUNGLE

Through me you enter into the city of woes,
Through me you enter into eternal pain,
Through me you enter the population of loss.

Justice moved my high maker, in power divine,
Wisdom supreme, love primal. No things were
Before me not eternal; eternal I remain.

Abandon all hope, you who enter here.

The Inferno, Canto III: 1-7, Dante Alighieri,
Robert Pinsky, translator

Jesse's hands shook. He stuffed them into the pockets of his black nit pants and pulled his black cap down farther on his head. With the safety and reassuring hum of the inside of the ship twenty yards behind him, he felt jittery and exposed, like the two moons of Terria would turn into a search beacon and home in the three teens snaking a path toward the outer circle surrounding the Demark ghetto: the jungle circle.

Landing the ship and cloaking it in the grassy plains of the Outlands, just beyond the jungle rim, had been easier than they had expected. Kate gracefully set the behemoth down when darkness came on, only after her mental signal from Eruk and Palk. Eruk and Palk would not be able to communicate with Kate after they entered into mental and physiological hibernation; they would appear dead to the Shaari guards, leaving a few berries and a suicide note stating that they were finally together in death, where they could love freely.

The "free love" note seemed a bit over the top to Jesse, but he bit his lip when Kate had relayed what the two gay Terrians had done. She'd said it in such a whispery, mesmerized tone that Jesse had known better. He'd nodded, saying, "Well, let's get on with this, so they really can be together." Kate had beamed.

Now Jesse felt he may implode with nerves. He, Hayden, and Kate crouched behind a stone archway that had crude letters carved across the top. Jesse couldn't make out what it said in the dark, and he didn't want to risk shining any light from his light lasso onto it. Even though there wasn't supposed to be any surveillance, he still wanted to blend with the night.

"Can you read it?" Hayden asked.

"Abandon all hope, you who enter here," Jesse quoted from Dante's *Inferno*. Kate shuddered next to his left shoulder, and Hayden harrumphed. "Don't get nervous," Jesse added. "I just quoted the *Inferno*. I was joking a little."

"So now you become the comedian," Hayden said. "No offense, but your timing is off."

"Okay. Sorry," Jesse said. "I can't see what it says."

HERRR-OOOOWWWW

HERRR-OOOOWWWW

HERRR-OOOOWWWW

HERRR-OOOOWWWW

"What the heck was that?" Kate asked and leaned into Jesse's shoulder. The orb was in a nylon backpack slung across her shoulder. She was so close; he felt it slide in the bag and knock against his back.

"I don't really want to venture a guess," Hayden said even lower. "Pick a hybrid, any hybrid, pretty lady."

"Look, from my calculations, we need to go through this archway," Jesse said and pointed up. "Then we move through about one mile of jungle, and then we hit the desert circle. Once in there, and thanks to Kate's great parking job, we should only be about two hundred yards from the rocks surrounding the Valley of the Beasts."

Kate took a deep breath and leaned in closer. The whites of her eyes were visible. Jesse smelled the tangy scent of her hair; she said she'd put some oil in it to mask the perfume of the lotions and sprays they used after their non-showers. He breathed it in three deep breaths and focused.

Jesse opened his eyes and saw both of his friends looking at him expectantly. All through their train track path along the Chicago suburbs, Jesse had been the leader. Despite his rages and obsessive behavior, they still wanted him to lead them to the Valley. Somehow this reassured him.

"Okay, since I can't make these lassos do anything but make a dull shine, this will be our light source only if we absolutely need it. You too, Kate, light the orb up only if you're really in deep trouble. Stick to knives and daggers if we need to fight anything. The atmosphere is different here, so if you use your super skills, you could get really weak afterwards. At least that's my guess," Jesse said and padded the inside of his jacket, which was laced with his weapons.

"Fine, I'll use my superpowers only in case of emergencies," Hayden said with a nervous laugh.

"Okay," Jesse said, thrusting a knife forward like it was a shield, "let's go."

Instinctively, he crouched passing through the stone arch because he had a tickly feeling that once through it, the rock may collapse because they breached a border. But no alarms went off, and no beasts charged. In fact, it was eerily quiet. Almost like entering one of the environmental domes he had visited with Michael in Milwaukee one time: The Mitchell Park Domes had three habitats, a show dome, an arid dome, and a tropical one, each displaying plants from different places. Once in the tropical dome, a spray of humidity had engulfed Jesse. He'd loved it: the banana plants with thick green fingers of growth, the hulking trunks of unknown trees, the rich red flowers hanging from vines like panting tongues. He and Michael had done the "search for the plants" activity, ate humongous burgers at Miss Katie's Diner, visited Michael's mother, and then went home. It was a father/son day. Jesse wiped sweat from his brow and choked back the memory. This wasn't a game, or a benign dome of display vegetation. They had no idea what some of these plants could do.

"Don't touch any plant or tree," Jesse whispered. "Remember what I told you I read?"

"Remind me one more time, bro," Hayden said; his voice quivered a bit. "No offense, but sometimes I tune out the long discussions on Terrian plant life."

Jesse rolled his eyes in annoyance, and then said: "There's a fleshy quality to all the vegetation, even the trees. They're, well, think of them as animal-like, and some may be meat-eating, so stay away. They aren't made of wood and bark. That's for sure."

"Sounds almost as charming as the gooey enhanced inhabitants," Hayden said. "Are you sure I can't just put us in a bubble and float to the Valley?"

"I really think it'll expend too much energy. We're in a totally different atmosphere here. Save it for Eruk and Palk. They won't be able to move," Jesse said.

Jesse turned and signaled for them to follow. A flowery scent mixed with something— maybe mold and mud—assaulted Jesse's face, and the ground squashed beneath his feet. After they moved away from the shadow of the arch, wild strands of iridescent blue, green, and yellow vines cascaded from plants the size of pines back home. The plants' trunks shot like arrows into the dark night, their shimmery pink bodies swaying slightly in the gentle wind. No bird sounds or small rustlings danced in the canopy, only a creepy whistle of the wind could be heard, and Jesse tried hard not to make any squishing sound when he stepped down.

Kate was directly behind him, and Hayden brought up the rear, his dagger ready. They walked as quietly as possible, and even though they were on a different planet, in an uncharted solar system, and surrounded by fleshy plant life, Jesse felt a familiar surge of normalcy with the three of them being in open air and marching toward a destination. He realized that the confines of the ship had made everything, especially Sofia's capture, more maddening and claustrophobic.

As they moved deeper into the jungle, the plants seemed to rustle with knowledge. It spooked Jesse so much he had to stare at the ground to watch each footfall, to force his legs to move forward. Roots in the muck, thick as whale tongue, had sinister twists and a luminescent pinky-peach color, but Jesse appreciated them as markers to help him see they were still moving in the direction of the desert ring. The hardest part was they looked so much like a white human's skin he cringed when his boot touched one. Some roots snapped back, like an animal in a trap, and retreated into the mud.

Jesse regained his normal breathing and crept ahead. He sensed his friends behind him but didn't look back.

Good thing there are two moons and the weird glow of some of the plants. It helps guide the way. Kate sent a message directly to Jesse's mind. He still wasn't used to her growing ability to speak to him in his head. He and Hayden could only send two, maybe three, words to each other or to Kate, but she had mastered full sentences.

Yep. Helpful, he sent back and felt like an imbecile.

If the sound we heard earlier turns into a hybrid, I could make a smoke shield with the orb.

No, he answered and concentrated to say more, but the mushy terrain and the eerie quiet distracted him. He also kept his eyes open for any more visible plant roots.

Too much energy, he mustered after several minutes.

A sound, something like a drill, whirred in the distance. Jesse crouched, and Kate and Hayden nearly toppled over him.

Whirr, tick, tick. Whirr, tick, tick.

It sounded mechanical and menacing, but they couldn't see anything. A breeze shook the plants in the canopy; they twirled like prom streamers dangling from high beams in a gym. Shadows danced on the path in front of Jesse, and the sound grumbled on somewhere in front of them.

Whirr, tick, tick. Whirr, tick, tick.

Whatever it was, it wasn't coming right for them, and even if it was, Jesse had no other choice but to continue forward. Soon Eruk and Palk would be put out with the trash, and their lives depended on the Triumvirate being there, waiting and watching, for the right moment to move in and save them. If their timing was off, then whatever mechanical thing was making that sound could get to them first.

Whirr, tick, tick. Whirr, tick, tick.

Whirr, tick, tick. Whirr, tick, tick.

Jesse kept walking, a little faster. The mechanical sound resounded frenetically for a few seconds and then stopped. Then it would start again, and each time Jesse's pulse quickened.

Whirr, tick, tick. Whirr, tick, tick.

It was definitely farther away, maybe in the desert area. Great, he thought, something to look forward to. After a few tense minutes of walking, it stopped completely, and a low hum, something like a tuning fork, took its place. The atmosphere thickened with humidity as they moved along the muddy surface, avoiding fanning leaves the size of flattened beach balls. The underside of one heavy, limp leaf dripped a sticky substance on the back of Jesse's hand. He scrubbed his knuckles against his jacket for several seconds as he led the group. Sweat poured down his face and back, and he wished he'd left the jacket back on the ship. But then the knives in the pockets ticked like silverware, and he tapped them again, a reminder of one defense. He also ran his fingertip along the daggers holstered to his thighs. He was ready.

Though he thought the jungle was almost completely silent, except for the low hum in the distance, he realized that there had been slight whooshes of slow air, or minute movements in the swaying vines and fanning leaves. In an instant, there was no sound. It was as if a giant dome closed over the jungle and hushed it. No gurgles of mud, no ticks of insects above them, no whistle of an occasional wind. And then,

WAM!

Something sliced across their path, something huge and scaly and slithering like an anaconda.

"Whoa! Back up," Jesse shouted and shoved his back into Kate. She toppled into Hayden, and the three did an awkward crab walk backwards as more lightning-fast hybrids snaked out of the jungle and slithered into the path, up the trees, and circled behind them.

Hissssssssssssssssssssssssss. Hissssssssssssssssssssssssss. Snuff, snuff. Hisssssssssssss.

Their call was constant and reverberating; it sent Jesse into immediate chills. He stood, his knives up, but all he could see were shadows along the path or on the fleshy pink trunks of the plants. He'd get a flash of pink roots burrowing into the ground, a flicker of purple scales, and then nothing. Kate and Hayden panted behind him; both were on their feet and holding weapons in the air. Hayden made large circles with his Terrian blade that glowed blue. He pumped his arms, and he started to glow as well. His light wasn't as brilliant as it had been on Earth when he fought the Bull of Heaven, but it was enough to show them some of the terrific, reptilian figures that were hanging on the trunks above them.

Enormous creatures, some kind of mix of a small dinosaur, snake, and a ram with hollow black eyes stared down at them. One twisted its massive body around a tree trunk, letting its snake tail cascade down. Claws on four feet clung to the pink trunk, causing something to ooze out of the plant and slide down like maple syrup. Its broad, muscled back and shoulders looked like a giant Gila Monster's, but a sail of scales stretched from its neck down its spine. The scale wall heaved up and down with the creature's rattling breaths. Book-casing a hideous and furred face on the ram's head were swirled horns the size of truck tires. Its teeth snapped up and down, and in one horrifying second, it dipped one claw in the plant ooze and drew it up to its mouth, slurping at the syrup like its claw was a salt lick. It moved its blank, black eyes in the direction of Hayden's light, stretched its arms out, and sailed down. Right toward Jesse.

CHAPTER EIGHT
HELLO, HYBRIDS

In many cases, Terrian plant life and animalia have been tampered with, in a fundamental genetic way. This began with Shaari domination over two thousand Earth years ago. Shaaris took over Liquid Light control by force and instituted planetary changes in terms of genetic modification. The most notable was the coded changes to eye, hair, and skin color to match factions (yet, it was the Gelf leader, Impala, at the start of their regime in the middle of Earth's 20th century, who chose the reddish hues to signify Gelfs). This penchant for altering genetic coding was not new because it is the basis for our abilities to alter our body molecules with the catalyst of Liquid Light for space travel. Furthermore, the Shaaris began instituting genetic modification and cross breeding in animalia and plant life. The results are multifarious, some beautiful, some horrific, and some truly terrifying. Beasts and vegetation on Terria are true originals, and in some cases, terrific, as in the Earth meaning of 'exciting terror'.

"On Terrian Animalia and Vegetation,"
Keepers Data Update, Earth 21st Century,
Jesse Woods, translator

The hybrid, reptilian body with a ram's head sailed down from the fleshy plant trunk; its fanned back caught air and propelled it in circular motions toward the ground, right to Jesse's location. He started to run forward, but the thing picked up speed and whirled like a helicopter with its snake tail whipping leaves on its way down. In seconds, the hybrid was on top of him. He stabbed with his knife, hit air, and groaned. The thing's belly collided with his chest, and he fell backward, struggling to regain balance but righting himself to a standing position. He glimpsed his friends, who had moved in both directions in the jungle, fighting their own ram-headed lizards.

"Aurrgh," Jesse hollered and ran back toward the hybrid. Once on the ground and straddling the path like a Komodo Dragon, it didn't look as big. But then it chomped its jaws and dug its claws into the mud, and it didn't matter how big the thing was—maybe the size of a jacked-up tiger with a double-length of tail—Jesse feared the horns, grinding jaws, and talon-like feet.

After dropping the shorter dagger to the ground, Jesse reached to his thighs and grabbed both knives. He pointed the blades and charged, which he regretted the instant he started. What would happen when he slammed into those curled horns? The words "battering ram" echoed in his head as he sprinted toward the beast, which was now pawing the path and breathing out thick swaths of smoke.

Great, he thought, smoke could mean fire.

The hybrid started to trot on its wide legs, and Jesse thought he should make for the flank, away from the ram's head and the snake's tail. He looped right, tripping momentarily on a vine, regained his foothold, and charged. He stuck one knife into the side, just below the sail, but the tail lashed around and slapped his back while the beast let out a hiss and groan, a sound like a cow's moo, but distorted and rattled, like something got knocked loose in its stomach. Jesse made the mistake of hanging onto the knife rather than withdrawing it and falling to the ground. Now that the beast stomped and trotted, he wasn't sure how to get off it. It ran forward, frothing at the mouth and yowling in pain. Its tail whipped back and forth, sometimes knocking Jesse on the back so hard he slammed into his knife handle and the scaly muscles. His head throbbed with pain, and a trickle of blood ran into his mouth. He had to get off the thing, but it shook so hard, he had to time his fall. On the backswing of the tail, he pushed his legs against its side and yanked the knife out. He fell to the ground with a thud and rolled to clear the beast's claws.

Jesse scanned the area for Kate and Hayden, but all light from the tubers and roots had retreated with the plant creatures. Hayden's glow was gone as well. Where were they? He took a fast breath and faced the hybrid a second time. Despite its injury it was readying to charge again, so Jesse put both knives in front of himself. Within seconds the beast was upon him.

Flash. Bang.

The ram head hit him in the gut, and he flew—one, two, three—why was he counting? The jungle twirled above his head, and he flipped awkwardly in the air before hitting something. His sight went to black and then spotty yellow flashes before he realized he didn't hit ground. His jacket had caught on the left horn of the beast, and it turned its head in odd revolutions to try to shake him free.

Jesse tried to fixate on some point to gain control, but everything was spinning like on a tilt-a-whirl. He had managed to clutch his two knives, so he focused on shoving his flailing legs around the hybrid's neck. After five kicks and swings, he clamped his thighs around the neck and wiggled his jacket off the horn. It wasn't running any longer, but it squirmed and slapped that tail, pissed as anything.

What now? Jesse wanted to kill the frigging thing and find his friends. He glimpsed more shadows skulking in the jungle, but he couldn't focus long enough to see exactly what lurked there. Finally, exhausted and barely hanging onto the horn and neck, he thought of his hands. He lit them as if healing and placed his right hand on the beast's back. In his mind's eye, he saw the rollercoaster of intestines, five stomachs, blood surging through pipe-sized veins, and then the delicate pumping of the beast's heart. He knew this was where he wanted to strike. One of its stomachs was already compromised from his first attack; he wanted to slice the heart out of it.

Without thinking too hard about it, Jesse wrapped his arms around the hybrid's neck and slid his body along the sail on its back. It was slowing, maybe because of the extra weight or the injury, and every few steps it huffed, spitting pinkish foam from its maw, and then it fell belly down to the ground. In an instant, while it rested with feet splayed, Jesse cupped his fingertips on the rim of the sail and dropped his feet down. He crouched low and when the beast hoisted itself again, Jesse stepped under it, just below the head, and drove both knives into the heart. He meant to leave the knives in the thing and roll out from under it, but he was in an awkward backbend position. His hand went back just as the hybrid groaned and fell, nearly smothering Jesse. Luckily the knives were there to break the fall, the handles making an odd tent, but Jesse's legs were jammed under the dying beast.

Gross, he thought. The hybrid's jowls quivered, sending out blood and foam right next to his face. How would he get out of this? The only thought he had was to heal it with his hands, so it would get the hell off of him, but this seemed counterproductive because then he'd have a refreshed and newly mended monster to kill again. He tried to concentrate hard on a message, but his mind was numb and worried. A slithering sound echoed from the jungle and that same *Whirr, tick, tick* he had heard right before the hybrids descended. More were coming.

The hybrid's breathing grew labored and erratic. Jesse knew it would die in minutes. He looked up in the canopy and saw enormous bird creatures with monkey-like faces. They circled and cawed a haunting trill. He shivered and closed his eyes.

In trouble, he sent a message to Hayden and Kate.

The beast let out one last wail and died. More weight pressed on Jesse's legs and its girth settled on the teetering knife handles. Soon all its mass would sink down. Jesse tried to conjure the rage he had felt when he set his command chair on fire, but then what? He'd hurl fire and black goo at the beast's dead body, which would only catch him on fire as well.

Crash!

The monkey birds were dropping like hail, and soon more ram-reptile beasts were surrounding the body. Jesse tucked his head beneath it and struggled to get a knife from his jacket pocket.

I'm coming, Kate said in his head.

Jesse couldn't see anything but flashes of color as the ram-reptiles and the monkey-birds fought. Hisses and snaps echoed somewhere behind him. This was it. He was going to be picked over like a dead carcass. The feather flapping from the monkey-birds whooshed air on the right of his face. He struggled to free his feet again, but now the dead hybrid seemed even heavier.

One nasty little ram-reptile, maybe a younger one, slid next to Jesse and started chomping on the dead beast's side. Jesse yelled and twisted his body away from the jaws as much as possible, but its pointy claws easily tore at the flesh. Every couple of times it dug into the hybrid it sliced Jesse's shoulder, drawing blood. The smell of blood and spilling organs was so thick in the air Jesse gagged on bile in his mouth. He was afraid to vomit it up in case the beast liked puke, so he swallowed it back down and nearly passed out from the taste.

"AAHHHH," Hayden yelled somewhere behind Jesse. A blue light flashed and faded, flashed and faded.

Suddenly the blue light scaled a tree. Jesse craned his neck to the left and saw Hayden digging two daggers into a tall trunk. He made a quick climb up as three ram-reptiles started after him. The plant swayed and screeched like an animal dying; thick pink syrup, or blood, oozed down its sides. Hayden struggled in the slick, cursing and kicking his feet at the beasts.

Then out of nowhere cloud cover filled Jesse's line of vision. Everything was amber-purple-pink smoke. He coughed at first and thought a fire had engulfed everything. He struggled more beneath the creature, his eyes stinging, his shoulder throbbing, and his feet trapped and cramped.

The smoke stopped smothering him. He breathed normally and miraculously the hybrid lifted. As soon as he could manage it, Jesse rolled out from beneath it. He put his one hand over his head for protection and grabbed for a knife with the other. But he didn't need the knife. He looked up and saw that each beast was cushioned in a puff of smoke. Kate held the orb in one palm, her other in the air, and somehow managed to put each beast, whether monkey-bird or ram-reptile, into a smoke puff. Even the ones pursuing Hayden drifted off in their own clouds.

"That's what I'm talking about, Kitty-Kat!" Hayden shouted and slid down the wailing plant trunk. "We can't fight these things without using our powers."

Jesse looked up and saw brilliant circles of purple and shimmery red circling in the sky above them. Dragons.

He tried to stand, but his ankles were broken. He lit his hands, placed them on his ankles, and healed them in seconds. Kate's eyes were closed, and her body started to sway slightly from her efforts. Hayden rushed up to Jesse. Blue sweat from *The Glow*, mixed with a little blood from a few cuts, poured down Hayden's face. His pant legs were torn, but other than that both of Jesse's friends appeared unscathed.

"Kate, can you hear me?" Jesse asked.

She nodded.

"Can you move?"

Another nod.

The dragons above them screeched and roared, making reverberations like thunder.

"Come on, we have to get to the desert circle," Jesse shouted.

"I wonder what lovelies await us there," Hayden said.

Jesse guided Kate by the arm. She opened her eyes, but they stared straight ahead in concentration. Her lips quivered, but she followed as Jesse pulled her forward through the jungle.

Hayden took the other arm. The two hunched together and moved as fast as possible with the meditative Kate between them. As soon as a beast made a motion toward them, Kate instantly flicked her free hand and put them in smoke puffs. Soon hybrids were hovering in clouds all around them. Some floated just above the ground, some coalesced near the tops of the tall plants, and others drifted like odd talismans right in front of them.

"Okay, this is creepy," Hayden whispered.

"Yeah, I just worry about the strength this is draining from her," Jesse said. "And she can't put those circling dragons in smoke puffs, can she?"

"Dunno, but for now, they're only circling. Maybe they'll stay away."

"Doubt that," Jesse said. After a loud roar and a peculiar mechanical clicking ahead of them, he added, "Let's see if we can pick up the pace."

Though Kate didn't answer, she responded by jogging between Jesse and Hayden. Each cradled an arm while she balanced the orb in one palm, and the three did a panicked run toward the desert rim. The circling dragons were descending with each wide loop above the tree line. Jesse chanced a longer glance as he jogged.

"What are we going to do?" he asked. "I count at least ten."

Kate's knees buckled, and Jesse grasped her by the waist. He lit his right hand and placed it on her forehead, hoping his healing powers would give her strength. But she had crossed into a deep trance-like state, and Jesse's efforts did nothing.

EEEEEEE – Pow!

One of the dragons shot daggers of metal from its mouth. The spears hit the ground a few feet in front of them.

Dazed and barely standing, Kate waved her hand to the sky.

"No!" Jesse pushed her hand down. "Hayden, she can't do any more. We need her to be able to communicate with Eruk and Palk."

"I know, I know. I got it," Hayden paused and closed his eyes. For several seconds, which felt like hours to Jesse, Hayden stood stock-still waving his hands in front of himself. More daggers came like rockets from the dragons, but they bounced in midair and spun off. Jesse saw a pack of them slice through one of the dragons after rebounding. The luminescent beast let out a screech like crunching metal, and then it fell and slammed into Hayden's protective barrier with a massive electrical crack.

"We need to run," Jesse said, looking at Hayden.

"Yeah," Hayden said and panted. "You were right about the different atmosphere thingy. This feels much harder here than it did in Chicago." Hayden opened his mouth to say more but stopped and bent over at the waist.

"You okay?" Jesse asked, his arm around Kate who lolled sideways in weird loops. "Damn, she's fading."

Hayden stood. "Let's run. You gotta carry her, bro."

Jesse squatted and threw Kate over his shoulders. A soldier's carry, he thought. She was light, but her unconscious state made her feel like wet clothes in a laundry bag. The orb dropped from her hands. Hayden picked it up and stowed it in his backpack. Like bursting soap bubbles, the hybrids in smoke puffs popped, their massive bodies dropping to the ground or hitting the barrier in heavy bangs. Hayden and Jesse couldn't help but flinch every time this happened. The ones within the barrier fell to the ground and shook themselves out, ready to charge and attack. Hayden quickly threw up mini shields, each effort an obvious struggle.

"You can do it, Hayden!" Jessed shouted, but he worried every time Hayden stumbled. "We're almost there. I'd say don't worry about the beasts, but we know differently." He cursed himself internally for thinking they could fight these creatures without more training. He bit down hard on his lower lip and concentrated on holding Kate in place; on his right side her slim legs dangled without life, and on his left her thick braid thwacked his chest.

Come on, come on, he thought. They had to make it. He pumped his legs harder and thought of Sofia. They had to make it.

Finally, they broke through the jungle circle by sliding down a slope of mud. Jesse balanced Kate awkwardly on his shoulders as he slid and paddled his feet in front of himself in order to have a little bit of control on the descent. Hayden collapsed and did a half-slide, half-roll down the hill. They stopped at the bottom, Jesse colliding into Hayden's back. Kate slipped to his right side, so he cradled her in his arms like a baby.

Kate's eyes were closed, and her face shone with sweat. Small cuts lined her neck. It was the first moment he had to examine her, so he unzipped her jacket and saw more bloody slashes along her collar bone. None were deep, but he couldn't help but light his hands and mend the wounds while Hayden caught his breath.

"I'm toast, bro," Hayden said. He slid his body into the sand. There was an actual line between the two habitats. The mud of the jungle pressed right up next to the sand. Hayden dug his hands in the sand and let some drop through his fingers. "So weird. All the sudden—desert."

"Yeah, and a nasty drop along some rocks if we're right about where we are," Jesse said. He put all of Kate's weight onto his right arm and squatting legs, and then he pointed. "The drop off to the ravine should be right up ahead. We'll need a little light so we don't fall."

Hayden dimmed a light lasso and aimed it in front of them. Jesse heaved himself and Kate to his feet. Every step toward the ravine felt like he was carrying lead in his feet and arms. Behind them he could still hear the electrical surges of dragons hitting the barrier Hayden had left secured, and beyond that the whirring ticks of the reptile-rams and the screeches of the plants sounded in muted tones.

The desert ring was silent.

A chill ran all along Jesse's skin. The sweat that covered his body because of the humidity in the jungle now felt cold in the arid, night air. Hayden must have felt the same because he shook a little as he held the light.

"Are you okay?" Jesse asked.

"Weak as hell," Hayden said. "Cold as hell, too."

"Yeah, Dante's hell was all ice," Jesse said. "Lucifer's giant bat wings made such a wind it froze everything. So he was the cause of his own demise—"

"Bro, I'm shaking like Jell-o, could you just—"

SQUAWK. SQUAWK.

The sound came from the ravine. Hayden and Jesse crouched but continued forward. Soon they came to the slope of rocks that led to the Valley of the Beasts. Both teens stood —Jesse still holding Kate — on the cusp and watched by the small glow of the lasso.

Horrific hybrids, mostly bird creatures, circled above the valley or ran along the base of it. The most in number were giraffe-sized flamingo creatures with rows of monstrous teeth sticking out of their beaks like the serrated teeth of angler fish. Their long legs had spiky plates running from their thighs to their large, webbed feet. They were bending and eviscerating some bodies, and then tossing their long necks back to swallow huge chunks whole.

Snakes as long as school buses slithered and made tunnels of sand while hissing and spitting out some kind of gooey substance. Half bears, half eagles soared and landed. They were fewer in number than the flamingo things, so they only struck at the carcasses that were already picked over.

"Isn't it beautiful," Hayden said. He huffed and sank to his knees.

"Here." Jesse lit his hands and held Hayden's shoulder. Heat ran through his friend's body until he stopped shaking.

"Thanks. At least now I won't shake to death."

"We need to wake Kate up, so she can send a message to Eruk and Palk, to let them know we're here, and they can go into hibernation," Jesse said. He glanced down at Kate who was still unconscious, looking like she could sleep for days.

"Well, you know what'll do it, our prince," Hayden said with a smirk.

"No, I don't. I already tried to rouse her with my healing hands."

"Kiss her. That'll probably do the trick."

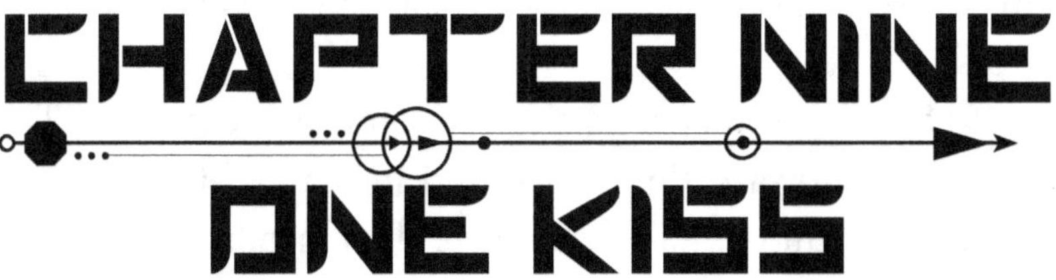

ROMEO [To JULIET]
If I profane with my unworthiest hand
This holy shrine, the gentle fine is this:
My lips, two blushing pilgrims, ready stand
To smooth that rough touch with a tender kiss.
JULIET
Good pilgrim, you do wrong your hand too much,
Which mannerly devotion shows in this;
For saints have hands that pilgrims' hands do touch,
And palm to palm is holy palmers' kiss.
ROMEO
Have not saints lips, and holy palmers too?
JULIET
Ay, pilgrim, lips that they must use in prayer.
ROMEO
O, then, dear saint, let lips do what hands do;
They pray, grant thou, lest faith turn to despair.
JULIET
Saints do not move, though grant for prayers' sake.
ROMEO
Then move not, while my prayer's effect I take.

Romeo and Juliet, Act One, Scene Four,
William Shakespeare

"I can't," Jesse said. He glanced down at the unconscious Kate in his arms.

"What do you mean, you can't?" Hayden asked. He flicked his right hand toward the jungle, and his tunnel barrier hissed. He waved his hands in a circle above their heads, and Jesse felt a surge of warmth. The domed barrier around the three of them gave off a shiny pale blue light.

"I can't kiss her. I said I wouldn't. I couldn't. Not until I resolve things with Sofia. And Kate agreed."

"What?" Hayden stood up and paced their sphere of protection in the desert circle. "You gotta be kidding me, right?" He didn't wait for an answer. He lit on, "You better frigging pucker up and drop the 'I need to be better than everybody' bull. Think of it not as kissing or some sin against your hostage girlfriend, but as fixing a problem. That should play right into your savior complex."

"What? What's that supposed to mean?" Jesse wanted to stand, but Kate rested awkwardly in his lap. Plus, he was afraid he might hit Hayden. Savior complex. "You can go f—"

"Don't. Don't say anything, Jesse. I'm sick of this. 'No powers, Hayden. No smoke puffs, Kate. We need to fight the hybrids with other skills.' And we listen to you. All. The. Time. Now listen to me, you proud-ass control freak, do whatever you need to do to wake her up: kiss her, feel her up, give her—"

"Stop. Just stop." Jesse took three long breaths and thought of the Tao. He had to calm down before he said anything to Hayden. "Okay, I know. She has to wake up. It's just, I can't betray Sofia again. And, dude, she isn't even awake to say she wants to be kissed by me." His voice was soft. He stared at the sand as he spoke. Outside their bubble there were more squawks and thrashes coming from the Valley of the Beasts.

Hayden stood over him. Jesse heard him breathe short, angry breaths. Then Hayden slumped to the ground next to him and started running the sand through his fingers. They sat there for a few moments in silence.

"One thing I've tried to do since we started chasing the Gelfs is put myself in your shoes," Hayden started. "I keep asking myself what if it was someone I cared about in that red bubble with the Gelfs? Since I've had many girlfriends, the closest I could get to sending me into total rage is my little sister, Norah. If anything happens to her in all this, I'll be certifiable."

More silence. Jesse focused on the sand running through Hayden's fingers.

"What I wish you'd do right now is stop thinking of yourself."

Jesse looked up, right into Hayden's eyes. He was about to respond, but Hayden put his hand up.

"I know you think you're only thinking about Sofia, but I'm your friend, bro, and you're not. It's about you, your inability to save her. You can't stand that. If I'm wrong, you would've had this whole chastity-belt-on-the-lips thing going on back on Earth. But where was this 'I can't betray Sofia' stuff when you and Kate were getting cozy in the janitor's closet? No, man, I'm shooting you straight on this one. Think for once that Kate and I have families, too. We have people we're fighting for just like you do. Ours may not be with the Gelfs, but honestly, we don't know if any our families are okay right now. We need to do this, and we need to do whatever it takes to fight these bullshit gods."

Jesse sighed. Everything felt heavy: Kate, his clothes, and his own muscles seemed to weigh him down even more. Was he really such a control freak? He never realized this about himself until now. But now was the perfect time to see it: Before Hallia revealed that the Shaaris were playing gods for humans he had a very structured life. He scheduled his time, whether work outs, practice, studying, and even time with family or Sofia down to units that filled the days. Why was he so dependent on such order?

He watched Hayden's hand making circles in the sand. He smelled sweat and a mossy, moldy scent coming from all of their pores.

It was his father. He didn't want to lose control. Ever. A lack of order got you killed. It meant you failed people. It meant that you were open to being hurt again and again. He wanted to be dependable and solid. Not temperamental and unpredictable like his dad was. How else would he succeed? How else could he fight his own genes and the worm in his thoughts, a buried fear that he could be unveiled as a hood. Or worse, deep down, if he lost his neatly ordered life, then the true Jesse would emerge, and that person was volatile, erratic, and quick to put himself above everyone else. That was what his dad did. Why else would he go cruising with his brother and his brother's friends who were so far into dealing smack they couldn't see their own asses? He hated himself for it, but no matter what, he didn't want to be like his dad.

"Okay," Jesse said, staring at Kate.

"Okay, what?" Hayden asked. He rubbed his hands together and stood up.

"Okay, I'll get her to wake up, but you need to turn around. Don't look at us."

"Right. No problem." Hayden turned around and stared out of their bubble at the Valley of the Beasts. Within seconds he was whistling.

"And no whistling. Please, this is awkward as hell as it is."

"I'm mum as a bunny," Hayden said and chuckled.

Jesse looked down at Kate and sighed. Of course, he wanted to kiss her. She was … beautiful. And smart. And sexy. And mysterious. He allowed his thoughts to meander even more. He let his eyes drink her image in: He studied the sheen of sweat and dirt smeared across her face, the stray hairs that had fallen out of her tight braid, her round eyes, long eyelashes, full mouth, aquiline nose, the fine bones and jaw line, the straight neck dipping down to her chest. And beneath the layers of clothing and weapons, her smooth skin waited for him to touch it. Her muscles and tendons were ready to tense or relax by the touch of his fingertips. He let himself really feel how her weight sunk into his thighs. His legs, his groin, and then all of his body started to feel electrical and energized. He slipped his arm under her shoulders and brought her face to his.

Her lips tasted like salt. At first nothing happened. Jesse had a small moment of panic, like he had trespassed on a territory he was no longer allowed. Why was it that all those fairy tale dudes could kiss any sleeping princess and act like it was the most normal thing in the world? In actuality, the act left a residue of violation. What if she didn't respond? He was the one who said they shouldn't kiss or anything because of Sofia. Kate had agreed right away. Maybe she was moving on. Maybe it was all an apparition.

Then she moved. Her legs rubbed the sand, and her arms came up. In one delirious moment, her hands grabbed the back of Jesse's head and neck, her fingers like lasers of heat and pleasure. Her lips responded, and she kissed him back. At first it was soft like running a flower petal along your lips, but then she picked up steam and kissed him hard. He was getting excited, too excited.

She pulled back and wiped the stray hairs from her forehead. Her blush was visible in the dim light. Her breaths were short and expectant.

"You kissed me," she said.

Hayden started whistling and examining the weapons in his leg holsters.

"Yeah," Jesse answered. "I hope it's okay. I had to wake you up."

"Oh." Her face fell for an instant, but then recovered its usual openness. She sat up and scooted off of Jesse's lap. He missed her as soon as she was gone.

Jesse wanted to say so much to her, but where to begin?

What should he say? He hated to see her downcast face even for a moment. Instead of saying anything new, or providing any words to make her feel better, he repeated, "I hope it's okay. That I kissed you."

"Yeah, it's fine."

"Fine?"

"Nice, oh, I don't know," she sputtered, and her face was beet red. "Jesse, I get it. It's what we do. I guess."

Hayden was humming loudly at this point. Hum. Whistle. Hum. Whistle.

Jesse played Kate's words in his head: *I get it. It's what we do. I guess.* She felt it too. She wondered if all this attraction only served one purpose: to bring about powers. Then what? Would they become like trick animals? Then they'd only kiss to blast aliens. It was all too weird.

Hayden turned around and saved them from more discomfort.

"Hate to interrupt, but we have a suicide mission to complete here," Hayden said.

"Right, I'll tell Eruk and Palk we're safe and waiting for them above the Valley," Kate said and shut her eyes.

Hayden gave Jesse a big smile, almost like he was proud of him. What was that about?

Several minutes passed while Kate communicated with Eruk and Palk.

She opened her eyes and said, "It's done. Now, we wait."

For what felt like hours, no one said a word. Hayden was getting antsy. He started to jog in place and then he ran in tight circles around their sphere. Kate sat cross-legged and occasionally closed her eyes. When she opened them, she stared straight ahead and took long meditative breaths. Jesse had gotten used to her trance-like states since they'd started out in space. He didn't want to break her concentration, but he was starting to get anxious himself. And gazing down at the shadows the beasts made or listening to their terrifying sounds only made the anxiety worse.

"Any news," Jesse asked when Kate looked less like a monk at morning prayer.

"They are in hibernation. I can feel them, but I'm not able to communicate," she said.

"Okay, glad to hear that the meditation hour is over because I want a clear, detailed plan. We obviously realized that no matter how much it drains us, we have to use shields to get them out of that snake pit. Agreed?" Hayden asked.

"Agreed," Jesse and Kate said at the same time.

"Jinx," Kate said and smiled like a kid. Jesse's tension eased a bit.

"Good, so we see Eruk and Palk being dumped, and I float in a bubble like the one I made in the Hall of Gems at the museum. Damn, that feels like years ago – the Hall of Gems. Anyway, with this darkness and the loose security I go unseen. I get the boys and float the three of us back through the jungle, hopefully, and to the ship," Hayden said. He bounced up and down, and their protective bubble quivered. Between breaths he said, "That means you two need to motor through the jungle in a smoke bubble, or I try to carry all of us. Sound like a plan?"

"I worry about the drain of energy for both of you. If we separate, what if any of the three of you need medical help? How can I get to you?" Jesse asked.

"We won't," Hayden answered. "We'll be cruising as fast as my bubble butt can carry us. I'll put it in Glow gear. Anyways, I can send a message if things get gooney. The more I think about it, taking all five of us, that freaks me out more. I've only expanded a sphere to float with the three of us. Now isn't a time to do an experiment. Don't you think?"

"True." Jesse had no counterpoint.

"I feel more energized than I have since Earth," Kate said and blushed again. She touched her hand to her face and coughed. "I'll be able to carry all of us if you want me to."

"Really?" Jesse asked. "I didn't think you could direct the smoke puffs like Hayden can the bubbles. Yours seem just to hover."

"Yeah, that is true. It is a different sort of risk. I've been working on directing them, but I guess I shouldn't say I could do it when I've never tried it with people inside of it. And look what floating the hybrids did to me. I should just shut my mouth." She smiled and stood.

Jesse felt odd being the only one in the sand, so he stood up as well.

"We need a tether," Hayden said.

"Right," Jesse answered. "I see where you're going. Somehow Hayden needs to tow us while we're in the smoke puff. That way we'll move faster and expend less energy."

"You two will move faster," Hayden said. "But not me because I'll be dragging your sorry smoke butts."

"I don't need you," Kate said and laughed. "And I might add you wouldn't have a butt to speak of if I hadn't saved it. Or it would be up a plant trunk in a hybrid's mouth about now."

The three laughed, but something caught Jesse's eye. He turned toward the Valley of the Beasts and watched two enhanced Shaaris struggling with a tarp that was the length of semi-truck. Each of them used one hand to pull it taut between the two of them. In the other hands they held long staffs with brightly lit tips. When the hybrids swooped in to attack the carrion on the tarp, the Shaari guards struck them with a crinkly current of electricity or some kind of charged power. Finally, the two enormous beings dropped the tarp unceremoniously and flew back to the ghetto complex.

"Hayden, go now!" Kate shouted. "Eruk and Palk are out there."

CHAPTER TEN
TOW ROPE

Breaking the deep sleep that filled my head,
A heavy clap of thunder startled me up
As though by force; with rested eyes I stood

Peering to find where I was – in truth, the lip
Above the chasm of pain, which holds the din
Of infinite grief: a gulf so dark and deep

And murky that though I gazed intently down
Into the canyon, I could see nothing below.
"Now we descend into the sightless zone..."

The Inferno, Canto IV:1-10, Dante Alighieri,
Robert Pinsky, translator

It all happened so fast. Kate yelled at Hayden to get to Eruk and Palk. Hayden began swirling his arms in dervish circles. There was a scurry of sound and flashes of shadow in the Valley when their light from the protective bubble went out.

"I'll get a tether," Jesse yelled. Without thinking, he dashed into the jungle realm, just on the edge of it, and pulled up a dead vine curled at the base of a plant trunk that looked a lot like a palm tree on Earth.

He struggled with the slick weed, and when he found it was attached to the back of the plant's trunk, he took out a knife and hacked it off.

The screams from the plant were so ear-piercing Jesse's body shook for a second.

"Come on, Jesse," Kate shouted.

He yanked at the final tendons, and gooey pink puss oozed from the wound. That word actually flashed in his mind: wound. These things were definitely more animal than plant.

"Dude!" Hayden shouted.

Jesse ran to the desert ring, tying one end of the vine around his waist and stumbling in the sand.

Hayden was already in his bubble and ready to go. Jesse had a real moment of panic when he saw Hayden drifting there. He could see Hayden. The Shaaris weren't like average humans who couldn't see the bubble. They really weren't certain Shaari guards wouldn't happen to look at the Valley just as Hayden hovered there and retrieved two dead Browns.

Jesse tossed the vine anyway. Hayden's hand materialized outside the bubble. He caught the vine, squished both back inside, and tied his end at the same time one of Kate's smoke puffs surrounded Jesse. Kate's power kept him secured in the smoke puff to an extent. Jesse couldn't see Hayden, but the pull on his waist jerked in sporadic and powerful yanks. He felt Kate behind him in the puff but found it difficult to speak. He wanted to tell her to hang onto him because he feared being plucked from the smoke puff, causing him to dangle from Hayden's bubble.

What kind of force would he have to strain against once Eruk and Palk were with Hayden? Jesse hoped Hayden already had them, but he couldn't see a thing. Kate's power was stronger since the kiss; he could feel her guiding the smoke just a little. He sensed her breathing behind him, letting out long breaths and small murmurs. Finally, he drew from her strength and spoke: "You need to hold onto me." He twisted in the vine to make the knot sit on his back. "I'm afraid I'll get pulled out."

"All right," she answered. Her voice was a whisper.

She leaned in and grabbed his arms. He grasped hers in the same manner. Once in a while, when the vine tugged, Jesse's legs drifted up, and Kate held tighter. They looked like two skydivers doing a stunt.

Just as when Kate had put him in the puff after his explosion in the main cabin, nothing choked him. The smoke engulfed him but didn't smother. Instead of smelling bitter, with a suffocating persistence, Kate's smoke was deceptively peaceful. And she controlled it—that was for sure. He doubted he could get free of her hold, nor would he want to. Her face came in and out of the smoky haze and had an airy look of serenity at one moment, and then stern concentration in the next frame. Several peculiar minutes passed in this manner: They floated; Jesse felt a tug at his waist, the plant goo smelled really moldy and coated his jacket through to his shirt, and often his legs drifted up until Kate opened her eyes and grasped his shoulders harder. Sometimes her nails dug in, the points oddly stimulating, and then she'd glance up to his face, her eyes half-obscured, but brightly lit like candlelight.

The vine tether started to slacken and then yank. A glob of goo soaked Jesse even more. His back ached, and his legs twitched uncontrollably from the force. His heart rate raced.

"Jesse, Hayden's fading."

"Does he have Eruk and Palk?"

"Oh, yes," she said, surprised, "we're almost to the ship. Should I try to move ahead and tow them?"

"No, you're doing a great job, but if you try to lead we could drift for a long time, and we need to wake those two up. Remember what they said about the risks of hibernation: Some kind of coma could come on if we don't get them up soon."

"All right, then what?" she said, holding tighter as the vine pulled and slackened, pulled and slackened.

What could they do? Should they simply ride it out? If Kate could monitor Hayden's progress and they held on like the devil, then maybe they'd plop down in front of the ship just in time. But what if Hayden totally passed out like Kate had done? It wasn't like Jesse's kiss would wake him up. Jesse bit his lip. That was it. Not a kiss, but a connection. Why couldn't he "heal" Hayden using the vine as a conduit? It was worth a try. His healing powers hadn't worked with Kate after she had passed out, but if he caught it early enough, maybe it would be enough.

"Can you hold me so I can send my healing stuff to Hayden through the vine, before he totally passes out?"

"Yeah, sure," she answered. "How about you twist around again, and I'll hold you while you're on your back. Kind of like how you'd learn to do the back float," she said. Her voice quivered with excitement or nerves; Jesse couldn't tell.

The vine's movement became more erratic more frequently. Jesse wiggled while Kate kept her hands on his shoulders, armpits, biceps, whatever she could grasp, while he turned to have the front of his body facing the knot around his waist. He leaned back into her arms and felt hot right away: Kate cradled him, her legs drifted in front, and his fell in line with hers. Once in position, she latched her body to his by putting her arms through his armpits and clasping her hands across his chest. If he thought too hard about where each part of her body connected with his, he would have an erection to match the vine jutting out of his abdomen.

"Okay, I got you, Jesse," she said.

Oh, yes, she did, he thought.

Jesse closed his eyes, lit his hands—the amber glow dim in the smoky air—and put them on the vine. The vine hissed and jerked. He imagined his power running the length of it and reaching Hayden's waist. He saw the light race along the plant like electrical current. He felt it hit Hayden's waist, and he actually saw Hayden then, just like Kate was able to. It was only for a few seconds, but there he was sitting in his bubble, slouched over, with one hand in the air. Eruk and Palk were unconscious on both sides of him. Their lifeless bodies swayed within the bubble. It reminded Jesse of Sofia. He concentrated more, and a thrust of power jolted from him, through the vine, and right into Hayden. Hayden's eyes shot open, and he woke, alert. Then Jesse lost sight of him.

Two things happened at once. The once dead vine began to shriek and move, and the velocity of their entire caravan increased double time.

"Augh," Jesse yelled and released his hold on the screaming, twisting vine around his waist.

"Is it the vine?" Kate asked. Her voice was so steady.

"It's got some juice again, that's for sure. It's going to break some of my ribs if we don't get there soon."

The strength of the vine's hold grew tighter and steadier. Could he suffocate this way? Or damage internal organs? A rib cracked, and then another. Jesse gasped and put his hand to his side. He tried to light his hands to heal the break, but more jolts came, causing him to buckle from the pain. Breathe, he told himself, but hardly any air seemed to come in. It felt like he kept having the wind knocked out of him, and there wasn't a damn thing he could do about it.

Vine trouble, Hayden sent a message to his mind.

Oh yeah, Jesse answered back after a few more seconds of excruciating pain.

"Hang on there, Jesse, we can make it," Kate said.

How was her voice so calm? Jesse wanted to tear at the vine and scream, but he couldn't do anything but writhe and try to "talk" to Hayden.

Cut it? Hayden asked.

Yeah. Cut.

Before he knew it, the plant was hanging like a loose belt. He didn't waste any time untying his end and flinging the thing out of the smoke puff.

"Are you okay?" Kate asked. She still cradled him like a baby, and all he wanted to do was sleep. He let himself catch his breath, and then he lit his hands and healed his five broken ribs in seconds.

"I'm okay," he answered. "Can you see Hayden? Is he all right?"

Kate closed her eyes for a few seconds.

"He looks hurt, Jesse. I need to guide our puff to the ship to help him."

"Right," Jesse said. Before he could move, she hugged him tighter to her body and kissed the back of his neck. Pin prickles ran from his ear lobes to his shins. He didn't want to move or miss anything.

"I had to," she said. But then she didn't say or do anything else for what felt like an eternity. Jesse stayed in a reclined position, paralyzed yet uncomfortably excited, waiting for her next move. It seemed that they were moving in the same direction they had been, but there was no way to tell.

No more kisses came, and soon Kate's hands fell from his chest. Her head, which had been behind his right ear, slid down and flopped onto his shoulder. He turned to hold her up because she was out again from the strain. Now what? He kissed her frantically, but nothing happened. Total panic set in after multiple tries with kissing, healing hands, and the combination of both didn't work. He was not at all aroused any longer. He was scared.

You there? He tried to reach Hayden.

He waited in the smoke puff for an answer while Kate rested lifelessly in his arms. No answer came. How was she keeping the smoke puff intact while unconscious? Her subconscious must be working in overdrive, and if Hayden was out, too, that meant he and Eruk and Palk were out of their protective bubble, or Hayden accomplished the same subconscious skill as Kate, making them secure in the bubble. This would really drain his friends, and reality sank into Jesse as being the only one conscious among the five.

What now? He couldn't even get out of the smoke puff. And if he could, then what would he do? Should he try to talk to Kate? Tell her to release them. Then he could at least haul them back to the ship. Through the jungle. Yeah, right, he thought. He'd never last without Kate's help with the puffs.

"Kate, if you can hear me at all, please wake up," he said. He remembered his mother telling him that she always spoke to coma patients in the ICU because she knew they could hear her. Maybe this was the same.

"Kate, you're asleep and I tried to wake you up, even my kiss didn't work," he said, trying to make his voice light. "Hayden's out, Eruk and Palk are out. Maybe out of the bubble. And I'm scared that if I don't find a way to get them back to the ship, they'll die. And if our puff pops over the jungle, I'm afraid ..." His voice actually quivered. This was so hard for him to admit weakness, to ask for help. Suddenly tears started down his face, and he didn't try to choke them back. He kept talking. Maybe talking would save them. "If we land in the jungle, Kate, I'm afraid I won't be able to save you. And I can't bear to think of that. I can't watch you die in that jungle, Kate. Please, wake up. We have to do this together. I need you. Please."

Jesse hated how he sounded almost whiney, like a petulant child, but he was desperate and alone. She didn't wake up. He gave up talking for a while and stroked her hair. He tried a few messages to Hayden, but he didn't answer. Jesse stared down at Kate and rubbed the dirt and sweat from her face. She looked so peaceful. Maybe he should try to sleep too. Maybe they could all slip into a dream state and never wake up.

He wasn't sure how long they drifted until he finally dozed off. He went in and out of sleep and then woke to an odd sensation. The contours of the puff were changing. At first he thought the sides were contracting, and they were for a few seconds, but then they expanded. He floated up with Kate in his lap. Was it dissipating? This was it. They were dead in the jungle. Then the smoke puff grew so much, Jesse saw that there was something in front of them. He tried to move to it, but there was no controlling his movements in the puff. He simply waited until he could make out what it was.

Hayden's bubble came into view within a minute. The smoke pulled it toward Jesse and Kate until Jesse could touch the iridescent sheen. He saw all three boys slumped inside of it.

"Great work, Kate!" Jesse shouted and hugged her lifeless body. He was so proud of her. She did hear him. And she managed to move the puff unconsciously. Were they out of the jungle rim now and near the ship?

Before Jesse had another thought, the puff evaporated. Jesse and Kate plopped to the ground; she was still out. He looked up and saw the marker for where they parked the ship. Hayden, Eruk, and Palk were out of the bubble and smoke as well. The three teens lay in random sleeping poses in the furry moss just on the edge of the jungle circle.

Jesse heard movement behind him. The hybrids were coming.

CHAPTER ELEVEN
STIM MACHINE

Terrian brain chemistry is similar to human, but we have opened pathways humans have not explored. Humans only use thirteen percent of their brains. Mind expansion, in combination with catalyst agents such as genetic modification materials or Liquid Light, enhance brain activity and propel kinetic, telekinetic, or linguistic abilities to what humans view as godly powers. Our roles as humanity's gods for thousands of years fell in line with our superior technological and anatomical advancements. And yet, there is much to learn from the human brain. There is resilience and an untapped emotive center Terrians have lost sight of in our years from the Ancients' ways. We have become the lost ones. For all the opened pathways in our brains, we are soulless and searching.

"A Note on Brains," Keeper Data Update, Earth 21st Century, Jesse Woods, translator

Jesse wasn't sure where his strength came from. The whirring, ticking sounds from the jungle realm spurred him on that was for sure. Right away he closed his eyes and opened the ship door with his mind. The blinking lights from within the belly of the entryway beckoned him. He kept his eyes on them as he hauled each person to safety.

Without thinking, he picked up Kate first. He ran with her in his arms, set her down just inside the main cabin, and ran back for Hayden. Hayden was thin, but pretty built. With all the weaponry, he weighed even more. Jesse slung him over his shoulders and ran as fast as possible. He practically flung him in the door because he heard a screech above him.

Eruk and Palk were both light. Jesse guessed they hadn't had enough to eat in a very long time. He had one on his shoulders and was about to take off when two ram-reptiles lumbered out of the jungle. They spat and huffed at Jesse. One pawed the ground, and Jesse knew it was readying to charge.

"Not this again, you mixed-up cow," he said and pulled on either Eruk or Palk. He didn't know who was who, but he knew he had to haul them in together before they were attacked.

His body pulsated with adrenalin as he back peddled toward the ship. He had pure determination and the slow komodo dragon legs of the ram-reptiles on his side. One was faster than the other. It ran toward Jesse, its teeth chomping close to Eruk's or Palk's feet.

"Augh," Jesse yelled and turned. He sprinted up the ship's ramp and threw both Eruk and Palk into the main cabin. The ram-reptile was right behind him on the ramp. Jesse pulled a knife from his jacket and threw it. It stuck right between the eyes of the beast. The creature shook its head back and forth. The other one was doing odd circles around the base of the ramp; Jesse feared it would charge next.

"Get off!" he yelled and clapped his hands together. The ship shook in response. The ramp quaked so hard, the injured hybrid fell on its backside and slid down the ramp.

Jesse didn't stop. He ran to the main cabin, concentrated, and closed the hatch with his mind. In a flash, he saw outside the ship, an image in his mind, where the ramp retreated back into the bottom of the ship.

The next problem was getting all four to the medical room they had set up on level two. Terrians apparently didn't need stretchers because there was nothing like that on any part of the ship they had explored. He put Eruk or Palk over his shoulders and took off to the lift to level two.

After about one minute of running, his legs gave out from fatigue. He stood and focused on the lift at the end of the long, sterile hallway on level one. How would he ever get them all there? Why hadn't he planned for this?

"AAAHHHH," he shouted and sprinted again. He reached the lift and leaned his entire body against the cool metal wall while it sped to the next level. Thankfully, his destination was two doors down on level two.

Once at the door to the medical room, he slapped the control button and the door unsealed with a welcoming blow of air.

"Here, I'm going to call you Eruk until I know who's who," he said while lifting the slight body of the Terrian onto one of the beds. At least the room was enormous and set up to sleep about twenty people if needed.

Jesse had all of his equipment prepared on trays below monitors and buttons. Everything was written in Terrian text, but he read that like English now, so it didn't matter. He felt for Eruk's pulse but was not surprised that it wasn't there. He found the pads that connected to the electrical stim machine and hooked them to Eruk's brain and heart. He hoped that there was no miscommunication with Kate on all of this, or he would have a dead boy on his hands, and no way to save everyone else at this point. A chill ran through his body at the idea of being alone on this ship on Terria.

"No way, Eruk. You're coming back, dude, or I'm going to die trying." He started the machine and waited a few seconds to be sure Eruk didn't go into cardiac arrest. Then he found the largest bed sheet he could and ran back to the main cabin.

This time he dragged Palk on the bed sheet all the way from the main cabin to the medical room. The Terrian's thin form sat on the end of the sheet, and Jesse wrapped the other two corners around his shoulders like a cape and ran. His make-shift sled moved fast on the sleek floors. One time Palk rolled off, but Jesse righted him quickly and took off again. An image of his little brother Dorian flashed in his mind. The night before the tornado on Earth, Dorian wore a towel like a cape and slid around the kitchen on baking pans. He was getting ready for Halloween. Was it Halloween on Earth now? It should be. They had been traveling for over two weeks, give or take. Was his family safe? Please, he thought, as he bent over on the lift with Palk slumbering in the sheet, let them be alive.

He got Palk settled and went back for Hayden and Kate. He was determined to be finished, so even though it slowed him down, he put both of them on the sheet and hauled them to the medical room.

Should he hook them up to the stim machine as well? He could only guess if it would work, but he figured he would hook Hayden up first and monitor his vital with his hands lit for healing. If anything went wacky, he would heal him and come up with a different plan. Hayden was the logical one to go first, because of his strength, The Glow, which aligned him with Terrian physiology to some degree, and he wasn't Kate. Jesse couldn't risk losing her on top of all of this. He felt a little guilty when he hooked Hayden up, the guinea pig, but Jesse did it anyway.

Jesse's hands were lit with one placed on Hayden's head and the other on his heart as the stim machine thrummed. Hayden's vitals were normal, except his brain activity was in a cycle very much like REM sleep. It stayed this way for several minutes, but Hayden also didn't wake up. Eruk and Palk had told Kate it could take them several hours to regain consciousness. Would it take as long for Hayden and Kate? Would it even work? Hayden wasn't dying from the stim machine or becoming brain dead, so Jesse went ahead and hooked Kate up.

Jesse lingered over Kate's heart, letting his palm rest there, feeling its even beat. Her skin was clammy and cool. He wanted so badly to let his fingers slide down to her breast. He could trick himself into believing it was an attempt to wake her. But he knew the move was cheap and out of bounds. But he wanted to do it. He really did.

He stuck the stim leads to her chest, ignoring her breasts, and hooked up her head as well. Then he sat down to wait and monitor everyone's vitals on the screens lining each one of their beds. For a while he read their vital results one after the other, but his eyes got heavy, and his stomach growled. A worry that the ship somehow became uncloaked during their rescue mission ate at the back of Jesse's mind. He didn't dare leave his patients, so he started by taking his com-link out and placing it in his ear as if Hayden or Kate was at the controls. It seemed like a silly move, but it got his mind right about searching the main computer terminal in the medical room. In his previous study, Jesse thought it was kept with Terrian anatomy, genetics, and history of epidemics, but he wondered if there was something he missed. He first looked at the main database of all the readings the Keepers had stored. His hope was that from there, he could access the main controls. If something went terribly wrong, he wanted to be able to see it.

Not one of them had thought that this could happen. Jesse felt the level of their arrogance acutely. Of course, it was a possibility that all or most of them would be injured beyond Jesse's ability to heal. He vowed to read more and learn more so that this would never happen again. More than anything he wanted to be able to save his friends. Always.

After an hour of searching, Jesse did it. He hacked the main computer to feed into the medical room station. They were still cloaked, and there were no readings of any lingering hybrids outside the ship. The creatures had retreated to the jungle rim, and Jesse hoped they'd stay there. He checked everyone's vitals again and sat down. His entire body throbbed with soreness. The sweat on his clothes had cooled and now he shivered. He looked once more to be sure everyone was indeed still unconscious, and then he stripped down to examine his own body, using one of the mirrors in the locker area to check on his face and neck. The one little nasty hybrid had got him really good there. There were slash marks all down the right side of his face and deeper scratches on his neck and upper pectoral muscle. He absentmindedly healed those, wondering if any would scar, while he rummaged through his locker for clean clothes.

After finding some black pants and the least girlish black pullover, he put his healing hands on his abdomen, analyzing the fused ribs and sewn tear of his stomach. Everything looked good inside, but he had a whelp as wide as a tire ringing his torso. He smoothed his hands up and down from his chest to his pant line and around his lower back, and then he put on his clothes.

He devoured five packs of Terrian food: one supplement bar he had gotten used to on their trek on Earth and four other packs that were labeled as *Fortica* and *Vegimma*. After reading the nutritional information on the back, he surmised they gave him some protein and some kind of vitamins. Both tasted dry and brittle. The *Fortica* in particular had a terrible aftertaste, like he had eaten some bad seafood. He chugged two cylinders of water, checked everyone for the umpteenth time, and sat down to read more on Terrian anatomy.

He read an entire booklet on blood flow in Terrians and was ready to move onto the nervous systems, especially the brain activity in relation to sleep, when there was a tap of metal hitting the floor.

Jesse sprang up to face either Eruk or Palk sitting up in his bed. He was the one who looked a little Asian by Earth standards. His brilliant almond-shaped eyes blinked, and his shortly cropped hair stuck to his scalp. He didn't say a word but pointed to his mouth. Jesse rushed over and handed him a cylinder of water. The one he had been calling Palk sipped it and nodded a thanks.

"Can you speak?" Jesse asked.

Palk coughed and cleared his throat. He drank a few more sips of water.

"Yes, thank you, Jesse. We are indebted to you and your friends."

"You're welcome. I have to ask. Are you Eruk or Palk?"

"Eruk."

"Oh, I had it wrong. I didn't know who was who, so I had to call you something," Jesse said and found he had no idea what else to say to this very sincere-looking Terrian.

"Yes, I am Eruk. I need to check on Palk. Oh, and Kate and Hayden, are they all right?" he asked, straining to rise from his bed.

"Easy there. Palk is fine. I've been checking his vitals constantly, and if you woke up, he should do the same really soon. I didn't know what to do with Hayden and Kate. They were totally out from all the strain of using their powers. My err, my healing hands didn't work, so I connected them to the stim machine as well." His face got hot. He felt like Eruk could read his mind, which meant that when Jesse said, "healing hands," Eruk knew that kissing Kate didn't wake her.

"But they have not woken?" Eruk asked. This time he did put his feet to the floor. His naked feet were cracked and scarred. Jesse couldn't help by stare. It looked like there were open wounds that ran from the top of his feet and disappeared down the sides.

"Wait, Eruk. Let me see your wounds. See if I can heal them," Jesse said.

"Thank you, Jesse," he said and stood. "You may do this later. Now I need to connect with Kate before it is too late for your friends."

"What?" Jesse's heart raced instantly.

Eruk was at Kate's side. He didn't look up as he spoke, "As you have guessed, this atmosphere is different from Earth's, and so are many other things here. If your healing didn't bring them back, I fear that they may not come back at all."

CHAPTER TWELVE

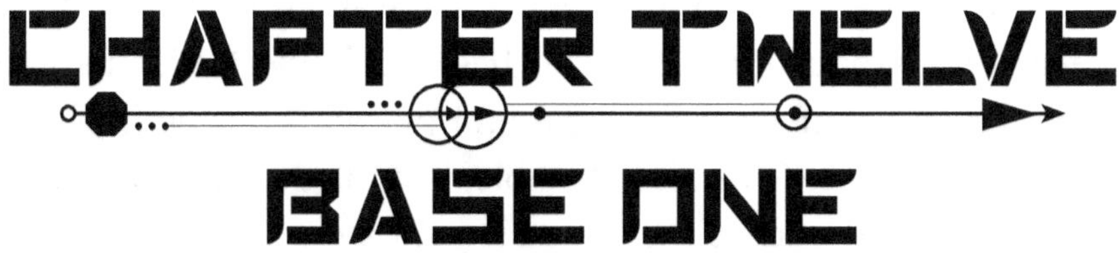

BASE ONE

THE WORLD is charged with the grandeur of God.
It will flame out, like shining from shook foil;
It gathers to a greatness, like the ooze of oil
Crushed. Why do men then now not reck his rod?
Generations have trod, have trod, have trod;
And all is seared with trade; bleared, smeared with toil;
And wears man's smudge and shares man's smell: the soil
Is bare now, nor can foot feel, being shod.

And for all this, nature is never spent;
There lives the dearest freshness deep down things;
And though the last lights off the black West went
Oh, morning, at the brown brink eastward, springs—
Because the Holy Ghost over the bent
World broods with warm breast and with ah! bright wings.

"God's Grandeur," Gerard Manley Hopkins

Maybe it was all the exertion on his body, or the news that Kate and Hayden may not wake up, but whatever the cause, the room spun so fast that Jesse had to hold onto the side of Kate's bed to steady himself.

Eruk put a hand on his wrist. Jesse wanted to rip away out of fear and exhaustion, but Eruk had the kindest eyes he had ever seen. Jesse lit his right hand and placed it on his forehead to stop the vertigo. Once he felt stable, he pulled away from Eruk, respectfully, and went to the other side of Kate's bed.

"They have to wake up. We'll find a way," Jesse said.

"May I have a moment?" Eruk asked.

"To do what?"

"Explore Kate's mind," Eruk said. His lips were dry and cracked. The olive skin of his face had small scars at the jaw line that could have been from acne if he was human. Kate was right; these two could definitely be two teens walking around on Earth. But there was an otherworld-quality to how Eruk held his head, slightly to the side, and his whole body moved so fluidly, almost like he was drifting just above the floor.

"Do whatever. If you think it'll help her," Jesse answered.

Jesse watched intently as Eruk placed one hand on her forehead and closed his eyes. Nothing happened for several minutes. Jesse got tired of doing nothing but stare at each of them, so he went back to reading. That didn't last long. His pulse was quickening and sweat dripped down the sides of his face. He peeled his pullover off and found a short-sleeved shirt to put on instead. Eruk didn't see any of it; instead, he stood immobile with his head tilted and his hand on Kate's forehead.

Palk stirred in the far bed. Jesse ran to his side and watched as the other Terrian twisted in his sleep, threw off the light blanket, and sat up, his eyes wild with questions.

"You must be Jesse," Palk said. This alien was thin, but Jesse could tell he did some kind of exercise to build what muscles he had. He had the same brown skin, hair, and eyes. His hair was also cut short, but he let some facial hair grow down the side of his face to make a half-grown peach-fuzz type of beard. While Eruk's nose was wide and his eyes welcoming, Palk's nose was long and pointed. And his eyes weren't kind; they were angry and combative. Palk woke up ready for a fight.

"Yeah, I'm Jesse. Hey there, Palk."

Palk scanned the room, his eyes resting on Eruk.

"Kate and Hayden are hurt," Palk said.

"Yeah, we have to wake them up. They used too much of their powers in the jungle and desert circles." Jesse could tell Palk wouldn't thank them for this.

Palk stepped off the bed, winced momentarily, but bit his lips and stood up. He went straight to Eruk's side and held his free hand. Eruk's eyes fluttered acknowledgment. Jesse felt itchy and peculiar. He did not want to watch them together; even the intimacy of two guys holding hands seemed so strange to Jesse.

Get a grip, Jesse, he told himself. It was only two people holding hands. Two people, no big deal. Then Palk lifted Eruk's hand and brought it, palm up, to his mouth for a kiss. Jesse cringed and hated himself for it. He was grateful both of them had their eyes closed. He wished he could just get over himself.

Jesse rocked back and forth on his feet for something to do. Eruk opened his eyes and hugged Palk.

"We made it," Eruk said. Tears settled in his eyes but didn't run.

"Yes, how is Kate," Palk answered. He was all business. No tears in Palk's eyes.

"We need to do all we can to help her get back to Base One," Eruk said.

"Base One?" Jesse asked, grateful they weren't touching any longer.

"Yes, Base One is the starting point of all mental acuity, where all humanoids exist most of the time. Telekinetics are able to go much deeper very often, but Kate has slipped too deep. If we don't get her back soon, she'll stay in this state. My guess is Hayden is the same, but it's different for him. He's a Kinetic. Palk, examine Hayden, and Jesse and I can work on Kate."

"What are Kinetics and Telekinetics? I mean, I can guess by the words. I've read some about this. I'd like to know more—"

"May I explain later, Jesse?" Eruk asked, his eyes soft and clear of tears now.

"Yeah," Jesse said. "Of course."

"I will check on Hayden," Palk said. "I suggest Jesse take the lead with Kate, considering their link."

"I am aware of that," Eruk said with an edge. It was the first time Eruk used anything but an even tone.

Palk looked at Jesse, "What is her most erogenous touch point?"

"Excuse me?"

"What is her most erogenous touch point?" Palk repeated and stared at Jesse like he was the village idiot. "How do you stimulate her the most?"

"I," Jesse started, but found he didn't know what to say. His entire body felt hot and tingly. How in the hell could he answer that?

"You mean you don't know?" Palk said.

"Look, I can't talk to you about that stuff. It's between me and Kate."

"Palk, they are new to all of this. Remember. Leave him alone."

Palk stormed over to Hayden and put his hand on Hayden's forehead.

"Please excuse him," Eruk said. "He has much he wants to accomplish."

"Yeah, well, so do I."

"We know. We will wake your friends, and then we will plan a way to retrieve Sofia." Eruk closed his eyes again to think. Jesse was sick of the whole meditative-state thing already with Kate. If these two did the same thing all the time, he'd really go insane.

"What about the orb?" Eruk asked. "Is it lost in the jungle?"

"No, it should be in her bag over here. I'll get it."

Eruk placed the orb on Kate's stomach and set her hands on top of it. He put both of his hands over her forehead. "Now, please touch Kate wherever you think it will be most effective for stimulation."

What the hell? Of course, Jesse wanted to do anything to wake her up, but he was more than uncomfortable. And what was he supposed to do? Casually slip his hand on her ass? Up her shirt? How did he get here? He was also troubled because he really didn't know where to touch her. He knew where *he* wanted to touch her, but what would she want? What did Kate like? Who was she? His yearning to discover her in that moment was so great, his own body felt like a black hole, a vast endless void of want.

"Okay," he said. He decided on her neck. She had kissed the back of his neck in the smoke puff, and it drove him out of his mind. Plus, her neck was long and perfect. He touched her neck. Heat pulsed at his fingertips.

The three were linked for a few minutes. Jesse sensed that Palk had finished with his assessment of Hayden because even though his eyes were closed, and his hands were on Kate's neck, he could hear a distant tapping of fingers and the click of changing computer screens. Palk wanted answers and had already started searching for them.

Soon Jesse's body got tired, like his muscles and tendons had relaxed so much they were atrophying. If he bent his knees, he was certain he'd fall to the floor. He was so intent on staying standing that he didn't realize Kate's eyes had opened until her hands were touching his and then Eruk's. She sat up and yelped with joy.

"You're here! We did it. You're all right, right?" She hugged

Eruk and as soon as Palk was at her side, muscling in next to Jesse, she embraced him to.

Jesse moved to the foot of her bed and smiled. He would have liked the first hug, but at least she was alive and speaking. He wanted to examine every inch of her, to be sure her below Base One state didn't damage any brain or system activity, but now seemed like the wrong time.

After the hugs and gushy sounds from Kate, the medical room fell silent. She caught Jesse's eye, and he thought his legs would give out again. How was it possible for her to look so radiant after everything they had been through in the last few hours?

"Thank you, Jesse. For everything," Kate said and blushed crimson.

"Of course," he answered. His voice cracked like a kid new to puberty. "But Hayden hasn't woken up." He walked over to Hayden and lifted his eyelids, to do something. He hoped he would see the usual gleam, but he didn't. "Eruk, is there any way to use his dagger, or something, like we did with Kate? Maybe he would feel strength from it and wake up."

"I know what would work," Palk charged in. "Liquid Light. He has *The Glow*. He's a Kinetic. It would work, I'm sure of it."

"Ah, yeah, I don't have any Liquid Light," Jesse said.

"I do not think that is the way, even if we had it," Eruk said. "It is the first and foremost corruption point for our people."

"Your refusal to use it will only make us weaker, less of a threat to the Inner Sanctum Shaaris and high-ranking Belites. We need it," Palk said and started pacing. His cat crawl around the room reminded Jesse of Hayden, making a heavy pit sink in his stomach.

"Arguing about the same point we have been debating for years will not help this situation. I highly doubt the Keepers stocked any Liquid Light on the ship," Eruk said.

"It's worth it to look," Palk countered and stopped inches from Eruk.

"Okay, you two," Kate said, "please stop. I agree with Eruk on the corruption thing, but if there is Liquid Light on this ship, then it'd be good to know about it. We can think about how or if we'll use it later."

Somehow Kate didn't miss a beat on the discussion between Eruk and Palk, but Jesse's head was spinning. He knew controlling Liquid Light, the Terrians' means to enhance and travel at faster-than-light speed, kept the Shaaris in power. Being able to travel to Earth so efficiently also gave them the opportunity to infiltrate Earth's population and guide its religions. Was there more he didn't know about? If so, if Kate knew more, why hadn't she told him?

The two Terrians nodded in silent agreement. So apparently Kate had the same effect on them as she did on Jesse and Hayden: Her *enough* voice shut them up, too. How did she do it? Just when he thought she couldn't get any more mysterious to him, here she was doing it again, making him think about her all the time. He had to get back to his very own Base One Rage, he thought. That way he wouldn't lose sight of getting Sofia back or killing as many Gelfs as possible. He also wanted all the god-pretending Shaaris to blow up in goo and fire as well.

There, he thought, he was on the way to rage again. Any more time near Palk would help too.

"We all have maps and inventories of the different levels and rooms on these hand-held screens," Jesse said. He found his and handed it to Palk. If there was Liquid Light to be found, Jesse had a feeling Palk would be the one to find it. "We haven't located any, and it isn't labeled anywhere on the maps."

Palk snatched the screen and began scanning it. He muttered

to himself and then spoke in a Terrian dialect to Eruk whose brow began to furrow.

"Yeah, I can understand you too, Palk," Jesse said. "To answer your question, we would have no reason to lie to you about the Liquid Light. And just so you know, you can throw Proto-Terrian, Ancient Terrian, Middle Terrian, and all faction dialects at me and I'll figure it out. I see you use a mix of a Belite dialect and some of the Ancients' linguistic colloquialisms. Like I said, it must be brain-use expansion, because you can put any text in front of me and I'll devour it in minutes, and with different languages it doesn't take any time at all to read it, hear some audios, and I'm damn near fluent. So, no secrets on this end, and none on yours. Sound good?"

Jesse relished in the looks of surprise. Kate knew he was reading like a fiend, but he hadn't gone into too much detail of how quickly he was picking up on other languages, including alien ones.

"Basheer," Eruk said, which was the equivalent to an "Amen" at his Baptist church back home. Palk scowled but nodded affirmation. For the first time since they got on the ship Jesse actually felt proud of himself.

"I'll find the hidden store of Liquid Light because I believe the Keepers would not have let us fight this war without it," Palk said.

"Oh yeah, since we're on the topic, and before you go questing for the stuff on this ship, I think it would be a good idea to track down a Keeper or two after we get Sofia. They could clear up a lot of questions, especially about the Shaari agenda," Jesse said.

Palk was already across the room and almost out the door when he answered, "Not possible, Lingua-Shaa, they're all dead."

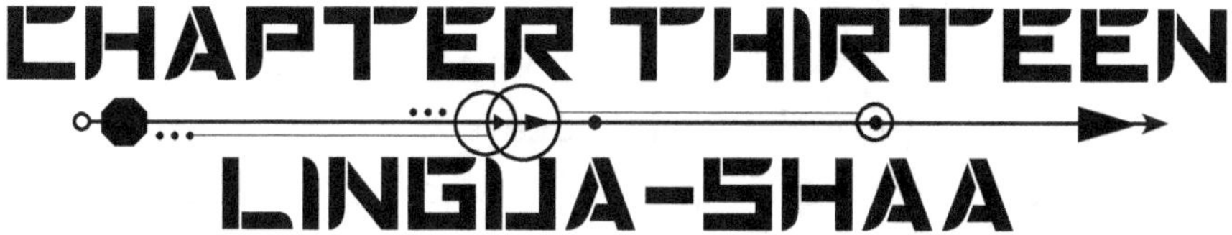

CHAPTER THIRTEEN
LINGUA-SHAA

Jesus said, "Let him who seeks continue seeking until he finds. When he finds, he will become troubled. When he becomes troubled, he will be astonished, and he will rule over the All."
Jesus said, "If those who lead you say to you, 'See, the kingdom is in the sky,' then the birds of the sky will precede you. If they say to you, 'It is in the sea,' then the fish will precede you. Rather, the kingdom is inside of you, and it is outside of you. When you come to know yourselves, then you will become known, and you will realize that it is you who are the sons of the living father. But if you will not know yourselves, you dwell in poverty and it is you who are that poverty."

"The Gospel of Thomas," The Gnostic Gospels

Palk's comment that all of the Keepers were dead sent a jolt through Jesse. Before he had a chance to ask anything else, Palk was out the door of the medical room with ship map in hand. Jesse turned to Eruk who was now doing his eyes closed/hand-on-the-forehead thing to the unconscious Hayden.

"I don't mean to interrupt," Jesse said.

"Jesse, don't," Kate said and hopped out of bed. "He's trying to reach Hayden through telekinetic speech."

"Didn't you hear what I just heard? All the Keepers are dead."

"Yeah, I heard it, but right now Hayden is the priority," Kate said.

He was getting tired of being told what to do. Kate scrunched her shoulders as if to say sorry in a sheepish way, and this infuriated Jesse more.

"Kate, I want Hayden to wake up just as much as you do, but Hayden would want to know this as well."

"Of course," she said in a whisper. She leaned in to watch Eruk like he was the frigging Buddha, but Jesse went on.

"There are so many agendas here. We need to figure all this stuff out. What happened to them? Do you think they died in battles?"

"Shhhhh," Kate shushed and watched Eruk more intently.

"No, I don't want to shhhhh. I want answers. Eruk, what happened to the Keepers?" Jesse raised his voice. Eruk's eyes fluttered. He opened them a slit.

"They were captured and tortured by Kerr, the Shaari leader. Not one Keeper would give up information on the power source. Most died under extreme torture methods. I heard of one who committed suicide. There is only one whose body is unaccounted for, but we do assume he is dead. You understand now why you were found in that tornado at your school. The Shaaris needed all the Youth Triumvirates to search for the power source because they had no way to find it."

Jesse scratched at his face and took two breaths to calm down. All dead. This Kerr sounded like a real crazed leader. Kate bit her lip and crinkled her brow. Was she mad at him for interrupting Eruk? A tendon of worry ran through Jesse, but he squashed it.

His priorities had to be getting answers, finding Sofia, and now helping Hayden. This list was growing, and he felt dizzy with the pressure.

"Wait a minute, how do you know all this? No offense, but you've basically been imprisoned in the ghetto," Jesse said.

"Yes, but you have to understand that despite the totalitarian control of Kerr, there is only one way for Shaaris to control Telekinetics. They have shields surrounding the ghettos, but we have found fissures to send out messages, like how we did with all of you through the orb. The resistance is growing. We have members in the Belite forces, one in the Elite Guard, and one, who is now dead, with the Gelfs."

"What's the Belite Elite Guard?" Kate asked. Finally, she was getting on board.

"Those are the Belite leaders who are trying to supplant the Shaaris. They want to take over god status for Earth inhabitants. They are just as corrupt and power-driven as the Shaaris. They are the ones you've encountered in battle. It is a small percentage of the Belites, but it has been enough to start battles here and on Earth," Eruk said.

"You add some Gelf nihilism, and you have the present Terrian factions. So the Browns are basically any Terrian from any of the factions who go against the present order in some way. Right?" Jesse asked. His mind was clicking at a furious speed.

"Yes, both Palk and I were raised as Belites in the Belite territory, rather than as servants for the Shaairs in their lands. We were made Browns the equivalent of two Earth years ago," Eruk said.

"Because of your love for each other, or was it more?" Kate asked, her voice shaky.

"Mainly for our love. Mono-loving, what you call homosexuality, is against the law. Also, my parents were Keepers, so they assumed I had sympathies for the Ancients' ways."

"So you're parents... they were tortured by Kerr," Kate said.

"Yes. As far as I know they both died while plants ingested their internal organs," Eruk said in a matter-of-fact tone.

Jesse was nauseated. He hated having the plant goo on his skin let alone inside his body.

"I'm so sorry," Kate said and embraced Eruk for a long time.

Jesse wanted to punch something. Nothing was available. Instead, he checked on Hayden's vitals for the millionth time. No change. Now he wanted the Liquid Light. He wanted to use it to wake Hayden up and then eat some to kill Kerr, Nosh, all the sanctums and inner circle Terrians. They had to die.

"Maybe if we try to talk to Hayden together, telekinetically, he'll wake up," Kate said to Eruk. Jesse felt invisible and ready to blow.

"Yes, it is worth the effort," Eruk answered. "Perhaps before we begin, since Hayden is stable, you will take a few moments to heal my feet. The pain has been excruciating," Eruk said to Jesse.

He had forgotten Eruk's bloodied, pus-filled wounds. "Of course," he answered, gaining some calm at the idea of doing something. "Sit back down and let me have a look at the bottoms as well."

Eruk sat and hoisted his legs up and pulled off his sandals, allowing the entirety of his wounds to show. Jesse had gotten used to some bad blisters and scorched skin with the burn victims at the Chicago battle, but Eruk's feet were heinous. Long cuts ran from his heels to his toes and wrapped up to the top of his feet. They hadn't been cared for, so infection had set in. Green and black pus had flowed and hardened around each section of sliced skin. Jesse immediately lit his hands and got to work. From what he had read, human and Terrian anatomies were similar enough he figured he could heal most wounds without feeling like he'd cause more damage. The internal organs made him nervous, but this obviously started as a superficial wound, so he thought he would mend it like the burn victims' skin he had grafted and repaired.

While Jesse worked on Eruk's feet for a few minutes, Kate brought him water and a few packages of food. Eruk sipped the water and nibbled on a package of what Jesse and his friends had started calling "Tree Bark Trail Mix." Eruk sighed with relief the whole time Jesse worked. His feet were healed with only a few visible scars before Eruk had finished his first pack of food.

"Thank you, Jesse," Eruk said.

"No problem. How did this happen?"

"It was a punishment. My pod leader found out I had been storing food rations for the Tens in our unit," Eruk said. He chewed more food in pinky-sized bites.

"Tens?" Kate asked.

"Yes, those are the children in the ghetto."

"Why are they called Tens?" Jesse asked. Maybe there were only ten kids there. He hoped there weren't many of them in the ghetto.

"That is the age of our youngest," Eruk said.

"You mean there are no smaller children than ten years in the ghetto," Jesse said.

"No, there are none who are younger. Children who are ten years, which are similar in age and maturation to children that age on Earth, are the youngest we have," Eruk said.

"Is it because of sterilization or because even Kerr has rules about kids? Does he let little ones stay with their moms?" Kate asked.

Jesse knew better, but he didn't want to bust in and answer that. He let Eruk explain.

"It is because of the enforced sterilization law Kerr put in place years back. It is also part of Terria's overall problem," he said.

Jesse knew about the sterilization from Kate, she must have forgotten, or her optimistic attitude wanted a different outcome, so she conveniently blocked it out. Why did this irritate him? What was wrong with him? His interest was piqued as well. Why else weren't there younger kids in the ghetto? He waited for Eruk to continue, but when he simply chewed more bark mix, Jesse had a snaking heat rise from his stomach to his head. He kept his voice as level as possible.

"Please, enlighten us, Eruk. What are you talking about?" Jesse asked.

"Enforced sterilization and reproductive damage due to overuse of Liquid Light has made it so there have not been any successful live births for over ten Earth years."

"So it's not just in the ghetto," Kate said. "You don't have any kids under ten on the planet, do you?"

"That's correct. But more on all of this later; we should really see to Hayden. Kate, you have a good idea. Let's both try to speak to Hayden," Eruk said. He hopped off the bed and tried his new skin out. His face widened in a smile. "You are an impressive healer, Lingua-Shaa."

"Thank you," Jesse said. "And just to make sure I understand you, what exactly is 'Lingua-Shaa?' I wasn't sure if Palk was insulting me or not."

"Oh, no. It is a high compliment. Our abilities fall into three categories: Kinetics, Telekinetics, and Linguists. We used to have Shaas, or healers, but not now. You are a rare gift, Jesse; thus, you import the rare name of Lingua-Shaa because you possess both healing and linguistic abilities. I wasn't certain of this until I met you, but there is no denying it. Terria has not encountered a species with your powers since the time of the Ancients."

CHAPTER FOURTEEN

ENKIDU AND GILGAMESH

> *"Hear me, great ones of Uruk,*
> *I weep for Enkidu, my friend,*
> *Bitterly moaning like a woman mourning*
> *I weep for my brother.*
> *O Enkidu, my brother,*
> *You were the axe at my side,*
> *My hand's strength, the sword in my belt,*
> *The shield before me ...*
> *Tiger and panther, leopard and lion,*
> *The stag and the ibex, the bull and the doe.*
> *The river along whose banks we used to walk,*
> *Weeps for you...*
> *What is this sleep which holds you now?*
> *You are lost in the dark and cannot hear me."*

"The Death of Enkidu," The Epic of Gilgamesh,
N.K. Sandars, translator

"The Tao gives birth to One./ One gives birth to Two./ Two gives birth to Three./ Three gives birth to all things./ All things have their backs to the female/ and stand facing the male./ When male and female combine,/ all things achieve harmony./ Ordinary men hate solitude./ But the Master makes use of it,/ embracing his aloneness, realizing/ he is one with the whole universe." Jesse read aloud from his hand-held screen. He had been sitting with Hayden all day, hoping the words of the Tao would wake his friend.

Multiple efforts with telekinetic speech, healing hands, and even setting Hayden's dagger in his hands hadn't made Hayden stir. Complete exhaustion forced Kate and Eruk to give up. One kept watch in the main cabin while the other slept. Palk had slept only a couple of hours and resumed his search for Liquid Light. He agreed to take a com-link to communicate with Jesse.

"Or maybe you want something else?" Jesse asked and flipped his screen to the *Epic of Gilgamesh*. He was so thankful the Keepers had included key spiritual and mythological texts from Earth's early civilizations.

"All right, I think we left off with Enkidu and Gilgamesh getting ready to fight the Bull of Heaven. Sound familiar? It should. You were in prime beast mode with the Belite bull back on Earth. Okay, here we go. 'When they reached the gates of Uruk the Bull went to the river; with his first snort cracks opened and two hundred fell down to death. With his third snort cracks opened, Enkidu doubled over but instantly recovered, he dodged aside and leapt on the Bull and seized it by the horns. The Bull of Heaven foamed in his face, it brushed him with the thick of its tail. Enkidu cried to Gilgamesh, 'My friend, we boasted that we would leave enduring names behind us. Now thrust in your sword between the nape and the horns.' So Gilgamesh followed the Bull, he seized the thick of its tail, he thrust the sword between the nape and the horns and slew the Bull. When they had killed the Bull of Heaven they cut out its heart and gave it to Shamash, and the brothers rested.'" Jesse scanned ahead and read that the gods curse Enkidu to die because the two friends killed a creature of the gods. He turned off the screen and put his head in his hands. He didn't want Hayden to hear that. Jesse believed Hayden could still hear him, and he didn't want to diminish any fight Hayden had in him to come back.

"You have to come back, Hayden," Jesse said in a low voice. "You can't leave me alone with all these meditating monks." It was the best Hayden-like line he could think of. He struggled more with something to say. He let his words ramble with the hope something would click in Hayden. "I used to play army men and make battlefields with Legos and wooden blocks. This was when I was five or so, when we lived in the city. One time I heard my mom outside my door, must have been a Saturday. I jumped under my dinosaur sheets and blankets and closed my eyes. You know that crazy feeling that someone actually doesn't see you when you play hide and seek, and you feel like you'll pee yourself. That was it. She was in nursing school at the time, but didn't have class or work, so I could smell the pancakes she'd made. Homemade. Damn, I'm drooling thinking about them, but hey, when you wake up you can try to make some. That bread you made was all right. Anyway, think pancakes, think cold tile floor in February, think hissing old-style radiators in those old-ass apartments. Mom walked in and instead of tickling me and saying, 'Made an army tank pancake for you, Jess-a-peak, you don't want to miss that,' her slippers dragged on the floor. She sunk into the bed, her weight like stones. She said, 'Daddy just got home, baby, and Uncle J.T.'s here. Let's stay in your room awhile. I'll play aliens and army with you.' I got out from under the blanket to see her. She looked tired. I told her I wanted to get up and eat. She said, 'Later. Not now. They're prowling out there and I don't want you near it. I'll make a double stack when they're gone.' I remember what I said to her. I said, 'You be the alien ship, and I'll be the hero.' I know this sounds weird, Hayden, but I can relive this memory like how I can see words I read in my mind after I'm done reading. Not all my memories are like that, but strong ones are. My mind is racing so fast since we've been on the ship; I can only calm it with exercise and reading the Tao. I wish you'd talk with me. It's weird cause I think maybe this memory was like foreshadowing in a book. Think about what I said. Strange, huh. Aliens. A ship, but me as the hero feels like a total stretch. Don't you think?" Jesse paused and breathed in and out. He wanted Hayden to wake up and laugh with him. Tell him he was one crazy Lingua-Shaa.

The room was silent with the occasional whirring sound from the stim machine they kept attached to Hayden even though it wasn't doing anything. Jesse put his chin in his hand and sat staring at Hayden's chest moving up and down.

"Wake up," he pleaded. Recounting the memory of his mother and facing the possibility of no Hayden made Jesse feel tired and actually scared, just like he felt that morning when his dad and uncle were drunk off their asses and whooping and hooting in the kitchen because pork rinds and beer were hilarious when watching cartoons. He cringed. Uncle J.T. was probably high as a kite. Jesse couldn't remember, and he never saw them. His mom had played with him in his room for a short time, and then she went out and kicked both men out. She'd teared up at the table, and Jesse had felt the weight of it all on his shoulders. He had vowed never to be like that.

Jesse felt like one of those decorated eggs his gran made at Easter. She poked these tiny holes on each end and blew out the yokes and whites of the egg. Then she decorated the shells with fabric and fake jewels. Keisha loved to help her. These solid people in his life made him feel safe. That no matter what everything would work out. Things would be all right. Hayden would make a laugh of whatever felt insurmountable or downright scary. His mom would stand up and kick out the bad guys, even if the bad guy was her child's father.

Jesse rubbed his eyes. His com-link buzzed in his ear.

"Everyone, this is Palk. I've located the Liquid Light. Meet in the medical room."

Jesse stood up in anticipation. "Great! Great, Palk. Yeah, bring it," he answered and turned back to Hayden. "Did you hear that? We have Liquid Light, and this is going work. I just know it."

Eruk was the first one to enter the medical room. "Is he here yet?" he asked.

"Ah, no. Not yet," Jesse said.

Eruk tapped his com-link. "Do not ingest the Liquid Light, Palk. Come straight to the medical room." Jesse heard Palk swear back over the com-link. Eruk cut him off and closed his eyes in the standard mental communication manner. He retreated to the far side of the room with a scowl on his face.

Kate appeared; she had dark circles under her eyes. Her hair was tied back in a long ponytail, but wisps popped out around her face.

"How is he?" she asked.

"No change," Jesse said. "I've been talking and reading to him. I hoped it would wake him."

"I'm sure it will help. I heard you when we were in the smoke puff, and I was out of it."

"You did?" Jesse said.

"Yeah," she said and twisted some of the loose strands of hair. "I heard you, and even though I couldn't show it right away, it gave me strength."

"I wondered. My mom always said her patients could hear her singing and talking to them in ICU," Jesse said.

Palk stormed into the room.

"I didn't ingest any Liquid Light," Palk said. Eruk walked over with his arms crossed over his chest. Apparently, body language was universal to the universe, Jesse thought. He almost smirked.

Palk went on: "I don't think any of you can argue with the need to give Hayden some. Correct?"

"Go for it. He's been out too long," Jesse said.

"I have concerns," Eruk said.

"Do the concerns have anything to do with Hayden?" Palk said. "Or are they on principle alone?

Jesse decided he kind of liked Palk. He was rough around the edges, but Jesse thought the edges had some heart.

"My principles do not fade away amidst individual need," Eruk said.

"Look, if this will wake Hayden, then we need to give it to him. He did fine with it in his system in Chicago," Kate said.

"Then most of us agree," Palk said and pulled out a metal case shaped like a tackle box. He opened it, and capsules just like Hallia had given to Hayden on Earth fit into layers of slots. The capsules looked a lot like the elongated bath beads in his mom's bathroom.

"Where was it?" Kate asked.

"On the weapons' level. One of the tables for cleaning and sorting weapons had a cross-section compartment. I came upon it by surprise. When entering the room, I observed thin indentations that were actually levers. Once I pressed those, the table opened, and the box was inside. There may be more tables like it, but I thought I'd bring this right away."

"Thank you," Jesse said and meant it. "How much should he take?"

"Again, I'd like to repeat that I have concerns," Eruk said. "Though Hayden had this on Earth, as you have all experienced, the atmosphere is different here, causing different effects to the same actions taken in your own atmosphere."

"I don't think it will be as much of a problem on the ship," Jesse said. "The climate controls are pretty standard, and they mimic oxygen levels similar to Earth. So if that's the case, then Hayden will be fine."

"There is also the question of corruption," Eruk said.

"You mean another dose of the stuff may make him sterile," Jesse said.

Palk cut in, "There is no evidence for such a reaction in humans, and it would take multiple uses over time to have such an effect."

"As you said, we do not know this for certain because there is very little data to draw from on the topic," Eruk said.

"You are being overly cautious," Palk said.

"And you too rash," Eruk countered.

"The Yin and the Yang," Kate said. "You need both opposites for harmony."

Jesse wanted to kiss her. Had she been reading the Tao as well?

"We are going to give him one capsule, Eruk, like we did on Earth. Jesse can monitor him. We'll all be here to try whatever it takes to bring him back. The three of us are a team." Kate took a capsule and handed it to Jesse.

"Can one of you show us how to inject this since he can't swallow it? I saw this done during a battle on Earth," Jesse said.

"Yes, of course," Palk said.

Eruk stood to the side while Palk poked a hole in the capsule with a syringe. After the contents were in the syringe, Palk went over to Hayden and injected the Liquid Light.

"Kate, Eruk, try mental communication again. Jesse, stay near in case something goes wrong," Palk said.

Jesse stood right next to Hayden's head and watched his eyes intently. Please open, he thought.

Hayden's body didn't react at first, but after several minutes, his skin took on a blue hue. It shimmered under the fluorescent lights.

Kate's eyes shot open. "He said your name, Jesse. I heard it in my head."

"Really? Great, okay." Jesse crouched next to Hayden's ear. "I'm here, Hayden, will you just wake up. You're giving all of us near heart attacks. Who's going to race with me if you're asleep? Although sometimes it's hard to tell if you're sleeping or not when we run."

Hayden's eyes flickered. His lips moved, but no sound came out.

"Sit him up and give him some water," Eruk ordered.

Palk rushed and handed Kate a full cylinder. She nursed some to Hayden's lips. Hayden's eyes opened, and he rubbed them hard with the palm of his hand.

"Better," he said. Jesse could have hugged him with joy. Instead he clapped Hayden on the back and smiled like a kid.

"Oh, Hayden, thank god you're awake," Kate said and held his hands.

"Doc, thanks for the stories," Hayden said. "And just so you know, I had no intention of being Enkidu to your Gilgamesh. Now get me to a training room so I can fly while this stuff is in my system."

CHAPTER FIFTEEN
GENETIC MODS

Large, multi-colored cats, ones that are larger than an Earth tiger on average, are popular pets on Terria, as are birds; the birds have vibrant plumage, and are not unlike Earth's male peacocks in incandescent feathers and size; however, Terrian pet birds fly like Earth's hawks. They can be trained to assist in battle maneuvers. These pets roam all habitations as freely as Terrians do.

"Pets," Keepers Data Update, Earth 21st Century,
Jesse Woods, translator

After spending a day recuperating, the group on the cloaked ship in the Outlands of Terria decided to meet in one of the cabins that looked like a conference room. Jesse was the first one to arrive. A long rectangular metal table sat in the middle of the room. There were fifteen chairs around it. He sat down. Why didn't the ship have any comfortable chairs on it? The best one had been his command chair, which was now a heap of burned metal. No cushions or wooden rockers existed anywhere on the monstrous ship. He tilted the springy back toward the ground and almost toppled backwards.

Hayden flew into the room. Jesse saw Hayden circle the ceiling and drift to the floor. His feet touched down like a superhero from a movie.

"Still flying, I see," Jesse said and sat up.

"Bro, this is so cool. I can understand the addiction to the stuff," Hayden said. "It's wearing off though. I can tell I'm done for awhile. May be done for good. Then it's back to feet all the time. Total bummer. Hey, but at least I'm here, thanks to you." Hayden slapped Jesse on the back in the manner that had become their signature sign of affection.

"Like I told you, Palk was the one to find the Liquid Light. And Kate and Eruk did their mind-talk thing with you. I just stood there."

"You were the one to sit and talk to me and read to me like I was in some kind of ancient texts seminar. I heard you, and I'll never forget it. Your voice led me out of the fuzz."

Jesse didn't know how to respond so he said, "Any time," which seemed more than lame. It was way too nonchalant, like something you say when you fix someone's tire. He was grateful when Eruk, Palk, and Kate entered the room.

Jesse pulled out his hand-held screen. "I thought we could all have these out and set to monitor the main computer." There were nods of agreement, and everyone found a seat near Jesse's end of the table and put their computers in front of them.

"I know I've been in the training rooms most of the time since I woke up, so thanks again everyone for helping me back to Base One," Hayden said and beamed. Jesse was so relieved to have that face back.

"Well, we need someone to figure out the laundry thing, and what would we do about food?" Kate joked. She also got up and hugged Hayden for about the fifth time. He'd been counting. Jesse hadn't gotten one embrace since back on the ship. They were in the

No-Fly Zone on touch again, and Jesse knew it was his doing, so it shouldn't bother him, but it did.

"Should we get started?" Jesse asked, mainly to get Kate back in her seat.

"Yes, we know you are all anxious to get Sofia back. Let's start the planning process," Eruk said.

"We have no way to plan without your help," Jesse said. "We had been trailing the Gelfs when we entered your atmosphere, but they disappeared right after we exited the Worm Hole. Our trail has run completely cold. And from what I've read, their headquarters are unknown and underground."

"You witnessed the phenomenon that has helped the Gelfs stay undetected since their inception. They have devised invisible tubular slides that move them from Terria's outer atmosphere to wherever they need to go to enter their domain," Eruk said. "We do have some information from a Gelf who was in the Demark ghetto for a few days. We took care of him between his torture sessions. He knew we were resistance members who follow the Ancients' ways, so he decided to tell us a few things, mainly because we showed him kindness, and he was nearly delirious at the end."

"What do you know?" Hayden asked. He couldn't help himself. He was making his body float up and down above his seat. Soon he hovered above the table like a genie just sprung from its bottle.

"We have coordinates of a possible entrance in the Outlands," Palk said. "But the coordinates only get us so far. Once in their complex, we have no idea how to find Sofia. The security will be strong. Nothing like the lax system in the Demark ghetto."

"I wouldn't call the hybrids lax, my friend," Hayden said and plopped into his chair from two feet in the air.

"We have the cloaked ship, but any shields we can make are seen by other Terrians. How will we move through the complex?" Kate asked.

"That is something I've been working on for the last day," Palk said. "You've met some of the Gelf creatures."

"You mean the friendly seven-headed dragon and the chimera. Such lovely pets they have," Hayden said.

"From what we learned from our informant, the Gelf headquarters has many menageries to house their beasts. Often, some of their tamer creatures, mainly bird-like or cat-like ones, roam the complex freely," Palk said.

"So they are like pets," Jesse said. "I've read something about that."

"Yes," Palk answered. "If we looked like some of these free-roaming creatures we could move about the headquarters unbothered."

"And I was missing Halloween," Hayden said. Palk gave a quizzical glance and continued.

"As you know, Terrians have advanced genetic modification capabilities. In fact, they are part of our birth rituals, or it used to be. For example, both Eruk and I were Belite born, so right after birthing our coloring – hair, skin, eyes – was modified to match the Belite standard color, which is gold. These hues were removed once we were captured and put in the Demark ghetto. Terrians can modify our bodies on a much larger chromosomal and structural level. I found such technology here on the ship."

"You're saying we can become a creature, say a cat or whatever the Gelfs might have as pets, and they won't know we're human or Terrain," Jesse said.

"Yes, that's exactly what I'm saying," Palk said.

"How long do the modifications last?" Hayden asked. "I can tell when the Liquid Light is starting to wear off, and then it's just – gone."

"This type of modification requires a partner to administer the injections for formation and the ones for re-formation. At least one of us would have to stay back to be ready to change us back to our present forms. It will not wear off. Some of the beasts in the jungle or the desert circles are actual Browns who have been altered."

"That's horrific. Do they remember who they are?" Kate asked.

"We can only guess. At first, yes, it is apparent from the modification demonstrations we witnessed that the Browns knew what happened to them. But if they become a new creature and live for more years as that beast, then we can guess they fully adapt to the creature's mental and physiological traits. No one knows for sure," Palk said.

"So, yeah, at least one of us has to man, or wo-man, the ship," Hayden said. He got up and started pacing the length of the room. Once in a while he surged upward and glided for a few seconds, but his time in the air didn't last long.

"Okay, so we change form. We move the ship to the coordinates, stalk it, and gain entry. Then we move around the complex, find Sofia, but then what? How will we actually get her out?" Jesse was sweating profusely at this point. He wiped his brow with the sleeve of his shirt. "I mean, this ship has weapons that could tear the complex apart. We obliterated some enhanced Terrians at the end of the Chicago battle."

"We must conclude that there would not be the same outcome if you used the weapons," Eruk said.

"What do you mean?" Kate asked and leaned in.

"The days after the Chicago battle, before we reached you telepathically, Kate, we did receive communications from our liaisons from both our Shaari and Belite contacts. There was a mad search for you, but more than anything else, key scientists in both camps actually came together to adapt to the weapons' strength. At this point we must assume that Shaaris and Belites have genetically modified, most likely because of the pliability and versatility of Liquid Light. Thus, the soldiers fighting will have stronger shields and even weapons to attack this ship. The only elusive strength we have is the cloak on the ship."

"Can we do that too, adapt our weapons like that?" Jesse asked. He hated the idea of not having the ship's weapon strength as a means to destroy whatever Terrian he needed to. He had spent a great deal of time fantasizing about blowing Nosh up with the ship's weapons.

"I could study the Liquid Light we have and see what I can do," Palk said, excited.

"And we would be no better than our oppressors," Eruk said. "The Ancients who constructed this ship and left it for you three to find did so because they foresaw a future where humans and Terrians work together to heal both of our planets. Though the Keepers have updated its capabilities over the years, those of us who are a part of the resistance follow the way of the Ancients and believe that one only takes up arms for a just cause. We do not attack for the sole purpose of destruction. Many in the Gelf compound have been kidnapped and forced to live there if they have abilities the Gelfs need. Would it be right to attack them? And what if we have just as powerful a weapon with Liquid Light as the Shaaris, Belites, or Gelfs, then what? We will all destroy each other in this war, and there will be no Terrians left. Is that your intent, Lingua-Shaa?"

All the heat and anger inside of Jesse dissipated. This was the language and truth he had touched on when he read the Ancients' text back on Earth for the first time. It was about peace and unity, not the biggest weapon. He thought of the Tao.

"No, that is not my intent," Jesse answered. "First, we get Sofia, and then we'll work from there."

"Can't get used to the 'Lingua-Shaa' thing, bro, but I got your back," Hayden said.

"Okay, back to what we do once we get Sofia," Kate said. It was still hard for Jesse to hear her talk about Sofia. It was much easier for him to keep each girl in her own compartment.

"I suggest we have a means to alter her once we find her. It will not be easy, but I have no other ideas. Once she is a creature, she can slip out with us," Palk said.

"Isn't that going to be really hard with paws or claws, and where will we keep the injection stuff?" Kate asked. She was twisting her hair around one finger, so Jesse knew she was getting nervous about the plan.

"We will have to move in two teams, each wearing a collar or handkerchief holding the modification items. We doubt these things will stand out in any way. Our pets, which were similar in the Belite territory, usually had some kind of accessories on them. For administering the injections, we will have to practice handling the tools while in our altered states," Palk said.

"Hopefully, we'll be able to convince Sofia to let a giant cat or bird shoot something into her arm. Yeah, no problem there," Hayden said.

"I think we should all be trying to send telepathic messages to her once we're inside the complex," Eruk said. "Especially you, Jesse. My guess is her time in the Gelf bubble has made her susceptible to Terrian telepathy. Nothing long, just short repetitive messages. Then she will have some warning, and she may be ready and fully prepared to be modified once we find her."

Jesse felt like vomiting. No one was saying it, probably for his benefit, but what if Sofia had undergone some horrendous type of modification? What if she was a hybrid or if she had been raped or mutilated? What if her mind was altered and she wouldn't know who Jesse was? Everything spun. Jesse had to lean over and pretend to tie his shoes to get control of his nerves and emotions.

Sofia, he thought, you have to be the same. If she was near death or unrecognizable, then what?

CAT PAWS

When rich speculators prosper
while farmers lose their land;
when government officials spend money
on weapons instead of cures;
when the upper class is extravagant and irresponsible
while the poor have nowhere to turn –
all this is robbery and chaos.
It is not in keeping with the Tao.

Tao Te Ching, Stephen Mitchell, translator

The baseball mitt-sized cat paws were proving to be a problem. Jesse had spent the better part of a day as a giant cat. He was larger than a tiger or lion from Earth, but the basics were the same: teeth, fur, long tail, paws, claws, and an amazing ability to leap halfway across one of the training rooms in one bound. He really liked the growl and roar. Swirls of green, gold, and black colors covered his body. Instead of a mane or even thicker patches of fur, he had skin like a pachyderm around his neck. Eruk had tied a pouch there, and Jesse had gotten to where he could bite it open, letting the genetic mod tools fall. The trouble was being able to handle the stuff with his chunky paws, and the three-inch extendable claws were no help. He ended up knocking the syringe around like it was a cat toy.

Try teeth. Hayden sent him a mental message while he flew in high circles above Jesse.

Hayden was a bird. He looked a lot like an eagle, but again, the colors were off. Brilliant blue feathers covered his body. Jesse knew eagles were huge on Earth, but Hayden was bigger. When he stood at rest on his talons, he was a good seven feet tall, and his wingspan must have been twenty feet, give or take. The sight was impressive. Hayden could pick up the syringe easily in his talons, but he had no more luck than Jesse being able to simulate injecting anything into anyone.

Palk and Kate practiced on the far end of the training room. Palk was a similar cat, but his markings were huge spots of purple and black; Kate was a magnificent red bird, smaller than Hayden, but fast in flight, and she was the best at snatching the syringe. She had been the first to use one claw to successfully inject the placebo into Eruk.

"I'm sure you're all hungry and thirsty," Eruk said and waved everyone into the center of the training room. He had poured four large bowls of water and unpackaged various food supplements, heaping them into piles.

Jesse was ravenous. It felt so weird to lap up water from a bowl and hunch over to eat. He devoured his pile in minutes, but found he was insatiable.

More? He sent a message to Eruk.

"Yes, I have more," Eruk answered. He unwrapped more packs and set them before Jesse. Jesse gobbled and purred. That was better. He drained his water dish and did more leaps around the room while the others finished. Kate and Hayden played around by tossing a food bar in the air for the other to catch and eat mid-flight. Kate did slow circles above Jesse, and he felt her bird eyes on him. How was this possible? He still sensed their connection even as a different species. He thought about the Browns in the jungle or desert rings who had been altered, and a sinking feeling overwhelmed him. He hoped they forgot what it was like to be a humanoid species. He hoped they simply crossed over.

Eruk checked his hand-held screen. "Everyone, there is some activity at the coordinates we've been monitoring. If there is an entrance to the Gelf underground, we may be able to witness something. Let's move to the main cabin."

An odd parade followed Eruk out of the training room and to the lifts that brought them to the level with the main cabin. All four creatures couldn't fit in the lift with Eruk, so they went in shifts. Once back to the command station, Eruk put the view of the outside on a larger screen. Everyone stood around and stared at the image. They had flown the ship to the coordinates, which were in the middle of nowhere. All that was out there was a bunch of rock and sand. Some plants jutted from the massive rock formations. They fell from gigantic crags, but nothing else sprouted from the rolling dunes of sand.

Suddenly two Gelfs appeared on the backs of winged reptiles. They swooped and dove. They were not enhanced, so it was difficult to make out faces, but Jesse could see flowing red hair on one Gelf and a short shock of red hair on the other. The two flew their beasts high into the sky, circled, and charged the ground. Soon one hurled a disk-shaped object at the other. The man caught it in a bubble similar to the one that had carried Sofia. He swirled the bubble until it combusted into a fire ball.

"These are impressive displays of kinetic abilities. I have not witnessed this in the Belite territory and certainly not in the ghetto," Eruk said. Palk growled and pawed the metallic floor. Hayden took off for flight and did a tight figure eight above all of them. He landed, his talons clinking like silverware.

Kate sat stock-still and perched in her command chair. Jesse glanced her way and though she was a massive red bird, she carried herself with the same grace and quiet resolve that she did when she was human.

The fire balls made by the Gelfs were growing, their intensity sharper. The woman Gelf flew with the ball in front of the beast's mouth; she moved her hand in up and down motions until the fire changed shape. A slender wall of fire preceded her flight path.

"A fire shield, the size and duration of her control has not been accomplished, as far as I have learned, from the resistance," Eruk said. His brow furrowed with concern. "The Gelfs are a mystery to all Terrians. Their ability to mark humans, like they did with you, Hayden, while completely cut off from Shaari technology, is mind-bending. Here we have these coordinates, but where did these two come from? According to the readings, they appeared out of nowhere. It is most likely the invisible tubes they've constructed, like what you experienced right after exiting the Worm Hole. No readings or any kind of gateway in the atmosphere are showing up." Eruk closed his eyes while Palk nestled his head against Eruk's leg.

Jesse took a step closer to the screen to avoid the touching. Even with one as a cat he felt uncomfortable by their connection. What was wrong with him? Now one dude was not only a dude, he was a cat-creature dude. He was thankful he was a cat, too, so no one could see his blush or worse, his cringe. Love was love. That was what Hayden had told him back on Earth. Jesse got a small sense of that idea in the moment Kate had looked at him. She was a bird, but she was still Kate. Her essence soared above him, and he couldn't keep himself from feeling her. So if Kate was a guy would he feel the same way? He felt itchy again, but he pushed his thoughts. Maybe. Whatever her form, he was compelled by an unseen force to touch her, be near her, learn about her.

"Palk thinks we should exit the ship and be ready to follow these two into the complex," Eruk said. "I do not see this as a sound possibility. Instead of me translating what messages everyone says to me, we need to link as a group, even if Hayden and Jesse can only say a few words. Go to your mental places where you are able to send and receive messages; this should be pretty routine at this point."

Jesse watched the Gelfs burn up the sand with blasts of fire from the bubbles they had created. He stared at the mesmerizing flames and focused on a clear mind. He had only had mental conversations with Kate and Hayden, and those were damn near monosyllabic on his end. But he wanted to be able to hear what everyone was saying, so he blocked his mind to any clutter.

There isn't much out there. If two cats and two birds show up just hanging out near the Gelfs, that will look strange. Kate sent the first message.

We land the ship right under their noses. When they make a move to leave, then we exit the ship. We will follow them in. Palk said.

Little time. Hayden said. Jesse was relieved that Hayden was still at the same level of telepathic communication.

Send out Hayden and me. We can fly around and get a sense of the area, maybe even see how they enter the tube. Kate said.

No! Jesse didn't have time to censor his response.

It is a strong plan. Eruk said. *Hayden, are you willing as well? There must be some life out there. I can do a scan for bird life.* Eruk checked the computer. *Yes, flying creatures are in the area. You two could blend in with the environment well.*

I'm in. Hayden said. His feathers rustled in a burst of movement.

No. Jesse repeated with more calm.

Jesse, it's our best plan. Otherwise we could sit out here for a very long time waiting for another opportunity. I'll be fine. Kate said.

Jesse let out a low growl. He hated the idea. Kate could be engulfed by a bubble so easily. They could capture her just like they did with Sofia. He scratched at the remains of his chair and shook his head.

I go. He said.

There are no signs of cats out there. Also, you and Palk are the most favored of pets among Terrians. It would be strange to see you in the wild. Eruk said.

Jesse paced a few times and nodded. He didn't want to agree with them, but they were right.

Okay. He said.

"Let's relax for a while, and I'll bring the ship out of visual range, so when Hayden and Kate exit, they can take off, and it won't look like they materialized out of nowhere," Eruk said. He took over Kate's seat and touched the orb. The power source glowed, and the ship moved. Eruk used the lowest gradation of juice to lift the ship. Drifts of sand shifted beneath them, but Jesse watched the viewfinder carefully, and the Gelfs continued their fire throwing in the distant sky. Eruk piloted the ship at an incremental speed. They finally touched down between two high dunes and behind a crest of red rock.

Hayden and Kate stood at the entryway. She cocked her head to the side and blinked at Jesse. He roared, actually roared, back at her. He wanted to leap over to her and pin her down with his paws, but he kept on roaring instead.

I'll be fine. I promise. Kate said.

Come back. It was all he could manage through the clamor in his head.

Stay cool. Hayden said. Even though the message was only two words, Jesse got it. It translated to, Don't blow up any chairs.

Then she and Hayden flew off. Eruk closed the door behind them, and Jesse scanned the viewfinder for the two to show up. And there they were: one red blur of color and then a blue. They spun and swooped around, and the Gelfs kept on practicing.

Now we wait. Palk sent a message.

This was the part that Jesse hated, more waiting.

An hour went by. At first Jesse didn't take his eyes off of Hayden and Kate, but after a time, he learned that his feline eyes tired of tracking the birds. He grew a little distracted and was more interested in cleaning his paws or jumping from chair to chair. Then his mind would kick in, and he panicked that he was becoming too much like a cat, so he forced himself to focus on Kate.

She was perched on a rock for a long time; Hayden continued circling; he started on the ground and made the same funnel pattern up to the level the Gelfs were. The two Gelfs never seemed to tire. Their fires got bigger, and their beasts kept them in a dance in the air. The man made a fire circle, much like Hayden's ring, but his was smaller. Jesse wondered if they got the idea from Hayden. All of the Terrians at the Chicago battle seemed surprised and baffled by Hayden's fire ring.

The man Gelf directed his fire ring to fit around the woman's neck. She laughed at this and made five spouts of fire shoot off from the main wall. He threw up a shield with the flick of his hand. Then he made a fist; the noose tightened.

Kate was flying off her perch in a flash and approaching the woman. Don't do a thing, Jesse thought. He tried to send the message to her, but he was in a panic. He growled at Eruk.

"I see her. I'll talk to her. Don't worry," Eruk said.

If Kate got a message, it didn't change her actions. She flew right up to the woman and hovered near her shoulder. She made unsuccessful attempts to pick at the fire ring.

No, no, no! Get off, Jesse tried to say, but another roar came out.

"I sent a message, but let's see what Kate accomplishes. I'll put on the audio, maybe we can pick up something. Proximity is good," Eruk said.

A garbled sound echoed in the main cabin, and then strong winds roared. Soon some words came through. Jesse recognized an accent to the Terrian speech; it must have been a Gelf dialect.

"Looks like you have a new pet, Amoxa," the Gelf man said.

"I'm taking her home. She's trying to save me from you. I think that's smart," the Gelf woman answered. The man laughed and opened his palm. The fire noose dissipated. Hayden swooped in and let out a musical trill.

"How about a matching set? We could use more pets," the Gelf woman said.

"No, I don't want a weakling bird," he said.

"I insist, or I could surround you in four fire walls all night," she said and laughed. "You know I can do it."

"Fine, if you want it, come on, bird. But don't you dare perch on me," he said. Kate chirped a melodic string of sound.

The Gelfs directed their beasts in the exact spot where an entrance should be, according to the coordinates. The woman allowed Kate and Hayden to flap and hover at each of her shoulders. The woman made a motion Jesse couldn't fully make out with her hands, and then in a blur of sand, all were gone.

"The soul answered and said, 'What binds me is slain, what surrounds me is destroyed, my desire is gone, ignorance is dead. In a world I was freed through another world, and in an image I was freed through heavenly image. The fetter of forgetfulness is temporary. From now on I shall rest, through the course of time of the age, in silence.'"

"Mary Recounts Her Vision of the Soul's Ascent,"
The Gospel of Mary

Dark soon. Jesse sent a message to Palk and Eruk. He had just devoured a heaping stack of protein bars and lapped up three bowls of water. Palk was to his left. He drank from his own bowl and then went back to a corner of the main cabin where he had been practicing injecting the placebo of genetic mod material into Eruk's leg.

Any messages? Jesse asked both Eruk and Palk.

No. Come and practice with us. Since Hayden and Kate had to look like birds from the wild, they have none of the genetic mod material with them. It's up to us to be able to administer this. Palk sent a mental message.

Jesse lumbered over and fumbled with the syringe for the hundredth time. Palk had grown adept at holding the syringe in his mouth and using the thick skin around his neck to push the stopper down. He had two successful injections, so Jesse gave it a try with the same technique. It worked. He leaped around the cabin and purred; his great tail sent the water bowls sliding across the room. Jesse checked out the viewfinder, hoping to see two birds streaking in the twilight, but nothing but an orange sun was out there. Within minutes it dipped below the horizon of sand. Everything went black.

"Let's get sleep in shifts. We'll all stay here, but we need to rest," Eruk said. He sat in the command chair and motioned for Palk and Jesse to find a place to sleep. Palk went right to Eruk's feet and curled there like a dog might. Eruk stroked the skin on Palk's neck and then the fur down his back. Palk purred rhythmically and fell asleep.

Jesse wished sleep would come that fast for him, but he knew better. His mind raced with worry. Was Sofia alive? Was she hurt? Where were Kate and Hayden and why hadn't they sent a message yet? How in the world would Jesse and Palk get into the complex? One question led to another, and though he licked his paws until they glistened with saliva and closed his eyes, sleep didn't come.

We are fine. Finally, a message came from Kate. The words echoed in Jesse's mind; he sat up and paced the room. Palk was up, too, and standing erect next to Eruk who sat with his eyes closed and his head tilted to the side.

If it's dark outside, you two should exit the ship and move to the coordinates. Amoxa said they didn't use any shields for all of us when we went in because they had Hayden and me with them. Did you see her hand motion? Use your paw and make a circle, a cross, and a diagonal slash slanted to the right. A keypad will appear for an instant. I couldn't read the markings, but hit the top far right button, the bottom far left, and the center button. It will feel like you're sucked into a vacuum. Amoxa did something for landing, and we were taken right to her cabin. I can't tell you where or how to exit. I've waited to send this message with the hopes that we could figure out where Sofia is, and then you could exit there. But we've been with Amoxa this whole time. You better get in here though, something is happening. Something big. Lights are blinking and instructions are coming over the loudspeakers. You might be able to slip in undetected because of all the activity and preparations for whatever is happening. If Amoxa has talked about it, we can't understand her. Be safe.

Jesse was already at the ship's door.

Eruk kneeled in front of Palk, and they put their heads together. Palk nestled in and Jesse looked away. It didn't make him uncomfortable any longer; he just wished he had said a proper goodbye to Kate and Hayden. All he had managed to do was roar. He nodded to Eruk who went back to the command chair and opened the door.

The air outside was cool and arid. Just as when he had exited the ship for the first time outside the jungle rim, Jesse felt relief, even though unknown dangers were in front of him. He ran up a sand dune and slid down it. His night cat eyes worked great! He bounded forward and chased Palk who couldn't resist running after him. They even rolled and pawed at each other for a few minutes. Jesse felt extravagant and a little guilty about the burst of play, but the feline in him took over. It would have been easier to stop himself from blinking than to resist frolicking in the sand.

You're almost to the coordinates. Eruk said. *I'll tell you when to stop. It must be precise.*

Palk and Jesse raced into the night. Jesse's paws struck the sand in powerful thrusts. He roared and held his mouth open to let the wind charge into it. He was beating Palk by several strides.

He heard him panting and growling behind him. Jesse pumped his four legs harder, making his muscles tighten and throb.

Stop. You are at the coordinates. Eruk said.

Palk caught up, and the two cats hunched over catching their breath.

Palk, move one step to the right, and you will be in position. Eruk said. *Good, now make the motions Kate told you to make: a circle, a cross, and a diagonal slash slanted to the right.*

A keypad materialized in front of Palk. He had his paw ready. Eruk's voice reminded them of the code: *Hit the top far right button, the bottom far left, and the center button.*

Wind whistled in Jesse's eyes, and he flew forward, roaring and thrashing his paws to try to gain a footing. There was no ground, no walls, nothing but patterns of colors all around him. Once in a while he saw Palk's paw or tail, and he heard his roar a few times, but otherwise he lost all orientation to what was up and what was down. Everything spun around, and the force of the wind was worse than hitting a tidal wave of water. Jesse shut his eyes in tight slits because he thought he may vomit all the water and protein bars he had eaten earlier. A sickening acid rose up his throat, so he locked his sharp teeth into a bite as tight as a tourniquet.

Their flight through the vacuum ended with as much of a jolt as it had started. They drifted now in a haze of pinkish orange. Jesse found his legs moved in reflexive steps, but there was still no ground beneath his paws, only air. Each march propelled him forward or in circles through the air. Palk's tail swished in front of his eyes and then disappeared. Jesse tried to use his own tail to direct his body one way, but it only flapped back and forth.

Where do you think we should we get out? Palk said.

No clue. Jesse answered. He felt like the answer took a long time, but he had no idea if this was accurate; everything had slowed.

The better question is how to get out. Palk said.

No clue. He was a parrot, not a cat. He tried to focus and make a message longer than two words, but his thought never complied. Right now, a three-word phrase, which he had managed a few times, seemed like an epic poem.

Look for any sign of a portal. Palk said.

Portal?

A doorway or hatch. Or maybe another keypad will show up. Palk said.

No code. Jesse added.

I know, we have no more codes. Palk said. *Just look and feel for anything besides this color. My guess is if we feel something solid, then we have a way in.* Palk said.

Okay. Jesse answered and concentrated more on pushing his front paws in all directions to try to make contact with a solid object.

This drifting, pawing, circling went on for some time. Jesse wasn't sure how long, but he was amazed his cat body wasn't tiring from all the exertion. Were they in some kind of suspended animation? Were they displaced in space and time, something like the Worm Hole? It didn't have the same violent pull of the Worm Hole. This was a peculiar feeling, kind of like an imaginary trip as a cloud on Earth. A continuous low rumble escaped Jesse's clenched jaws. If he were in his human shape, he thought he would have been humming to pass the time.

I hit something. Palk said.

Jesse barreled right into Palk's side. They collided and rolled a few times. Palk's front paw clung to something Jesse couldn't make out, but Jesse knew he had to hang on to Palk somehow.

Sorry. Jesse said and dug his claws into the wrinkled skin around Palk's neck. He hoped the flesh was a lot like human elbow skin where you could poke and needle it without it hurting too much. Palk didn't wince or complain about Jesse attaching himself there; he kept working his own front paw at whatever solid object was in front of him. Finally, Jesse made out a cable; a thin wire swayed while Palk hung on with all four paws.

Now what? Jesse asked.

I think this is a pulley. Palk said.

Whatever that meant? Jesse had no idea. He kept his paws in Palk's hide and was ready for anything.

The cities in the Belite territory have these to move between locations. We pull, hold on, and then we fly along the pulley to a destination. It's not as fast or exhilarating as Liquid Light travel, but it's a common means of transport. Palk said.

Jesse wanted to ask why they weren't going anywhere yet, but he didn't have the words.

Palk's body jerked forward, and Jesse dug his claws in deeper. They whizzed along the cable with colors flashing around them. Jesse let out a roar, but Palk was silent and clinging to the cable with unknown strength. How did Palk hold on to the pulley? He couldn't dig his claws into the metal. Jesse had no way of knowing and was grateful he had something porous to dig into, even if it was poor Palk's neck skin.

Sorry. Neck. Jesse said and really felt like a moron.

Don't worry. I've found our claws can curl around things. I've made a clasp around the cable.

Good job. Jesse answered and roared as they sped up.

I think we should let go soon. My guess is we'll drop and land somewhere in the headquarters. Palk said.

Okay. Tell when. There, he had managed three words. Finally.

They raced along the cable for a while longer. Without warning, Palk said, *Now!* and Jesse not only grasped his neck harder, but he also dug his back paws into Palk's haunches reflexively. Palk let out a loud roar but didn't send a message. Jesse tried to loosen his grip, but the force that was yanking them out of the color tunnel was too great to make any changes in his position.

They plopped down and rolled on what felt like astro-turf. A familiar jungle sound, Whirr Tick Tick, echoed overheard. Jesse jumped to his feet, Palk to his left, and surveyed an outdoor scene like on Earth. There was fake grass and fake trees, but it looked like real water was in a pool in front of them.

Don't drink yet. Palk said. He must have been as thirsty as Jesse was because that had been his first thought as well.

Giant birds flew across the "sky" which was only a fake ceiling tinted blue and pink in places. Bear creatures rolled out from behind a group of rocks and lumbered up to the watering hole. The ominous sound was actually the birds clutching long metal chains that other creatures rode like swings. The little sloth-lemur-like things made joyous clicking sounds as the birds ascended and circled in the room.

We are in a menagerie. Perfect location to land. Palk said.

How? Jesse said.

I sensed the creatures. Don't forget we're animals right now. Our senses are different.

Now what?

We drink. Palk said. They didn't waste any time running to the water and slurping it up with the bear creatures that had heads that looked a little like horses, but the snouts were shorter. The creatures sucked up water through the snouts and pawed in the water. They pulled up handfuls of plants they shoved in their mouths. Their teeth made ear-piercing grinding noises when they chewed.

Palk was already surveying the room. He moved with a cautious gait, creeping around corners and staying clear of the other animals. Jesse followed his lead and explored the other end of the menagerie. The pool trickled into a stream that Jesse splashed in, bending his neck once in a while to lap up more water. The stream petered out and Jesse faced a metal wall. This one had no designs or paint to mask the metal surface. He sniffed and listened. There was something on the other side of the wall.

Found something. Jesse said to Palk.

Within minutes, Palk had hunted him down and began licking and smelling at the base of the wall as well. He stopped and scratched at one section.

This is a doorway. He said.

Jesse didn't see anything. He wanted to ask Palk how doors opened in the Belite territory, but he didn't have the words. Most doors on the ship just opened when you stood in front of it, unless it was locked by the occupant on the other side. Palk hunched over with his eyes closed. Jesse kept glancing behind them to be sure no one came upon them by surprise. For the most part, the menagerie was peaceful; he liked it and felt he could lose a lot of time exploring the textures under his paws or the alluring smells coming from the pool or lush knolls of vegetation.

Palk found a way to open a doorway that slid up almost as high as the ceiling. Jesse was alert; his nose tickled with new smells in the passageway. Lights blared, and words echoed over a sound system. He wondered if in his feline state he would have trouble deciphering the Gelf dialect. Palk motioned for them to move into the passageway, which was a long metal hall like ones in an institution of some sort. It was empty save for lights lining the walls. After they moved into the corridor, the door hissed closed behind them. The information being repeated sounded like garbled vowels. Jesse tried to concentrate, but a scent like cleaners on Earth assaulted his nose; he couldn't do anything but shake his head with the hope of escaping it.

What word? Sending messages seemed close to impossible, but he wanted to know what was going on. It took more time than usual for Palk to answer, so the smell may have been bothering him, too.

This way. He said and signaled with a turn of his head. *Kate was right. Something is happening here. They are moving into full alert with everyone sequestered to their cabins. We'll draw attention if we are roaming around.*

Why? Jesse managed.

They slipped down the hall and turned a corner to see a large room of Gelfs lined like soldiers. Some were mounted on riding beasts Jesse hadn't seen before. Others were standing, broad shoulder to broad shoulder. Their blazing red hair made an impressive row of flame. All eyes glowed red as well, which Jesse hadn't seen in the Gelfs in the Chicago battle. He remembered Nosh having black eyes. Luckily other beasts stood in one corner of the room. Without communicating, both Jesse and Palk knew they had to slip to that corner with the other creatures, which included other cats like themselves, the bear creatures, and some reptiles that looked a lot like baby dragons.

The fuzz in Jesse's head was clearing. The Gelf dialect was becoming understandable words instead of gibberish. A built Gelf walked in front of the ranks and shouted out names and orders.

"Secure all labs, do rounds throughout the compound to be sure all members are in their quarters, and do not allow any movement along corridors or pulley systems. Kerr will speak to Nosh in his private menagerie. He cannot be left alive if he learns of our secrets. Be ready."

Palk shook with excitement, and Jesse felt that snake of rage curling in his stomach. Why was the Shaari leader, Kerr, here to speak with Nosh? They had to get into that meeting, and if Jesse was lucky enough, he could tear out Nosh's heart.

CHAPTER EIGHTEEN

MENAGERIE MEETING

> *And he exerciseth all the authority of the first beast in his sight. And he maketh the earth and them dwell therein to worship the first beast, whose death-stroke was healed.*
>
> The Bible, Revelation, 13:12

Jesse and Palk shoved within a group of cats that were being corralled to follow the built Gelf to Nosh's menagerie. A huge black and orange cat nipped at Palk's neck; Jesse swatted him away and muscled his way next to Palk. He wasn't good at telepathic speech, but he knew a punk when he saw one, even if the punk was a giant cat. Black and Orange slinked behind Jesse, and as soon as they crossed into another room that must have been Nosh's menagerie, Jesse urinated in the doorway to mark his scent before any of the other cats crossed in.

You're good at being a cat. Palk said.

All of the responses were more than Jesse could handle, especially with his heart racing and his stomach churning. He wanted to find Nosh. The other cats jumped through exercise equipment or lounged under fake trees. The floor was different in this room; instead of turf, there were stones; most were the size of pebbles, so Jesse often had to shake them out from under his paw pads. Enormous mesh nets lined the ceiling and waterfalls rushed down from hills and rocks. The entire room spanned more than a football field, or at least it looked that way. Jesse wondered if the size of the trees or land formations were an optical illusion. Just then an eagle-sized purple bird flew to one of the far rocks and perched, so that answered his question. Everything was real in a Gelf-made sort of way. Why had they made fake Earth trees like maples and oaks? Jesse knew they didn't have anything like those on Terria. Why mimic Earth if they wanted to destroy it? Or did they? From what he had read, no one really knew the Gelf agenda.

Palk and Jesse stayed near the built Gelf, until he shooed them away. They crept to a tree and curled up, licking their legs and watching intently. The Gelf instructed two others to set up a table and chairs in the center of the menagerie, not far from where Jesse and Palk lounged. Jesse figured that if they used regular speech, and not telepathic communication, they would be able to overhear something. Soon a group of soldiers entered the room in two lines. A red bubble floated above them with someone inside. At the back of their formation, Nosh strutted. Palk set his paw on Jesse's leg to remind him to keep still. It took all of Jesse's control to stay in place and act like another pet in the group. His claws could tear Nosh's throat so easily. He could dig out the black eyes and scrape off the red hair. He stopped his dark thoughts and focused on cleaning his fur. He refused to look up at Nosh until he heard that voice; it rattled from deep within Nosh's windpipe.

"Set Kerr down here," Nosh said.

The bubble dissipated, and Kerr slumped in the chair. One of the soldiers injected something into his neck and Kerr woke.

"Call off your men," Kerr said and stood.

Jesse glanced up and shuddered. Kerr was at least a foot taller than Nosh. He was built like a swimmer and wore a full body silver uniform like most of the Shaaris in battle. He had the same silver skin and hair, but his eyes glowed white. It unsettled Jesse even in his cat form. This was the man Jesse had seen in his dreams! Jesse nibbled his fur and remembered the first time he'd had the dream of Kerr riding up on an elephant creature. Jesse, immobilized, listened as Kerr said, "You'll have to choose, you know. I've been watching you, Jesse Voshon Woods. You thought you could solve everything with a neatly ordered life, with regimentation. But you have no control over anything, except maybe what you'll do next." What Jesse wanted to do next was claw away Kerr's skin. Then Nosh's.

"Yer god eyes have no effect on me, Shaari-whore," Nosh said. His voice rattled like gravel under tires on an abandoned road. Nosh spoke English, and so did Kerr in response. Funny how their common language was an Earth one.

"We need to discuss things in private, Nosh. That was the agreement."

"And how many agreements have the Shaaris honored?" Nosh walked over to a barrel, opened the lid, and tossed meat out to Jesse and the group of cats lounging with him under the tree. They jostled to get to the food, even Palk, but Jesse sat immobile and transfixed.

"I have nothing to say, unless it is in private," Kerr said.

Nosh chucked more meat toward a waterfall where other cats drank and waved off his men. The soldiers lined up and left out of a door with a pulley. Jesse made a note of the exit code one punched into the keypad.

"You called this meeting, Kerr. What do you want? I'd be happy to keep on blowing up your Shaari scum here or on Earth without another word between us. Or maybe that's the problem? After you failed at securing the Triumvirate or the power source, maybe you are starting to feel your totalitarian grip slipping? That it?"

Kerr closed his eyes and placed his face in his hands. He stroked his chin like he was considering Nosh for the first time.

"I think we could benefit one another," Kerr said.

"No deal."

"You do not even know what I am here to offer you," Kerr said. Jesse had to look away from the white eyes.

"Offer me? If it is your carcass to feed to my cats, then yes, we have grounds for discussion." Nosh laughed. He wore the baby-grin that Jesse hated.

"We are wasting time. You wouldn't have allowed me into your headquarters unless you were interested in what I had to say," Kerr said.

"All right, Shaari Hybrid, speak." Nosh's face rippled red and pink.

"Let us form a union, just the two of us. Leave this underground movement and become a dual god with me."

"So that's all you have to offer? Make me a god to a planet of consumptive water bags?" Nosh laughed again.

"We both know this appeals to your ego," Kerr said.

"What else?"

"Liquid Light. You will have as much access as I. The only other with unlimited access," Kerr said.

"Now, Shaari, we also both know that this has some downsides. Our dwindling populous is testament to that," Nosh said.

"I have a plan for that, and with your technology, we could

remedy the population problem on Terria and have complete control of this planet," Kerr said.

"What else?" Nosh said. His voice was a rumble. His hands were locked in fists.

"Our genetic material will be passed on to subsequent generations more than any other on Terria. We will be kings and our descendants will rule a slave nation. Though the Gelfs have the lead scientists and engineers, your numbers are too low to ever be anything more than a pack of mole-brids vying for tunnel space. Bring your skills to me, and we will share knowledge and power," Kerr said.

"And you need information on our experiments with breeding," Nosh said. "Because you and your Shaari legions can't do anything without Liquid Light. Yer weak and stupid, yer only strength has corrupted you."

"You are one to speak of corruption, Nosh. This is my offer. Leave the Gelfs, bring the ones most loyal to you, and join forces with me, and we will be invincible."

Nosh scooped out more meat from the barrel and looked over at Jesse. Blood coursed through Jesse's body. Did Nosh recognize him? Of course not, but the black eyes on him made Jesse pant.

Nosh walked over. He petted Jesse's neck and held his jaw in his hand. It would be so easy to snap that hand off. Jesse could smell Nosh; a mix of blood and some other musty scent rose off of him. One bite, one bite and Nosh's neck would split open, and he would gush blood like the Gelf trail when they had Liquid Light.

"Here cat, eat with the rest," Nosh said and slapped meat in front of Jesse. Jesse devoured it while imagining it was Nosh's face.

Nosh went back to the table and sat down. "I need more details, Kerr. What's your plan to boost the population? Where's this 'slave nation' gonna come from? We're a generation away from extinction."

"True, but I've heard rumor that you have scientists working on breeding techniques that are compatible with Liquid Light use. Is this true?" Kerr said.

"Nothing is conclusive yet," Nosh offered.

Kerr added, "Aren't you tired of this rag-tag group of misfits? They will never come together. You have a small number who are actually able to fight alongside of you. With each battle here or on Earth, we capture more of your soldiers and imprison them. Then you have dissent, I am sure. All leaders do. I've heard that some of your scientists think your methods brutal, and if they could leave your ranks, they would. What sort of a kingdom is that? You deserve better, Nosh. You deserve an entire legion of followers," Kerr said.

"Let's entertain the idea that I go with you. You need to tell me your breeding plan. If I give you our data, then what will you do with it?" Nosh asked.

"The war on Earth is not only a spilling over of our troubles here, Nosh. All of these battles are striking great fear in the human population. Most of the masses do not have Terrian gifts and cannot see through our shields, so they think they are witnessing horrific natural disasters. To some, the non-questioning minds of the faithful, Armageddon is in their midst."

"So," Nosh said.

"So, we will appear at a key moment, after we have taken from the planet what we need, and we will be the true gods who have come to save them," Kerr said.

"The entire human population will not believe it," Nosh said.

"We don't need an entire population. We only need a select group to enter our Heaven."

"Ah, I see where yer going with this," Nosh said and smiled.

"Very good. We are starting to agree. By selecting a base number of humans with whom we can breed, and we will be the two to have the first pick and the greatest number, we will start a new race here on Terria, our own human and Terrian hybrid population that will do whatever we want them to do," Kerr said. "What ignorant human wouldn't want to mate with a god?" Kerr stood and turned with his arms out. "All I ask is that you think about it."

Found Sofia. Hayden sent a message, and Jesse thought he might pass out from hearing Kerr's plan and Hayden's news. He couldn't hear any more of what Nosh was saying; his mind went fuzzy, and it took all of his power to concentrate on a return message.

She okay? Jesse asked.

Yeah. Hayden answered. After a few more seconds Hayden said, *Pulley cabin 889.*

Hayden, please have Kate communicate with us. Your skills are too limited, and we cannot risk a mistake. Palk said.

Jesse watched Nosh stand in front of Kerr. He injected something in Kerr's neck again and whooshed his hands in circular motions. By the time a red Gelf bubble surrounded the Shaari leader, Kerr already slipped into some kind of suspended animation. Two lines of Gelf soldiers entered the room and escorted the bubble and Nosh out of the menagerie.

Kate already communicating. Jesse knew those three words took a lot effort from Hayden.

Jesse could tell Palk was just as anxious as he was to leave the menagerie and get out of Gelf headquarters. A legion of human breeders! Jesse felt sick and disoriented. He longed to be human again, so he could get on with the next phase of taking down Nosh and now Kerr. If the two did join forces, their shared knowledge and powers would be almost unstoppable.

Who else is there? Palk asked. When no answer came right away, he continued. *Just answer yes or no to my questions,* Hayden.

Okay.

We see a door with a pulley system where we are now. Are you saying we should take that and punch the numbers 899 into the keypad?

Yes.

Is that where you, Kate, and Sofia are right now? Palk asked. Jesse paced along the base of the tree.

Yes.

Is 899 a menagerie? Palk asked.

No, cabin.

Is it the home cabin of the Gelfs you rode in with?

No. Hayden answered.

Is it Sofia's home cabin?

Yes.

Sofia had a home cabin in Gelf headquarters, and she wasn't hurt. This was good news. Jesse started strutting to the corner of the room near the door. Palk followed but kept throwing questions at Hayden.

Who is Kate communicating with?

Sofia. Rizzo. Hayden answered.

Who is Rizzo? Palk asked.

Gelf.

A Gelf? He must be a guard or something, but why was Kate talking with him as well? Jesse figured he and Palk would have the element of surprise to take this Rizzo out.

Do we need to kill Rizzo as soon as we exit the pulley into Sofia's cabin? Palk asked. Palk's stock just went up with that question. Jesse knocked Palk's shoulder in agreement and let out a loud roar.

Absolutely no. Hayden answered.

What? Why not kill this Rizzo?

Why not? Jesse burst in. He knew Hayden may not have the means to answer, but he gave it a try anyway.

Explain later. Hayden said. Then he followed up with. *Promise. No kill.*

All right, we promise. Palk said. *We'll get on the pulley system now and be there momentarily.*

Something else. Hayden said.

Yes, go ahead. Palk said.

Sofia's pregnant.

CHAPTER NINETEEN
SOFIA FOUND

After some time, the old woman perceived her daughter to be pregnant, but could not discover where the father had gone, or who he was. At the time of delivery, the twins disputed which way they should go out of the womb; the wicked one said, let us go out of the side; but the other said, not so, lest we kill our mother; then the wicked one pretending to acquiesce, desired his brother to go out first: but as soon as he was delivered, the wicked one, in attempting to go out at her side, caused the death of his mother.

Iroquois Creation

Palk and Jesse raced along the pulley system. The spinning and speed made Jesse's gut turn, but the real anxiety came from the game-changing news: Sofia was pregnant. How was this possible? She got the birth control shot; if fact, she was getting the shot the day the tornado struck. They were always so careful. It had to be a mistake. Did the Gelfs do something to make her delusional?

Or could she be longing for Jesse so much that she fabricated a pregnancy in her mind to connect to him? Or maybe she lied about her pregnancy to make the Gelfs lay off on the torture. All of these reasons made him feel sicker. Then there was the simple fact that if she was pregnant, then he was going to be a teenage dad. Jesse roared with anger and fear.

The two cats dropped with very ungraceful thuds into cabin 899 to face two giant birds, Hayden and Kate, a very pregnant Sofia, and a teenage-looking Gelf. His tall, lean frame contrasted with Sofia's short, round one. He had the genetically modified coloring to fit the Gelfs: red hair and pinkish skin, but his eyes were more of a brown-red. Jesse's mind did back flips when he really took in Sofia's form: She stood in front of him with the same expression she got when she was working something out while doing homework. Her hair was long and glossy, the color of obsidian marble, and her brown eyes sparkled. She had a rosy glow to her brown skin, and her stomach was huge. How was this possible? If Jesse was the father, then she wouldn't be that big yet. They had only been apart for a few weeks.

Is it safe for Sofia to speak out loud? Palk asked.

Yes. Kate answered in their heads. *Rizzo clouded the surveillance. We have not been disturbed. Sofia can hear within the mental circle of communication, but she answers aloud.*

"Jesse, is that you?" Sofia said and looked right at him. It felt like Jesse's fur was on fire. He wanted to take their genetic mod material and inject it in himself, so then he would be human and hug Sofia. She may be as round as a basketball, but her voice was the same, and she looked healthy, solid, and more than anything else, alive.

At first all Jesse could manage was a roar and a bounding fit that sent the few items in the Spartan room flying. A cylinder of water flew and crashed on the opposite side of the room. A metal chair slid and cracked the Gelf in the shins. He didn't even flinch.

Use your mind, Jesse, as best you can, to talk to us. Palk said.

This made Jesse stop and crouch. He concentrated for several minutes before he could say, *Yes. Me.* Sofia ran up and hugged him. He nestled into her neck and smelled powder and something else. She didn't smell like she had on Earth, and her skin glistened with a pink hue, but her solidity and curves were the same. Jesse felt Kate behind him. There was a flutter of feathers and a click of talons. He crept out from under Sofia who was now crying and wiping tears from her face.

Pregnant? Jesse asked.

"Yes, I'm pregnant. Jesse, there's so much we need to talk about, but later. Right now, your friends told me you're here to rescue us from this place," Sofia said.

Us?

"This is Rizzo. He's … ah, well, he's my husband," Sofia said.

What? Jesse roared and charged the Gelf who threw up a shield with a flicker of his right hand. Jesse bounced off of it and flew into the far wall.

"I'm sorry, I really am, but it was destiny that brought Rizzo and me together," Sofia said. She sat down on the thin cot and rubbed her stomach. "My last day on Earth, the day of the tornado, I was captured by Gelfs. In fact, they were the ones at my door when we were texting and you were heading out to practice. I couldn't put up much of a fight because two huge men did something to knock me out right away. The next thing I know I was having all kinds of bizarre dreams where I was floating. As you know I was floating across the universe, suspended in the Gelf bubble. But you see, all that time, after we left Earth's atmosphere, Rizzo was with me. When the Gelfs started off toward Terria, they put Rizzo in the bubble with me, and placed us on the same mental plain. We lived together in this mental world, and he became a friend, but then, over the years, we fell in love."

Jesse roared again and stomped his paws. He couldn't find any words to ask the questions he needed to ask. Then he heard Kate's calm voice in his head.

Hayden and I have been talking with them, so I can explain what she's saying. The Gelfs made it possible for Rizzo and Sofia to exist in another level of reality, one of the mind. This was a highly experimental effort for them. In the parameters of this reality, time moved more rapidly, and so when Sofia says they fell in love, to her, it's been several years. For Sofia, she has not seen you in what feels like five years, when in physical reality, it's only been a few weeks. The Gelfs also gave them maturation drugs to accelerate the growth of their bodies. They did this mainly to make the gestation cycles of Terrians and humans more compatible.

Kate was about to continue, but Jesse vomited the meat he had been given by Nosh all over the pristine metal floor.

"Oh, Jesse," Sofia said. Her voice sounded like a mother's already. There was a hush-hush quality to it that made Jesse growl instead of roar.

We need to get out of here. Palk interrupted. *We can work all of this out later.*

Rizzo had signaled for everyone to move away from the sick, and he unclipped a vacuum-like machine from the wall. The mess was sucked up and gone within seconds.

What about the Gelf? We hadn't planned on a hostage. Palk said.

"I won't leave without Rizzo," Sofia said. "We are united through not only the bonds of a mental marriage; he is the father of my twin sons."

This time Jesse urinated on the spot. How much more could

he take? He felt more than unequipped to handle this news in his regular human form, but as a cat, he felt crazed and more than a bit incontinent.

We can't trust him. Palk said.

Okay, I think. It had taken Hayden all this time to get this out. Jesse longed to be back on the ship and working out next to Hayden. Hayden would help him laugh about everything, and then it wouldn't all be so terrifying.

I agree with Hayden. Kate said. *We have been speaking with both Sofia and Rizzo, and I believe she will choose to remain here if we refuse to accept Rizzo into our group. From all Rizzo has told me, he has wanted to escape from Nosh's compound since he fully understood what they were using him for. He's a medical and scientific genius, has been since he was a small child. They kidnapped him from his parents in the Belite territory when he was six. The Gelfs murdered his parents, but he only learned this a few years ago. Since then, he has been waiting for an opportunity to escape.*

Then why use a possible dissenter in their breeding experiment? Palk asked.

Sofia winched at the words and harsh tone. Jesse snapped at Palk in her defense.

He insisted. Rizzo made his case as the best and only candidate from data from his research. After realizing what the Gelfs planned, Rizzo didn't want Sofia matched with someone, well, who was cruel. Kate said.

Jesse started to run in a circle around the tight room. He couldn't help himself. He had reached his limit. After two dangerous loops, Hayden swooped down and latched onto Jesse's fleshy neck.

Gotta chill. Hayden said with effort. Hayden was clicking his beak with the strain of keeping Jesse from darting forward.

Finally, Jesse slumped to the floor and lay like a lion might after a hunt. His body ached with fatigue; he wanted to curl up on the cold floor and sleep forever. Screw the escape plan. Why plan anymore? Everything went out the window each time they planned a damn thing. No more plans. No more trying to control anything. It never worked. Ever.

"We cannot administer the genetic modification injections with Sofia. It would harm the twins," Rizzo said. It was the first time he had spoken; his voice was as level as ice. Jesse didn't trust him, didn't like him, and really wanted to chew his limbs off. But there he was squeezing Sofia's hand and nodding to her. She beamed back at him like he was Jesus himself. Jesse wanted to yell, "He's not a god, but his lowlife, deceptive species likes to play god!" right in Sofia's face. He gnawed on a sore paw pad instead. This time Sofia was like humanity, and the Terrians, specifically the Gelfs, were playing god, trying to see if humans and Terrians could produce offspring because their species was damn near extinct.

Let me first express my discontent with taking the Gelf with us, but if we must, then we have no other means to get Sofia or the Gelf out of this underground compound without genetic modification. Palk said.

"His name is Rizzo," Sofia said. There, Jesse thought, Sofia finally had some of her Puerto Rican fire back, instead of all this glowing new mother bull.

"It's all right," Rizzo said. He had a lilt to his speech, probably a result of adapting to the gentler tones of human English. The Gelf dialect was the German of Terrian languages. "The Gelfs, and all of the Terrian factions, have much to answer for. I can get us out of here. The light above Sofia's door has returned to operation-red, so the annex to quarters is lifted. Whoever was here is now gone, so standard movements around the compound will be allowed.

Sofia has very limited access to any area within the compound, but I have asked for occasional clearances for recreation. I tell Nosh and his underlings that her diversions and exercise are vital for the development of the twins. With this argument, they agree with reasonable requests. We have gone to two menageries and to the practice grounds a few times. The practice grounds are outside."

We can give you the coordinates of where we entered with Amoxa. Kate said.

Rizzo went to the far wall and detached a hand-held screen much like what they had on the ship. "Can you enter them here?" he asked. Kate quickly tapped them on the keypad with her beak. A visual map of the entire headquarters, or at least what the Gelf higher-ups allowed Rizzo to see, was in view on the screen. Jesse couldn't tell how big the entire complex was, but there were hundreds of quarters and other rooms labeled "menagerie," "exercise," "weapons," "labs," and other things in Terrian, but Jesse didn't have a chance to read them all. Plus, his eyes were really tired. His head throbbed too. Was the genetic modification causing him to lose himself? Had they been this way for too long?

Let's go. He said and bit at the air.

"A few things need to happen," Rizzo said. "I need to remove the trackers that are embedded in our ears. We need clearance to go to the practice grounds. I'll send a request to Lima, my watcher, and if she grants the request, Sofia and I will be able to exit at your coordinates because they are within the boundaries of the practice grounds." Rizzo had already typed in the request and sat down next to Sofia on the cot.

The six of them made a motley group. No one said anything. Rizzo and Sofia held hands. He made sure she was drinking a lot of water. Jesse watched him fill a cylinder and eye it like he was taking in the volume. He probably had to be sure she got so many liters of water, or his precious test wouldn't work. Sofia just smiled up at him and sipped her water like it was a sunny day at the park. Why wasn't she pissed as anything about all of this? She was going to be a mother of an alien half-breed, and she acted like it was her life's work to do it? Was his Sofia completely gone?

Rizzo leaned in and whispered in Sofia's ear like a lover would, and this made Jesse's stomach itch. He circled and curled to the floor, licking his body clean and eyeing the Gelf the entire time. Sofia nodded somberly to Rizzo who stood.

"While we wait for clearance, I need to go to my lab to get instruments to remove the tracker. I also need some of my data," he said.

You will not be allowed to go alone. Palk said it, and Jesse roared in agreement.

I'll go with him. Kate said in a hurry.

"You will not be admitted to the lab. But there are often perches nearby for the scientists to tether their birds," Rizzo said.

I don't like it. Palk said. *Could I get in the lab as a cat?*

"No, you would have to wait in another menagerie, and that would waste more time," Rizzo said.

All right, then. I'll go. Kate said.

Rizzo squeezed Sofia's hand and whispered something to her again. Jesse really wished he were human again. The pouncing and roaring was really cool, but the inability to express his thoughts drove him crazy. He wanted to have a real conversation with Sofia. But what would he tell her? She was obviously mentally married to the pink Gelf, and there wasn't a thing Jesse could do about it.

Rizzo left with Kate flying to the left of his shoulder. Those remaining in Sofia's cabin fell into silence, partly because Jesse and Hayden could only have toddler-like conversations in their heads, and Jesse wondered what Palk would talk about with Sofia. He was surly and restless, pacing and growling.

I am going to meditate over in the corner to send a message to Eruk. He will need to be prepared for us. Palk said finally.

Sofia sat on the edge on her cot and smiled serenely at Jesse. Though Hayden was a bird, Jesse could have sworn that he was giving him an encouraging face, something that said, *Go ahead, talk to her, bro.*

As if he could talk, but he couldn't. Jesse worked his front paw with his tongue. Sofia rubbed her stomach and sighed.

"Thank you for coming for us," Sofia said.

Jesse concentrated for several minutes and then sent the message, *Came for you.*

At this point all were linked together in the same conversation, so he knew Hayden heard. Hayden didn't let on he was listening. He pruned his chest feathers and whistled a low trill through his beak.

"Jesse, I know. I know this is hard to accept. I can't imagine the tables being reversed, but to me, I've had years away from you. I've learned all about Terria and Rizzo. He wants to change things. He wants to save his people, and I think humans can help. I know we can, especially if my babies live." She parted her lips to say more.

Jesse had no way to respond, nor did he want to. Thankfully, Rizzo and Kate returned. Rizzo pulled out a smaller case with a scalpel in it from the satchel strapped across his shoulder. His lanky, tall frame stood in front of the small mirror on the far wall. He turned his face to the side and sliced his ear lobe. Blood poured from the cut, but Rizzo put some foamy cream on it that absorbed and cauterized the wound immediately. He found another device in the case, a circular object that looked like a poker chip, and held it under the lobe. A tiny piece of metal stuck to the chip. Rizzo took the metal, stuck something on it, and fastened it to the back of his ear.

"The survey team will not notice the difference," Rizzo said. "This magnetic chip has not been altered or damaged the tracker, so we will show up on their grid until we don't want to. Sofia, I'm sorry to do this, but it will only hurt for a moment. If there was another way to accomplish the same end, I would do it."

"I know," Sofia answered. "I trust you."

Rizzo did the same thing to Sofia's ear lobe, and she gripped her knees, but didn't call out or cry. What happened to the girl who still cried over splinters?

Beep, beep.

Hayden clicked over to the hand screen on the end table and picked it up in his beak. Rizzo did a delicate step over the sprawling Palk and took the screen.

"Lima has granted our request. Sofia and I will be able to use the pulley system and exit at your coordinates. I cannot say if anyone else is out there, but it's early so the practice grounds have a good chance of being empty. It's not strange for pets to be let out, but all of you exiting at once will draw suspicion. I suggest Sofia and go first. We'll act as if she needs air and exercise, and we'll head to the edge of the grounds nearest the coordinates of your ship. Once all of you are out, we will need to break through the barrier."

There were no barriers when we entered. Palk said.

"You most likely didn't register because you are animalia. We will register and draw attention as soon as we break through. We will have a short time to get to the cloaked ship and depart if necessary. Sofia cannot move quickly, and I worry about a fall if she rides with one of you."

Do you have a way to cloud their surveillance, like you did in here, so we could talk freely? Kate asked.

"No, creating a fuzz, as I call it, is easy in a small space. It's much like your clouds, Kate, but I cannot do anything in something as vast as the practice grounds," Rizzo answered.

Wing it. Hayden said.

"Pardon me?" Rizzo said.

Wing it. Hayden repeated.

Hayden is saying that we're used to adapting to variables in plans we make. If we say we're going to 'wing it,' it means we'll go with the flow. Kate said.

"I am still unclear," Rizzo said, looking nervous.

"They will do their best, my love, and we will make it to the ship. I just know it," Sofia said and kissed his cheek.

Jesse stood and growled. *Let's go. I'm done with this Gelf underground.*

Everyone was so shocked by his use of sentences that they mobilized. Jesse watched Sofia hold onto Rizzo and disappear through the door. The pulley yanked them quickly, and she was gone again. Out of sight.

CHAPTER TWENTY
ESCAPE FLIGHT

*The cry I bring down from the hills belongs
to a girl still burning inside my head.
At daybreak she burns like a piece of paper.
She burns like foxfire in a thigh-shaped valley.
A skirt of flames dances around her at dusk.
We stand with our hands hanging at our sides,
while she burns like a sack of dry ice.
She burns like oil on water.
She burns like a cattail torch dipped in gasoline.
She glows like the fat tip of a banker's cigar,
silent as quicksilver.
A tiger under a rainbow at nightfall.
She burns like a shot glass of vodka.
She burns like a field of poppies at the edge
of a rain forest.
She rises like dragonsmoke to my nostrils.
She burns like a burning bush
driven by a godawful wind.*

"You and I are Disappearing – Bjorn Hakansson"
Yusef Komunyakaa

Riding the pulley system behind Palk had become old hat to Jesse.
The biggest difference was they whizzed upward at the end, the
pull fierce. It felt like tiny pins yanked the fur on Jesse's face back;

his eyes watered so much he had to close them, relying on his hold on Palk's neck to guide him to the right exit. They shot up into fresh air and plunked out of the underground maze in the sand, under a hazy sun that looked like melted butter. Jesse and Palk tumbled down a small dune together but got their footing and looked for the others.

Hayden and Kate were circling in wide arcs above their heads. Rizzo and Sofia held hands and strolled on a path Jesse hadn't noticed before. A crude zigzag cut through the sand hills. It wasn't a grassy path through parks like on Earth, but at least it was level. Rizzo, who was around six feet tall, had to bend low to talk with Sofia who was only five-foot two in shoes. Her round ball belly stuck out in front of her. She looked at least six months pregnant, but that was a guess. Jesse tried to recall what his mother looked like when she carried Dorian and Kiki. Big, really big. Jesse remembered tying her shoes for her at the end. And he always stayed close to pick up things she dropped. His eyes watered more. It wasn't because of the wind from the pulley, or from the sand that whipped up in small gusts and faded back to the ground. It was his mother. He wanted her so badly at that moment his cat muscles quivered.

Now what? Hayden said in everyone's heads. His caw, a squawk and chirp blend, sailed over the group. Kate's trill called back to Hayden, but she didn't send any mental messages.

Jesse and I will head to the ship and re-form to humanoid shape, so we are more prepared. Palk said. *As the Gelf said, once he and Sofia break the barrier, the complex will be alerted. We will have to move fast. We have the advantage of a lead, and the ship is not only cloaked, it's sitting at the bottom of a slope between dunes. Kate and Hayden will cover us and distract the Gelfs if needed.*

Don't like. Jesse said. Palk didn't say how Hayden and Kate would distract the Gelfs.

Come on. Palk insisted and nipped at Jesse's haunches. *We need to move fast.*

They raced across the sandy hills. The sun hung low in the sky, and the air tasted gritty in Jesse's mouth. Palk nipped at him a few more times until Jesse bared his teeth and bit back. They sped along and crossed the barrier area Rizzo had spoken about. When they reached the massive dunes surrounding the ship, they slowed and pounded up the unforgiving sand hills. Jesse worried about how Sofia would get her girth up the hill fast enough. Once at the top, he started to slide down toward the ship. Shrill bird cries reverberated in the distance.

Go back. Jesse said to Palk.

No. Palk said and tried to bite Jesse's neck to hold him down.

Jesse was too strong for Palk. He shook him off and tore up the hill opposite the commotion.

Alarms are going off in the compound. It was Rizzo sending a mental message for the first time. *I dropped our trackers in the sand. I'm staying back to fight.*

I'm with you. Kate said.

Pure adrenaline pulsed through Jesse. He was grateful for the strength and speed of his cat body. He reached the crest in no time to see Kate running as much interference between Rizzo and the five oncoming Gelfs who poured from the invisible shoot like berries shook from branches.

Despite Rizzo's warning not to have Sofia hitch a ride with any of them, Hayden had already grasped her clothing in his talons. Sofia dangled below him as she clung to his thick legs, avoiding the spikes. The two did an awkward flight that sent Jesse into near fits. They flew straight, dropped a few feet, shifted a little, and got back to a height that allowed Sofia not to drag her feet in higher sand mounds.

Don't worry. Hayden said in Jesse's mind. A few seconds later came, *Got her.*

Jesse was in a raw panic. He knew Palk wanted him at the ship, and now that Sofia was on the way there with Hayden, he almost turned. But there was Kate circling three Gelfs.

Jesse could hear one yell, "You two follow the path and see if something hit the barrier on the opposite side to set it off."

Spit ran out of Jesse's mouth when he sighed with relief. The Gelfs didn't know it was Sofia who set off the barrier. One cut Gelf the size of a WWF wrestler didn't know what to make of Rizzo at first. He signaled to him, but Rizzo stood back. The two Gelfs went in the opposite direction along the path. If Jesse were human, he may have laughed inappropriately at the scene. The three pinkish-skinned, red-haired Gelf men stood around waiting for Rizzo to say something. Rizzo didn't move a muscle but must have been dying to look over his shoulder at the retreating image of a giant bird performing a nauseating flight in the distance. Jesse stood on the hill and willed Hayden to keep flying.

Don't look back, Jesse thought, *keep moving.*

From the Gelfs' angle they couldn't see Sofia's clothing clenched—the fabric on her shoulders to be exact— in Hayden's claws and her hands gripping his bird legs, but from Jesse's vantage point on the hill, he saw Sofia's belly coming at him full blown. The pair made an odd parachute and passenger formation. They might just make it!

Kate circled and sent out her signature trill.

Come back. Jesse sent Kate a message. Jesse didn't want to leave her with Rizzo. Why wasn't she coming, too? Hayden and Sofia were just above him and ready to dip below the horizon line. Jesse turned to follow them down the slope when he heard one of the Gelfs shout, "Something's on that bird."

Then the real commotion started.

Hayden nose-dived toward the ship, and Jesse ran in pursuit. Jesse skidded to the marker for the ship just in time for Eruk to make the door yawn open. Hayden was above Jesse and panting. Some of his feathers flew off with the strain, and Sofia tried not to yell out, but finally she shouted, "Drop me, the sand is there."

Jesse nodded, and Hayden let go of Sofia. Bursts of fire were shooting up from behind the hill. Kate had no abilities beyond being a giant bird. What was she thinking?

AAARRRRR! Someone yelled from the battle. More fire and explosions crackled. Sofia started sobbing; she clutched her stomach and screamed, "RIZZO!"

Eruk ran down the ramp, took Sofia by the elbow, and guided her into the ship. He murmured something in her ear that made her stop screaming. But tears streamed down her face, and she looked right at Jesse. She mouthed the words, "Help him." Jesse didn't care much for Sofia's new mentally married husband, but he never could refuse that face when they were together. Plus, Kate was out there. Hayden and Jesse stood sentry for a few seconds, and then took off for Kate.

Wait. Palk said in their heads. *We cannot help them in these forms. Get on the ship.*

No. Jesse said. Hayden took off in flight, and Jesse ran after him. Palk roared behind them but did not pursue. Jesse glanced over his shoulder and saw the ship doors close. That'd get back. They had to.

Hayden stayed directly above Jesse up the hill.

CAW, TWILL, CAW, TWILL. A bellowing even song came from Hayden while he flapped furiously, and Jesse ran like the devil.

More fire and smoke shot into the sky ahead of them. He couldn't hear Kate's song, and no messages came from either Kate or Rizzo. Were they already dead? Had the Gelfs captured them? What if they found a legion on the other side that would chase all of them down and then find the ship? Jesse blocked the thoughts and said, *Go, go, go* to himself and Hayden.

At the top of the hill, he paused to see Rizzo, strained beyond belief. He held up both hands making a shield as the five Gelfs threw fire balls at him. Kate circled high in the distance, but her bird gaze zeroed in on Rizzo. He nodded something to Kate. *What were they saying?* Jesse roared.

What now? Hayden asked in their heads. Kate didn't answer but flapped higher and sang louder than before. What was she thinking? Should they abandon Rizzo and head back? No, Jesse would never be able to face Sofia again if he left Rizzo down there to die.

"Give up!" The cut Gelf shouted at Rizzo. "More are coming, and some will be enhanced. You're dead, or you'll be tortured and then killed slowly. Come back with us, and we'll make a bargain."

"NO!" Rizzo yelled, and there seemed to be a little extra something to his shield because one flame shot back and scorched one of the Gelfs. The burning Gelf ran in circles screaming horrific sobs, crying "Help me," but none of the others stopped to help him.

The screaming was distracting. Two of the Gelfs shirked away from the flames, one about to redirect efforts at helping the one on fire, but the cut Gelf yelled, "No, keep firing. He'll tire all right, and then we'll have reinforcements."

Kate took that moment to dive from high. Her beak led the way, and her body formed a streamline pose, red feathers like flames themselves.

Head back. We're coming. She said to Jesse and Hayden.

Her speed and accuracy were phenomenal. She plucked up Rizzo by the straps of his satchel and his jacket and took off again, flapping at furious speeds along the base of the hill. Rizzo swung back and forth and tried to maintain his shields against the fire, but the up and down motion made it difficult. Hayden had already started flying back. Jesse didn't want to stand on the hill slack-jawed and immobile, but he didn't want to leave in case Kate lost Rizzo.

The shields were breaking and the Gelf fire advancing. Bursts of red and orange broke through and snapped at the sand. Geysers of flame shot high into the air.

Go back. Kate said again.

Come on. Jesse said back, willing them over the hill like he had done with Hayden and Sofia just moments before.

A few things happened at once. Three more Gelfs, one woman and two men, dropped out of the pulley tube at the same time a fireball broke through Rizzo's shield. It caught Kate's tail, and she flapped harder with Rizzo beneath her trying to douse the flame with his hand. Or maybe he was redirecting his shield to Kate's tail. Whatever the case, more fire streaks slammed into the hill where Jesse stood. He jolted. The three new Gelfs ingested Liquid Light and enhanced in seconds. They shot up high into the atmosphere.

Jesse sprinted and slid into the marker. The ship's door opened, and he ran up the ramp. The scorched and still-smoldering Kate was right behind him. She cawed and scuttled into the main cabin with a wheezy screech.

"Shut the doors," Palk said. Jesse felt dizzy and confused by Palk in his humanoid form again. He shook his head back and forth.

Get me back! Jesse said to Palk who came right over and injected the genetic modification material into Jesse's back. A fit of fur, teeth, and writhing took place. But seconds later, Palk handed Jesse his pants, and he slid into them and lit his hands.

"Work on Kate, I need to get us out of here," Eruk said and took the command chair.

Kate splayed across the floor of the main cabin, her wings wide and her breathing irregular. Rizzo had managed to put out the remaining fire, but her tail was burned off and her back was scorched and blistering.

"Wait," Rizzo said and touched Jesse's arm. "Bring her back to form first."

At first Jesse didn't register what was being said. What did Rizzo mean? Then it hit him. Kate was still a bird. Sofia walked around the cabin, opening and shutting cabinets like she was searching for something.

"Okay," Jesse said. Palk was right there with the materials.

"Be ready," Palk said. "This will hurt her with the burns, I think."

Hayden was already back to himself and dressed. He stood next to Jesse, his face tense.

"They're looking for us," Eruk said. "I'm going to take us out of the Terrian atmosphere."

When Palk injected the material into Kate, her bird scream reverberated through the cabin. Her body twisted and contorted so much Jesse wanted to put her back in bird form to keep her from more pain. Some bright feathers fell away, but five re-formed into her fingers. Her legs grew, toes and feet extending. Her head and face morphed back to her human shape.

"Aaaaaaaa," she yelled and rolled, naked on the floor. Sofia had found a blanket and threw it over Kate. The back of Kate's hair was burned away, and Jesse couldn't see all of her, but it looked as though the back of her legs and her back were already blistering. Hayden and Rizzo stretched the blanket beneath her and started to the medical room, carrying Kate, face down, as if on a stretcher. Before they dashed off, Sofia folded a corner over Kate's backside and caught Jesse's eye.

Jesse re-lit his hands, to get the most power, and started around Kate's jaw line and neck.

"Go!" Jesse shouted. "I'll work on her as we move."

He wanted to cry, but he kept his head during the awkward hustle to the medical room. Hayden hummed something; what was it? A Christmas tune of all things, but it seemed to settle Kate who was crying so hard and whimpering like a hurt puppy.

"It's all right, Kate. Let me see," Jesse said, mimicking his own mother's voice as best he could.

"Jesse, my face. Is it burned?" she asked.

They were at the lift and shuffling in. Jesse had already healed the burns on her neck and jaw. He gently turned her face while they rode the lift. Flame and heat must have reached her right check. It wasn't a bad burn, but it must have hurt. Jesse took his healing hand and placed it there. Somehow the usual warmth cooled her cheek. Instant tears ran down her face; he wiped them with his thumb.

"Remember how you held me like this on the train on Earth?" Jesse said. "You're always there for everybody. Now we're here for you. It's gonna be all right."

"You came for me," Rizzo said, "and saved my life. I will always be indebted to you."

Kate made a small squeaky sigh and passed out.

"Let's get her to a table. Place her face down," Jesse said. "Carefully."

"Oh yeah, bro," Hayden said, his voice crackly and ready to break. "You need to work your magic on our angel here." Tears started down Hayden's cheeks. He wiped them on his sleeve and stepped to the corner of the room to let Jesse work.

"I can help you," Rizzo said. "In your language I'm a medicine man and a scientist."

Jesse gave a half smile, "The word is doctor, but okay. I'll use all the help I can get in the skin grafting. And we can speak in your Terrian dialect if it's easier for you."

Rizzo's eyebrow went up. "You're Lingua-Shaa."

"Yeah, so I've been told," Jesse answered.

"That's my cue to check on the jelly monsters outside and see if our buddies need help up front," Hayden said. He paused at the door. "I'll put my com-link in. Tell me if anything changes with Kate."

Jesse nodded and lapsed into Rizzo's language. The two worked side by side. He used his hands to heal and look inside at Kate's blood vessels, nerves, tendons, and ligaments. Her lungs were damaged because of all the smoke inhalation. So Jesse rolled her to her side and placed his hands on her chest, closing his eyes for concentration.

"Her lungs are clear," Jesse said after a few minutes.

"You'll need to repair nerve damage to the backs of her legs," Rizzo said. "I have a salve that will heal the blisters and re-grow skin in the most damaged areas."

Rizzo opened his satchel and pulled out various pocket-sized instruments and vials. He also had balls in liquid form. He squeezed two and put them on a prep table. They started to form into longer tubes of substances just as their backpacks had formed way back on Earth, when all of this started. At that moment Jesse would have given anything to have his ordinary life back. He wished for ignorance. Whether Kate was right and there was a god out there for all of them, or if it was all an alien hoax, Jesse simply wanted to be a regular kid in a regular high school where his biggest worry was wanting to ask another girl out when he already had a girlfriend.

Jesse pushed aside these relived moments of his everyday life, and he examined and healed Kate. *Achilles tendon. capillaries, muscle, cells.* He worked on her legs while Rizzo spread the salve on Kate's back and neck. Her skin didn't return to its former whiteness in an instant, but Jesse could tell it was working. Kate woke and breathed in and out. Then she mumbled, "It's cooling. Oooooh, thank you, guys."

The entire back part of her hair was gone, so the sides hung down with some of the ends broken and burned. Before Rizzo applied the salve to Kate's face and jaw, he took her singed hair in one hand and twisted what was left into a ponytail. A smell of charred skin and hair wafted through the air.

"My hair," Kate whispered. Tears dripped onto the floor and pooled right below the bed.

Jesse finished repairing the fascia and heel skin and scooted beneath the bed where he could look up at her while lying on the floor. A tear splashed on his nose.

"Sorry, I'm being a baby. It's only hair," Kate said. Her head hung over the top of the medical bed for Jesse to see her eyes brim with fresh tears.

"You've been through a trauma," Jesse said.

Rizzo finished mixing something from his magic case. He stopped and went around the room opening cabinets and organizing medical supplies.

"Don't do too much re-org," Jesse said to him in the Gelf dialect.

"I won't, but there is an apparent flawed logic to how you've ordered things," Rizzo said.

Jesse wanted to say, "Bite me, asshole, we just saved your pink ass," but he didn't. Instead, he answered, "We can go over it later. How about you check on Sofia? Kate's stable, I'll stay with her."

"Yes. Fine," Rizzo said and left the room.

"I'm a back sleeper," Kate said after a few minutes passed.

"What?"

"I sleep on my back, not my stomach. It's going to be hard to sleep like this," she said.

"You want something to help you sleep? I can help—" Jesse said and started to get up.

"No, it's all right." Kate waved her hand at Jesse to stay put. "I thought I saw everyone get to the ship okay, right?"

"Yeah, we're all fine. We got three enhanced Gelfs dogging us, but I'm sure that won't be for long. Eruk and Palk are taking us out of Terria's atmosphere," he said.

They fell into silence for a minute; Jesse's feet were falling asleep, and his hands were cramping. He was still getting used to being human again, and he had pushed himself by healing right away.

"You were crazy out there, Kate," he said. "Would you please stop playing hero? You're going to make me go into cardiac arrest."

"Oh, that's all right," she said and smiled a little, but winced and touched her cheek. "You can fix that, Lingua-Shaa."

"Well, I don't want to, and seeing you burn like that..." he trailed off and twisted on the floor. His stomach hurt from the strain, and he realized he was getting cold because he didn't have a shirt on, only a pair of the stretchy geek pants. "Anyway, if you set yourself on fire again, I'll just have to burn away, too." He took her hand. They stayed like that for however long it took Kate to fall asleep on her stomach.

CHAPTER TWENTY-ONE
HIDING OUT

> *"Matter gave birth to passion that is without form, because it comes from what is contrary to nature, and then confusion arose in the whole body. That is why I told you, be of good courage. And if you are discouraged, be encouraged in the presence of the diversity of forms of nature. Whoever has ears to hear should hear."*
>
> "The Disciples Dialogue with the Savior"
> The Gospel of Mary

Three days had passed in the quiet wonder of a nebula. Eruk and Palk had taken the cloaked ship far out of Terria's atmosphere and parked it in puffy gaseous clouds that swirled with pink and gold light. Jesse had never seen anything so beautiful; the clusters were constant bursts of technicolor explosions filling their view screen. He had spent many hours in the last days gazing out, letting his mind empty, allowing the beeps and soothing thrums of the main cabin calm his nerves. From what they could tell, the enhanced Gelfs could not find them. They scanned the area multiple times a day, and there were no signs of pursuit. But without the ability to tap into some kind of satellite, or what the Terrians called, conduit feed, they had no idea what was really happening on Terria, or Earth for that matter. Rizzo had confirmed that the Gelfs had advanced tracing abilities by using Earth's and Terria's satellites or feeds. That was how Hayden had been "corrupted" back on Earth. A lifetime ago.

Jesse, finally alone, sat in Kate's chair in the main cabin. Even though the ship was massive, with many compartments still unexplored, it felt very much like a hulking, drifting prison. He longed for real air and outdoor smells: the sky before a spring rain, fresh cut grass in summer, burning piles of dead leaves in autumn, evergreens under new snow.

Jesse flicked the screen to the *Tao Te Ching* and read, "Be content with what you have,/ rejoice in the way things are./ When you realize there is nothing lacking,/ the whole world belongs to you."

"Hi," Sofia said. Jesse flicked the screen off and turned to face her. Her stomach seemed even bigger. He knew not to say she looked huge; he had learned that much from his mother.

"Hey." He paused, not knowing what else to say. He had done a good job of avoiding Sofia and Rizzo the last few days. He split his time between the medical wing, his own cabin, and the main one. Jesse had no idea what to talk about with this Sofia. She was different; she often got this wistful, faraway expression, as if she was listening to the sounds within her own womb.

"Rizzo and Eruk made some real food for us, down in the kitchen." She walked over and flopped in the other command chair. Her feet dangled, making her seem like a small child. The phrase, "Kids having kids," went through Jesse's mind. And yet she seemed so much older now. She even regarded him with the same curious face some of his teachers used to, like she was trying to imagine him when he was all grown up. That face kept Jesse turning the opposite direction every time he saw her the last few days. Now he was cornered.

"What happened to the other chair?" she asked.

"Ah, an accident," Jesse stammered. "I was experimenting with my powers."

Sofia kicked her feet, and Jesse wanted to stand up and quiet them, saying, "Don't you see, you're still a kid. How'd you go and get pregnant by an alien dude?" But he didn't say that. Sofia tossed her sleek hair back in a sexy way. Jesse pretended to check the controls.

"Everyone said it'd be okay for all of us to eat together in the room that's next to the kitchen. It's set up like a dining room, and we finally have some hot food. The babies are dying for something more than the food packs." She rubbed her stomach, a new gesture, definitely not sexy.

"I think I should stay up here. Cover the screens and stuff," he said.

"I asked and Palk said you could all have a com-link on and carry those hand screen thingys," she countered.

"Since when is Palk in charge?" Jesse asked, his tone more biting than he felt. He liked Palk, especially after their time together as cats.

"Come on, Jesse, lighten up and come and eat. Kate's finally up and moving around. It'll be a little celebration."

"She's up?" His whole body felt lighter. Sofia crinkled her brow, and an unreadable expression crossed her face. It changed in a blink of time, her serene face back and expectant.

"All right, let me go over things one more time and get my stuff. I'll be down in a few minutes," he said. He went over to the far screen and went through the motions of a systems check. He felt Sofia's eyes on him for a few seconds, but then she strained to get up and shuffled off.

"See you," she said to his back. The words stung; two words wrecked him. Why? They sounded so much like before all this. They could have been going their separate ways after practice or their third period study hall.

"Yeah, see you," he said over his shoulder.

When the lift closed with Sofia in it, Jesse let out a long breath. He switched his com-link on and called the medical room.

"Yo," Hayden said. It was his shift to watch over Kate, but Jesse knew not to put it that way in front of Kate.

"Kate up and moving around?" Jesse asked. His skin tingled with anticipation.

"Yeah, doc, your patient is stubborn as all get out. Once she was up, there's precious little I can do to keep her down. I told her to save up some energy for the big dinner. Did you hear? Hot frigging food, bro. My mouth is pouring. I don't care what it tastes like. If it's hot, I'm ready to cu—"

"Dude, Kate's right there. Clean it up," Jesse said and entered the lift.

"Sorry. But she's behind the curtain getting dressed, and she doesn't have a com-link in," Hayden said. "She can't hear me."

"Still."

"Okay, okay. I'll clean it up, especially at dinner with the Madonna and all," Hayden said.

"Have you been saving all this up?" Jesse asked and laughed.

"That obvious? Yeah. Got a little cabin fever, bro. I need exercise, and action. You know, Earthly things. I got an itchy feeling," Hayden said but cut off when the lift moved.

Jesse exited and walked toward the medical room; Hayden's rambling started back up on the com-link.

"Mashed potatoes, Norah's smile, all kinds of things. I can't get them out of my head. And then I want the next move. Ya know? We accomplished what we planned – got Eruk and Palk and Sofia – now what? Then when you told us about the whole Kerr-Nosh, two-headed monster possibility, I got a major case of creeps—"

"I'm right here," Jesse said, and Hayden started.

"Man, you got me."

"I know what you mean. I want to go home," Jesse said. "But then, there might not be a home if Kerr gets what he wants."

"I need help with my shoes," Kate said from behind the curtain.

"Ah, yeah," Jesse said. "I got you." He jogged across the room.

Kate sat on a chair, her face red with exertion. She wore a loose dress. A dress? Jesse didn't know any existed on the ship. It was pale yellow, with long sleeves and a V-neck. Jesse couldn't help but want to smooth out the thin scar that ran along the side of her neck. There were two others on the backs of her calves. With all the healing, salves, and Terrian skin grafts, a few scars still bumped up. Kate must have felt him looking because her hand went up to her neck, her face in a grimace.

"You both did a great job, but I guess I'll always have this," she said. Her finger traced it.

"I only notice it, and the ones on your legs, because it bugs me that I didn't get it all right. It's nothing to do with you. You're beautiful," Jesse said.

She glowed, really glowed. The grimace morphed into one of her radiant smiles, and Jesse warmed. Hot prickles shot from his shaved head to his toes.

He cleared his throat. "And you're in a dress – where'd you find it?"

"I didn't. Sofia brought it to me. She went through drawers and drawers of the clothing to find things she could wear. She came across lots of stuff Hayden never found. Like open-toed shoes. Can you imagine?"

"Heard that, Sunshine," Hayden called. "Like I said, you two could have easily gone scavenging at the beginning. But no. Somehow all the domestic ship duties fell to me. At least now we have some others on board to help out. Let's motor. Get the shoes on or go barefoot, Kitty-Kat. I'm starving for that food. What do you think they have down there? Palk told me that Rizzo brought some 'germination nodules' that have grown into plants and maybe substitute meat we can eat. I nodded my head like that was the most regular thing in the world because all I really care about is eating real, hot food again. Shoes on yet back there?"

Kate and Jesse smiled at each other, and it was the best, most relaxed Jesse had been since on the ship. After they accomplished rescuing Sofia, relief should have followed. Instead, he'd been playing this odd avoidance game that made him feel more trapped on the ship. Being just with Hayden and Kate was like stepping into broken-in track spikes.

"I have a heck of a time bending over with the grafts on my back. It hurts real bad and itches like crazy. Plus I feel like I'm pulling the skin apart, like I might make it fall off or something," Kate said. "If you could hand the shoes to me, or slip them on, I can bend my legs up to buckle them. Or I'll try to. The bending the knees motion is new too."

"Let me," Jesse said. He slid her slender feet into the shoes and buckled them for her. Her feet, impossibly delicate and kissable, felt warm to his touch. He thought her hand hovered over the back of his neck, but maybe he imagined it. When he stood, she sat with her hands in her lap, crinkling the dress.

"Whoa, how about a date, you two?" Hayden said when Jesse and Kate came out from behind the curtain. "Seriously, I'd date both of you. The dress looks great, Kate. And, doc, you look a lot better without your face always creased in anxious study. You'd do well with a drink, too. Loosen you up. I wonder what they have to drink. I hope it's not blood or something gross."

"Hayden, they're not vampires. They're an alien species," Kate said and chuckled.

"Right, but they could have some weird habits and rituals our Walking Encyclopedia hasn't read about," Hayden said and laughed heartily.

"Oh, yeah, your witty-ass is really on a roll tonight," Jesse said with a smile. "Terrians beware."

"Why's it always my white ass and now witty ass; why can't it be my fine ass?" Hayden asked. "I know you're thinking it." Hayden winked and beamed. Jesse laughed and shook his head, the jokes a comfort after so much fear and worry.

It was clear Hayden had a hard time walking at Kate's pace to the lift. He kept bounding ahead and circling back like he was the lead on a team cross country run.

"Please go ahead, you two," Kate said. "I'll get there when I get there."

"No," Jesse said. "He can go, I'm staying."

"Hah," Hayden said. "That's all I need to hear. As long as you have guidance, Kate, I'll see you in the dining room. Whoot!"

"You can relax now," Jesse said. "Manic Man is out of sight."

Kate laughed and flinched, clutching her side. "I can't laugh too hard. I get this weird cramp."

"Let me see," Jesse said and lit his hands. He took her waist in both palms and slid one up to cover her chest, not breasts – the two distracting wonders – but the area over her lungs.

"Oh," she said, surprised.

A charge of electricity linked them. He closed his eyes and looked inside. Focusing proved difficult with Kate within smelling range. She had really doused herself in whatever heavenly scents she conjured from the shower rooms. He breathed in and saw the effects of her mended lungs. The muscles surrounding the lungs were weak but healing slowly. He let go and opened his eyes.

Sweat beaded Kate's brow. She had the two long flanks of hair that had not burned tied back in a ponytail. Wet wisps fell to her cheeks. She took an uneven lock of hair and twisted it around her finger.

"Will I live?" she said in a whisper, out of breath and flushed.

Did he really have this effect on her? He knew it was a stupid thought, but he had been so caught up in his own groin whenever they were this close that it was hard to think, really think, of what she felt. For once, he seemed to be the one who was more in control. Maybe there was still a little Earthly Jesse left, the one who didn't spring up at the pants all the time, the one who didn't blow up chairs in anger.

"You're sweating," he said.

"I am?" She wiped her forehead. "Yeah, I am. Am I sick?" She let out a nervous giggle.

"No, you'll be fine. But take it easy, Kate. Your lungs and the muscles surrounding them are weak. With all their advancements, you'd think we could find a stretcher or a damn ballpoint pen around here. I can carry you."

"No, I'll be fine. We're almost there," she said.

They moved slowly again. Once at the lift, it was a short ride to the kitchen level. Jesse and Kate exited to find Hayden and Palk at the door.

"You made it," Palk said and smiled. Was this the first time Jesse saw him smile?

"Barely," Kate said.

"Okay, time for some locomotion intervention," Hayden said. "What's the safest lift for her, doc?'

"No levitating bubbles while she recovers. We need to lift her.

Over the shoulder," Jesse answered. "Carefully. I should do it."

"Got her," Hayden said. He crouched, lifted Kate gingerly over his shoulder, her head and arms dangling, and ambled off before Jesse could object. Hayden smiled over his shoulder, his eyes dancing. "Hurry up, bro. I can smell the food. Let's eat!"

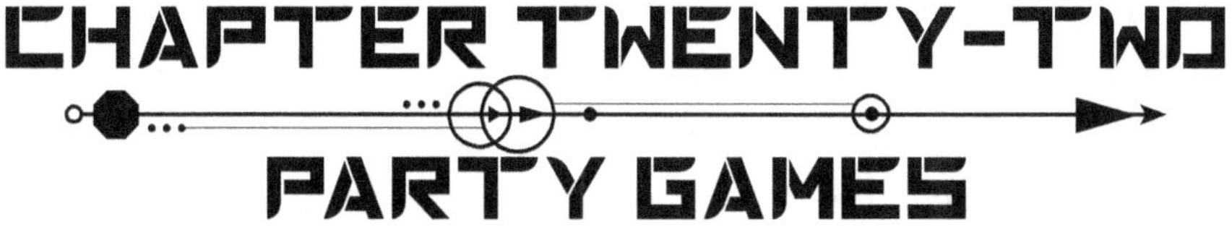

CHAPTER TWENTY-TWO
PARTY GAMES

*"This party," said Christopher Robin,
"is a party because of what someone did,
and we all know who it was ..."*

Winnie-the-Pooh
A.A. Milne

Jesse's mouth watered when he entered the dining room. The room smelled like spices that were familiar but off in an indescribable way. A meaty scent, and another like stewed vegetables, dominated the other aromas.

"Good. Sofia convinced you to leave the main cabin," Eruk said. His gentle eyes shined. He motioned for Jesse to sit at the table, a silver one someone had draped with a blue cloth much like the sheets in the medical room. More of the flexible metallic chairs surrounded the circular table.

Seven bowls and platters were heaped with food. Three had what looked like a vegetable and beef stew, two had some kind of bread, and the other two had long tan strips on them. Whatever it all was, Jesse couldn't wait to eat.

Hayden and Palk were already sitting with a seat between them. Kate sat on the other side of Hayden, and before Jesse could make it over to the free spot by her side, Sofia plunked herself there and tapped the free chair next to her for Rizzo. He raised a finger, "One moment, I need to get the *fraazooka*, or punch in your language." Jesse sat down in the free chair between Hayden and Palk.

"I cannot believe how good this all smells. My stomach is growling like you two as cats," Hayden said to Palk and Jesse.

Palk didn't smile, but said, "I'm glad to be myself again. No raw meat in the *kooloosh* Eruk prepared. This is a basic meal in the Belite Territory."

"So Rizzo grew the vegetables, or plants, whatever you call it, in a few days?" Kate asked, her eyes wide.

"Yes," Sofia said, looking proud, "he packed the molecular basics before we left. I'm so grateful he remembered. I don't think I could live on the food packages you all have been. They're so, so, synthetic."

"Well, it's all we've had," Jesse said. Why was his tone so hard? He tried to lighten it. "Hayden tried making bread, but I have to say these rolls, or should I say, *pannerria*, are really making me ready to dive into this."

Rizzo entered with a pitcher of water he placed next to Sofia and one with the *fraazooka*, which was a bright blue liquid with purple bubbles in it. Eruk stood and poured everyone a drink. Rizzo put his hand over Sofia's goblet and said, "Too strong for the babies." He filled her cup with water.

"A toast," Eruk said and lifted his glass, "to the Triumvirate, Terria's real saviors."

Jesse blushed. Kate twisted in her chair, but Hayden put his cup in the air and yelped. "The Triumvirate," Rizzo, Eruk, Palk, and Sofia repeated. Hayden, the first to drink, chugged half the cup.

"Whoa, this stuff is sweet as candy," Hayden said. "Much

better than the Christmas punch with the green sherbet my great aunt Carol serves. This is smooth. Now, what's to eat? Y'all have any special rituals we need to acknowledge, or can we pass the food and throw down?"

"Throw food?" Rizzo asked.

Sofia laughed, "It's an expression, dear, it means we plan on eating a great volume."

Ugh. Who was she? Jesse could hardly stand to listen to Sofia talk. The "dear" and "great volume" was such a front. Jesse knew she changed in her years of mental marriage, but he also knew when Sofia put on airs, like she was now. She wanted to appear to be this together couple with a husband who made the food and fussed over what she drank because she was the goddamned first mother for the frigging planet. Whatever.

"Yeah, if there isn't anything else, let's throw down," Jesse said, repeating the phrase not with humor, but spite. Kate gave him a look, something like, "Calm down, don't vaporize everyone with anger goo from your hands." This didn't help. There were enough mothers on the ship.

Palk slapped Jesse's back. "We couldn't agree more. Thank you Eruk, and Rizzo. There, I said your name. I'm making progress. Thank you for making this food. Do not judge me if I cry when I eat. I haven't eaten *kooloosh* since before we were put in the ghetto. It is a true gift to be here. To be free, and to share a table with all of you. And Gelf, I mean, Rizzo, if Kate was willing to risk her life for you, then I will too."

Another toast, glasses went in the air, and everyone said, "To Kate." Jesse smiled at her; she was so bashful, but also triumphant. He'd seen the face before, and it always made him warm with pride. He drank a fourth of his cup. The punch coated his throat and burned in his stomach. It didn't taste alcoholic, and that term didn't exist on Terria as far as he had read, but the effect was similar. His head got light; his muscles relaxed.

"Perhaps our hero party could include food now," Hayden said and smiled.

"You referenced A.A. Milne," Jesse said. "You're a lot smarter than you let on."

"Uh oh, come on, let's pass the dishes before Jesse starts quoting shit," Hayden said.

Everyone laughed, and Rizzo started the bread and stew by serving Sofia and Kate first. He let all the males get their own plates.

"What are these?" Kate asked, holding up the tan strips. They had the sturdiness of taffy, but when Jesse bent it, it snapped in half.

"Dried protein, in your language. Taste it," Rizzo said.

Jesse took a bite and his mouth exploded with flavor. Even though the strips were not warm to the touch, once they combined with saliva, they may as well have been a full bite of turkey and gravy on Thanksgiving. The bite became more and more tender, dissolving and warming Jesse's mouth with delicate tastes.

"Man, that's delicious," Jesse said.

"Amen to that," Hayden mumbled while shoving another roll into his mouth.

Sofia nibbled her food, "You may want to slow down on the food. Your systems are not used to the richness of the Terrian diet. Don't make yourself sick."

To this, Jesse shoveled in his biggest bite of *kooloosh*.

"Yeah, well, we've been through a lot too," Jesse said to Sofia, sloshing his punch in the cup before drinking a long gulp. "I think we can handle some home-cooked food, even if it's the staples of an alien species. Speaking of alien species—"

"Aaaaahhhh," Hayden interrupted, "this is so good. Pass the

punch, or the *frazooooooka*, Kate. Here, let me top you off."

Kate sipped hers and kept her eyes from Jesse.

"So Jesse," Sofia said, "what have you been doing? You know, since Earth." Her voice went up and down like a nursery rhyme.

"Oh, I don't know, saving aliens, sorry I know you don't care for the term," Jesse said and slapped Palk's shoulder. They had gotten into this habit since being cats. Lots of back slaps and shoulder shoves. "Saving Terrians, honing our superpowers. You'll have to come down to one of the work-out rooms and see us in action. You know, when we're not giant Terrian pets."

"So, it's funny how I'm here because of you, isn't it?" Sofia's tone wasn't funny at all. "I doubt I would have been picked out of the Earth population to be with a Gelf, but because of you – it was often because of Jesse back on Earth – here I am. With Rizzo." She kissed Rizzo's cheek who shot up and filled everyone's punch cups again.

"What do you mean?" Jesse started, but Eruk sprang up, too, and fetched more bread. His voice was louder than usual.

"Rizzo, I see you're in the reversal stage," Eruk said.

"Yes, I started the process yesterday."

"What's that mean?" Jesse asked. He had forgotten Sofia already and wondered what the reversal thing meant. His head floated a little, and his fingers tingled as he drank more punch and slopped up the stew with his bread.

"I'm stripping away the Gelf genetic modifications to my haploid cells," Rizzo said. "I want to be what I was born to be. I don't know what my eyes or skin or hair will look like. Right after I was born I was redesigned for Belite traits. Soon after the Gelfs kidnapped me, they gave me the rouge modifications."

"Yeah," Hayden said, "now that I look at you, you are less pink in the face and fire engine-red on top. Looking good."

Rizzo regarded Hayden for a few seconds and nodded.

"I only wish this could have been done before conception," Rizzo said.

Food shot out of Jesse's mouth because he coughed so hard at this. Sofia shook her hair out but readjusted in her seat in discomfort. Rizzo made it sound like the science experiment that it was for a minute, and they all heard it in his tone.

"I'm sure your twins will be like both of you, in physical characteristics and spirit. They'll be beautiful no matter what," Kate said. As usual, she turned things around by saying or doing the perfect thing. She placed her hand on Sofia's for a moment and squeezed it.

Everyone ate and drank in silence. After another protein strip that seemed to double in size in Jesse's mouth, he could have agreed with Sofia's warning, but didn't dare. His gut was stuffed to capacity, his head flying from the punch, and he feared he may collapse if he tried to stand. Hayden drained another cup of punch and tipped back in his chair. The pliant metal stretched back and nearly touched the ground behind him.

"Now, I say we have a game," Hayden said and snapped up in his seat.

"You've had a lot of punch, Hayden," Kate said, giggling quietly.

"And you've had your fair share, too, my darling," Hayden said.

Jesse was dizzy and excited. Now what? For the first time since his last supper on Earth, he felt sated. He didn't dream about spaghetti dinners, doughnuts, pizza, or roast after eating a freeze-dried pack of food. This food was good, more than good – divine. And the punch, well, he could handle another cup. Before he could ask for one, Hayden shot up and filled everyone's glasses, except Sofia who had already been given a hot tea-like liquid from Rizzo.

"How about we have an ice breaker game," Hayden said and

laughed. "We'll ask a question or something, or give a dare, and if we get it wrong we drink."

"I think you've confused about three different Earth games right there," Kate said. "You have Twenty Questions meets Truth or Dare meets What's Your Favorite Color for an ice breaker game."

"Yeah, that's what I mean. We'll make it up as we go, and we can keep drinking Rizzo's amazing *frazoooooooka*."

"The punch has not had the same effect on us as it has on you," Eruk said, smiling. "Whatever game you suggest will be much more entertaining to all of you, save Sofia, but nevertheless, I'm intrigued."

"Great. Here we go," Hayden said. "Hey, bro, help me out. Oh wait, never mind. His games will be too hard, and probably not that fun."

"Aw come on," Jesse said. He wanted to think of something witty to say back, but his mind was blank and more than a little fuzzy.

"How about we ask questions about each other's planets, or our powers, or experiences since all this started, and things like that," Kate said. "That way we can learn about each other. I still have so many questions."

"A wee bit vanilla, Kitty Kat, but you're on the right track," Hayden said. "The question is how to incorporate the *frazoooooooka*." Each time Hayden said the word, the vowel stretched more, and the volume increased, causing him to laugh hard.

Sofia smiled at Hayden, her skin and eyes glowing. "If it's that important to you, make it a guessing game. The person in the hot seat has something about themselves they want to divulge, and the rest of the group guesses. If they guess wrong, they drink."

"Excellent!" Hayden said. "Who wants to go first?"

No one volunteered.

"Okay, you chickens," Hayden said, "I'll go. I just need to think of something." He thought for a few seconds. "This is harder than it seems. What's the categories? I mean, if I think of my favorite movie, then the Terrians can't even make an intelligent guess, but if it's something about my powers, chances are Kate and Jesse already know the answer."

"No, do it this way. Get an image in your mind, and we'll try to read it," Sofia said.

"No offense, but you never used to read minds, Sofia," Jesse said. "Can you now, you know, after your mental marriage?" The effects of the punch veiled the harsh tone.

"We all can try," Sofia said. "You have been sending mental messages to each other. I've been working on it with Rizzo. It's worth a try."

"I'm game!" Hayden said.

"We have inherent advantages," Rizzo said.

"I don't think it matters," Palk added. "Let's begin. Go ahead, Hayden, picture something in your mind. Everyone else, close your eyes and concentrate on Hayden's thoughts."

Great, Jesse thought, a whole room of people meditating. This wasn't a game. Somehow it always came back to working on their skills. Wasn't this supposed to be a party? But he didn't want to be left out, so he closed his eyes and tried his best to think of Hayden's thoughts.

Nothing came. The backs of his eyelids presented nothing but darkness. Jesse wanted another drink of punch, so he shouted out, "Hamburgers."

"Nope, not even close, bro. Take a drink."

"Trees," Sofia said.

"Interesting, but no," Hayden said. "You'll need to sip that green stuff over there, Sofia. Anyone else?"

"This is too easy," Rizzo said. "You have an image of an Earth volcano in your mind."

"True," Hayden said. "But drink anyway, Rizzo. You need to loosen up."

Everyone opened their eyes.

"What volcano was it?" Kate asked.

"One in Hawaii, called Kilneau. I went there on vacation with my family last year. The thing has had a slow trail of lava coming from it since 1988, or thereabouts. My sister Norah kept laughing and saying, 'It's gonna blow,' when we were there." Hayden's face grew serious all the sudden, but quickly bounced back. "In fact, everyone take a drink because Rizzo couldn't name the volcano."

Kate giggled and drank again. She caught Jesse's eye and held it for the first time since they had sat down. Her face reddened from excitement and laughter. Her fingers went up to her ponytail, as if to check if it was still there, and then she traced her neck scar. Jesse couldn't take his eyes off of the V-neck of her yellow dress.

"I think Jesse should go next," Sofia said. There was something in her gaze Jesse couldn't name. Her voice was even, almost icy.

"Awright," Jesse said, his mood light. He held the *frazooka* up to the light. The purple bubbles popped. What image should he think about? He wanted something hard, something to stump the arrogant Rizzo. Should he imagine the outside of the ship? No, too easy. His house? No, too sad. What about a random football field or track he competed on during his old life? No, Kate would get that too quickly. Maybe he should imagine a random Earth animal like a cow or duck.

"I think I got something," Jesse said. He closed his eyes and pictured a group of yellow ducklings trailing their mother in a pond. Everyone else had their eyes closed, so he drank some more punch, his concentration iffy. The pond blurred to Lake Michigan, which became the alien battle, which went to people burning. He didn't want to go there, so he sipped his punch and tried to focus.

"Your mind is all over the place," Palk said. "Do you have one image? Anyone else sense this? Everything is jumbled."

Jesse harrumphed. "Maybe my Linguaa-Shaa brain is too much for you Terrians," Jesse said and laughed.

Hayden joined in. "Good one. My boy can talk trash when he competes, that's for sure."

"I have no idea what you two are talking about," Palk said, his voice light.

"I'll focus, I'll focus," Jesse said and tried to empty his mind to blackness, and then he attempted to see one yellow duckling.

"An egg?" Kate said.

"No, take a drink," Jesse answered, feeling good. The talking threw this mind off, though; it took another minute or two to get the duckling back.

"A yellow flower?" Eruk said.

"Drink."

"Mashed potatoes," Hayden said. "I have no clue, I just want some *frazooooooka*."

"Drink, you party fool," Jesse said and cracked up.

"A yellow shape," Palk said.

"Nice try with the vagueness, but no, Palk. Drink," Jesse said.

"You need to concentrate more," Sofia said. Jesse's eyes shot open. Hers were closed. She had her fingers laced across her belly. What was this vibe he was getting from her? He couldn't read her. Her tone was so condescending, and something else he couldn't place. He knew if he didn't feel so jovial from the food and punch, he would have snapped at her.

Jesse closed his eyes and tried to see the duckling. What a stupid image. Where'd he come up with this one? Yellow fuzz, duck bill, he thought. But he knew the image was murky, the yellow a blurry indistinguishable shape. Yellow, yellow. Duck, duck, duck, he said over and over again in his head.

"It's Kate's yellow dress," Rizzo said.

Jesse stood up with jolt and knocked over his punch.

"Naw, man," he said, trying to recover.

Everyone had their eyes open and looked at Jesse with a mix of expressions: Kate blushed; Eruk and Palk tried to stay neutral but acted like they knew some secret. Hayden smirked. Rizzo's eyes were cold, but honest. Sofia's mouth turned down; her hands kept tracing the rim of her cup.

"It was a duck," Jesse said. "Actually, a yellow duckling. A family of them. It's a nice dress and all, Kate..." This was getting worse. His hands began to sweat. He felt like he could pass out at any minute, and here he was trying to defend his yellow duckling that very well could have been Kate's dress – her lovely, smooth, soft dress that clung to her body just right.

"Maybe the party's over?" Hayden said. "Or maybe we should all head to a training room, take some Liquid Light, and fly all night. I'd kill for some tunes."

"It's time to clean up," Palk said. "Eruk and I will take care of it."

"I'll help, too," Hayden said. "I need to learn to make this stuff. It was great."

Jesse tried to mop up the punch, but his hands shook. Sofia glared at him now. Kate stood, nearly fell over, and grimaced with pain.

"I've moved too much," Kate said. "Palk, will you carry me to the medical room?"

Jesse moved to help her, but Sofia's gaze immobilized him. What did it matter to her? She was married to Rizzo and about to have his babies. But somehow that look, a mixture of rage and jealousy, kept Jesse in place. Palk picked Kate up and left the room.

"You just shared a snare with her, right Jesse? Allen set it up, that's what you told me," Sofia said. She wobbled from her chair, and Rizzo caught her.

"Time for bed," Rizzo said to Sofia. Her hands shook, but he steadied them. They walked hand and hand to the lift.

Jesse was alone in the dining room. What just happened? His mind clouded over, and his stomach churned. He closed his eyes, and an image surfaced like a whale on the water: It was a yellow dress with a V-neck. A simple dress. Kate's dress.

CHAPTER TWENTY-THREE
MEETING UP

*If you look to others for fulfillment,
you will never truly be fulfilled.*

Tao Te Ching
Lao-tzu

The day after the party Jesse woke in a daze. Before anyone could tell him what to do, he went to one of the training rooms to work out not only his body, but the fuzzy memories of the previous night. What really happened, he couldn't say. He had no idea what either Sofia or Kate was feeling. The thought of facing both of them made his skin itch and his hands sweat. Somehow, he was at a new level of the avoidance game he had mastered the last few days. Add Kate to the list, he thought, for reasons unknown. Was he running from everything else? Here he was the damn Lingua-Shaa, and he had no clue as to what to do next. He had no way to locate any of their families without being detected; he knew they had to stop Kerr and Nosh, but the question was how?

Jesse pulled a workout pad across the floor, making a rubbing sound like the stretch mats from track practice. Now that the adrenaline and anger dissipated, he had little else to keep away the thoughts of home. Where was his family? Were they already dead from some Shaari-Belite battle gone haywire? He started with one-hundred sit-ups and moved onto push-ups with the hope that movement would bring some clarity.

They needed to meet and talk about their odds, their strategy at stopping Kerr. Jesse stomped out an image of Kerr, silver-haired and imposing, appearing to average humans as a god. The thought was almost comical by today's standards, but Jesse also knew that given enough fear because of the destruction the Terrian battles brought, some would believe. Jesse saw lines from the Tao in his mind:

When morality is lost, there is ritual.
Ritual is the husk of true faith,
the beginning of chaos.

Jesse had found with his reading of the Tao that peace and spirituality came from within. Here he was though, on the inside of the story; he knew what the Terrians were about; he knew they were a screwed-up species on the verge of extinction. It was easy for him to see sense. Like his mom always said, "You go on and judge someone at the end of time, only after you've felt their pain." Where was she?

Jesse started his daily run but stopped. Sofia entered at the other end of the training room. She wore a blue dress that hugged her stomach, accentuating every pregnant curve of her body. Her sleek hair fanned out to hang in shiny streaks on her bare shoulders. He felt nauseated instantly and hoped the meal from the night before wouldn't show itself again on the training room floor. She didn't say anything, and Jesse couldn't stand it if they simply stared at each other across the room, so he put his hand up in a silent wave. Sofia regarded him for a moment and walked her pregnancy waddle across the room. Jesse jogged to meet her halfway.

"You said to come to the training room to see your superpowers in action," she said. Her voice was level, but Jesse could tell she strained to make it so.

"Did I?" he said. "Last night is a bit hazy to say the least."

"Hmmm, it's pretty clear to me."

They were two feet from each other now. Back on Earth they would have been holding hands or kissing. Now, he didn't even know how to occupy the same room with her.

"I guess my powers aren't much," he said. "I must have been showing off or something when I said it. I can heal people, with my hands. He lit them; they went from his normal dark color to having an amber-orange tint. When Sofia didn't say anything in return, he stopped and dropped his hands to his sides, not knowing what else to do or say.

After a full minute or two of complete awkward silence, he said, "How are you feeling?"

"Fine," she said in a steely tone.

"And the babies? They kicking a lot?" he asked. He wished anyone, even Rizzo, would enter the room. He wanted to move, to run, and to be anywhere but in the training room with Sofia.

"They're good," she said, allowing a small smile. "Rizzo gave me a check-up this morning."

Bet he did, Jesse thought. He said, "I'm going to do some arm work. Want to tag along? I mean, you can't lift anything, but we could talk or something." Do what, he thought, stare each other down in mutual hostile, jealous rages?

"Okay," she said and followed him to the weight area.

After a few reps with Sofia watching intently, he made another attempt at conversation. It felt like tiptoeing on a sheet of black ice; he didn't know if he'd hit a patch that could make him wipe out.

"Do you know if your mom and brothers are all right?" His voice was low, cautious. Sofia's dad had been out of the picture since she was two.

Her hand went to her forehead and eyes reflexively. She rubbed her closed lids and answered, "Nosh told me he spared them because I'm carrying the twins. He said he didn't want me to have any stress that could hinder their development." A note of bitterness broke through; she cleared her throat and continued, "Rizzo tells me the Gelfs could have altered the parts of their brains that contain memories, making them believe I'm in Puerto Rico with relatives. He says it with such confidence, I believe him, but I never did get a straight answer from anyone else. Then again, I've hardly seen anyone else. It's also hard for me to accept that so little time has passed on Earth. It's only late October, our senior year of high school, and that is so strange to me. But I can't help but wonder what will happen at Christmas. My mom will want me home, then what? It makes me feel scared and sick every time I think about it. Rizzo gives me stuff to calm my nerves, and I've been meditating with him a lot. That helps. I have to be strong for the babies."

Jesse stopped his reps. How was she handling all this? To Sofia so much time had passed, and now she was huge, ready to burst with two Terrian-human hybrids. He'd need a truckload of major muscle relaxers to get through it. Not to mention the whole who was God thing— Sofia and her family were pretty Catholic. A lot like Kate, but the Latina, not the Irish Catholic side of things. Both were clannish and clung to their rituals for solace. "You know Kate thinks the Terrians may have interfered with Earth's religions and stuff, but she really believes that there is a god out there for all of us. And she thinks fate brought our species together for a purpose, so we could heal each other," he said.

"She does, does she?" The venom was back. "I don't really care what she says, Jesse. In fact, I could give a fuck what she thinks for the rest of my life."

"Whoa," he said. "Where's this coming from?"

"From the Earth Sofia," she bit back. "You need to tell me the truth. Did you have something going with her when we were going out? I caught those looks, I'm no dummy." She started pacing back and forth, her brown eyes flinty.

"No!" His throat tightened; his insides bubbled. The remnants of last night's game stung his memory, and the punch came up for a second and went back down in a rancid bile belch.

"You're lying," she screamed and charged at him with her nails, one inch on each of them, aiming to claw his face.

He intercepted and held her wrists as loosely as possible. She yelled and clawed, once in a while catching some skin on his face.

"Stop, Sofia, please," he said. He didn't want her to get all worked up and go into early labor. "Please, calm down. We can talk."

"No, you lying sack. You macho, two-faced prick. Don't you dare tell me what to do. You were always telling me what to do. You controlling asshole. And when you weren't, then the sun rose and set on your damn life's schedule, your life plan. You were the frigging king of suburbia. How about that? Your ghetto black ass running the fucking show in suburban Chicago. Was that your dream, Jesse? Was that your life plan? Then you go and get yourself a white girl for your arm. You two will end up just fine in a big ol' New Franklin house with your little mixed kids that will never belong." She had crumpled to the floor at this point. Heavy sobs, ones like his mother had done when she'd found out his dad had died, shook her small frame. Her belly was solid, but Jesse could have sworn he saw a ripple of a leg or arm cross the crown of her stomach.

Sofia put her face in her hands; her hair draped it, sliding along her shoulder like gentle bristles on a brush. He placed his hand there, waiting for her to recoil, but she didn't. She kept crying. Carefully, he sat next to her and put his arm around her shoulders. She smelled more like the old Sofia, cocoa butter lotion and some kind of perfume.

Sofia turned her wet face into Jesse's shoulder, and he almost started crying himself. The position was so natural, and the memory of so many dates with her in this very place, save the sobs, flooded Jesse's mind. He stroked her arm with his hand and shushed her, saying, "It's going to be all right, Sofia. It just is. You're strong. You're so strong."

Somehow with his mother farther away than she had ever been in his life, he was closer to her by invoking her ways so often in the last days: first with Hayden when he was below base one, then Kate after being burned, and now with a pregnant and hurt Sofia. This made sense, though; his mother was a healer, too, after all.

Sofia calmed. Her shoulders relaxed, and her weight leaned into Jesse more.

"I'm sorry, Jesse," she said. "I didn't mean most of what I said."

"Most?"

He felt her smile into his pec muscle.

"Was I that much of a controlling prick?" he asked.

"Naw, you weren't," she said. She looked up at him, her face wet and clear. "You were just so regimented and disciplined all the time. It was hard not to fall in line like a soldier. And let's be honest, I was a little insecure, always following, never leading. Sometimes I wanted to be the focus of things, the star. But I never was."

"I didn't see it like that," he said, his voice shaky, "you meant a lot to me, Sofia. You always will. I've felt so guilty and crazy over you being taken by the Gelfs. I should have been there for you. I should have been able to protect you, but I failed you."

"Jesse." She took his hand. "There was nothing you could have done. And you did come for me. You did save me. And in typical Jesse fashion, you made room for my husband." She paused. The word "husband" sent a chill through Jesse, like fingers on a chalkboard. "There was a part of me, even after all this time, that wanted you to fight for me."

"You mean fight Rizzo?" he asked.

"Yeah – stupid, I know," she said.

"No, it's just that you're so ..."

"Pregnant," she finished and rubbed her stomach. "And married, and carrying a part alien set of twins, and years from us." The last word held all their shared sadness and regret. Jesse slipped his arm from her shoulders and faced her.

"I spent a year mourning you in my mind," she said. "I would hold hands with Rizzo, and we were getting closer, but I insisted you'd come for me. I said I wanted to wait for you, so we could be together again. But in my reality, years passed, and Rizzo and I fell in love. It's different from you and me. I'm older now in many ways."

"What was it like? You know, the mind-reality you lived in?" he asked.

"The landscape was a mixture of the best of Terria and Earth. It was just the two of us up until the end, when we found out I was pregnant. Anyway, that's another story. The Gelfs woke us up and we were in the compound like you found us. During our mental marriage, Rizzo and I spent time in various places – his Belite home with images, or reflections, of his family, but in reality, they are all dead. The Gelfs had killed them when they kidnapped him. Rizzo and I now have the freedom for him to deal with the memories of his family. Living in the mind-reality was a dream for him, too. We also spent time with mine, or the reflections of my family. Now that my mind is clearer, I see how I put a mist over everything, just to cope. I believed what the Gelfs wanted me to believe, but Rizzo was real. I don't really remember much of the beginning. It felt like I was in an egg being incubated or something. I guess I was in the Gelf bubble. A lot of that first year – I have no idea how long that was in actual time – I thought I was sleeping on my bed at home. I smelled my mom's Puerto Rican rice and other things she made. Eating her food in the virtual realm was so real – I really tasted it! But in reality, nutrients were pumped into my body through injections. It's very strange to think about. Anyway. Then Rizzo and I had separate houses on a beach. After dating for three years, we got married. It wasn't long before I got pregnant. Sorry, I'm skipping around in the timeline, but you have to know, everything is so—"

"Weird." Jesse shook his head.

"Yeah, weird. I feel like I haven't seen you in years, Jesse. But then I do get these moments when I feel like it has only been a couple of months. I hate those times, and I didn't have them until I saw you. Then I saw how you looked at Kate. Then the frigging yellow dress image, and I haven't been able to calm down much since last night. Rizzo said I needed to talk to you, and then he said he'd meditate with me until I relaxed and reached a healthier state."

"Sofia, is he nice to you?" Jesse felt like a grade school kid, but he had to ask. He couldn't stand the idea of her being with him if he was a bully.

"Oh yeah, he's protective and courteous. He's so smart, maybe smarter than you," she said, and Jesse cringed.

"He may be smart in a Gelf way, but he's not smarter than me," Jesse said and hated himself for it.

"Okay, okay. But yeah, he's nice. I just have to keep him from being too clinical with me and the babies. Other than that, I love him," she said.

"Good," he said, but it didn't feel good at all. He hadn't thought much past getting Sofia back, but he surely didn't expect this. He didn't think he'd be dumped for a pink Gelf.

"What about you?" she asked. She was back to the placid Sofia, the mother of the new world.

"What about what?"

"You obviously have feelings for Kate. Are you two dating?"

"If you call sharing packages of alien food and killing hybrid beasts dating, then yes," he said.

Sofia smiled. "I won't push, but I do want you to be happy."

"A few minutes ago, you were trying to claw my eyeballs out of my head, and now you want me to be happy?" He cracked a half smile.

"Chalk it up to raging hormones," she said. "So, what's up?"

"I dunno. There's definitely a ... connection," he said. He didn't want to say too much not knowing how quickly the nails could turn on him again.

"She's a good person. I knew that on Earth, and it hasn't changed." Sofia moved to stand, and Jesse shot up to grab both of her hands. They stood holding hands for several seconds. She kept his gaze for a long time before speaking again. "I don't know what's going to happen, Jesse, but they're all looking to you to lead, whether you like it or not. Rizzo even said as much to me."

"Really?"

"Really."

"What if I screw up?" he asked.

"Then you'll finally learn that you're human," she said and walked away.

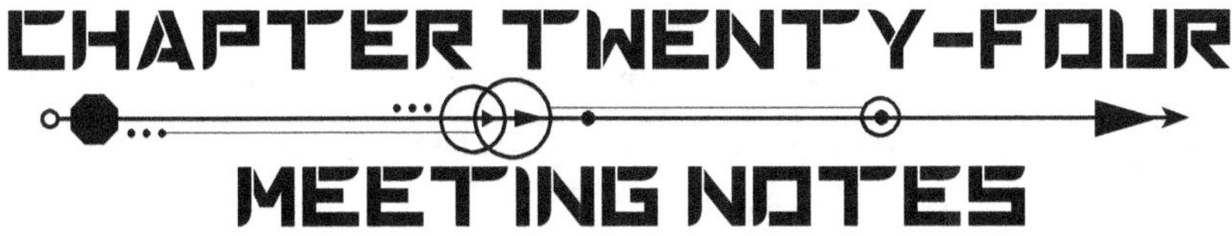

CHAPTER TWENTY-FOUR
MEETING NOTES

"Mr er – er – You never did tell me whut yo' name wuz."
"Ah sho didn't. Wuzn't expectin' fuh it to be needed. De
name mah mama gimme is Vergible Woods. Dey calls me
Tea Cake for short."
"Tea Cake! So you sweet as all dat?" She laughed and he
gave her a little cut-eye look to get her meaning.
"Ah may be guilty. You better try me and see."
She did something halfway between a laugh and a frown
and he set his hat on straight.
"B'lieve Ah done cut uh hawg, so Ah guess Ah better
ketch air." He made an elaborate act of tipping to the door
stealthily. Then looked back at her with an irresistible grin
on his face. Janie burst out laughing in spite of herself. "You
crazy thing!"

Their Eyes Were Watching God, Zora Neale Hurston

Jesse was on his way to what had become the meditation room
on the ship. He had already visited Hayden in the main cabin to
collect his input for the meeting. Jesse had sent notes to everyone's
hand-held screens saying that he called a meeting for the next day.

He also told everyone he would be making rounds that day to get their input on their main concerns or plans. He could have typed up Hayden's points on a running list on his computer, but instead Jesse opted to write in the one notebook with one of the scarce pens from their Earth packs Hallia had given them. Even though the Keepers hadn't supplied these things, Hallia knew to do it. What was she doing? Probably fighting Belites in Earth's atmosphere. She could be dead for all Jesse cared.

Find Families

Liquid Light Use

Next Move

How to Kill Kerr

Those were Hayden's main things. Jesse thought he'd deal with Rizzo and Sofia last, so he stood outside the meditation room and took a long breath. He hadn't seen Kate since the meal the night before, and he worried that there was some hidden tension he was responsible for, but clueless about how he created it. She had been meditating all day with Eruk and Palk because they thought it was safe for them to try to connect with their resistance partners on Terria. Despite needing to rest and heal, Kate meditated right there with them, and Jesse knew from experience that meditation proved to be just as strenuous as physical training, sometimes more so.

The door slid open to darkness, except for the familiar orange-pink glow of the orb. Kate, Eruk, and Palk sat cross-legged around it. Eruk and Palk held hands, their knees touching. Jesse approached quietly. He never liked to interrupt any meditation groove, but he was on a timeline all of the sudden. He decided to sit in on the circle. Maybe a message would materialize on the orb. He doubted any of the three would notice him. He could even think over more points for his list.

Jesse sat outside the circle, a few feet from Kate's back. In the faint light he watched her head tilt to the side and her body squirm.

"What is it?" Eruk asked.

"Jesse's here," Kate said.

Everyone opened their eyes.

"Sorry, I was trying to be discreet," Jesse said.

"You may as well be a giant cat with all the noise you make entering a room," Palk said. He stood and stretched; he rubbed his long, sharp nose and then his eyes. "I could use a rest anyway. What do you want?"

"I came to ask what each of you would like to see on the agenda for our meeting tomorrow," Jesse said, pen ready.

"I want to search for our families," Kate said. "I had a dream that my brother Patrick was saying something to me, but I couldn't make out the words."

"It's already on the list," Jesse answered.

"The ghettos," Palk said. "I want to make a plan to free the other Browns in the ghettos."

"Wow. Okay. Got it. Anything else?"

"I'd like to know the extent of Rizzo's knowledge base about the Gelf agenda," Eruk said.

"Good one," Jesse said.

"And we should have him talk about what it's like for humans and Terrians to breed," Kate said.

"I don't want to know that," Jesse said before he could think otherwise.

Kate reddened and looked away. Here they went again, no eye contact.

"Not the details, Jesse. We need to be prepared for Sofia to have the twins. We should at least know when. It is also important in terms of Kerr's overall plan to lure humans to Terria for breeding purposes." She sounded annoyed with him. He just wanted to catch a break in the girl department today.

"Kate's right. It's been so long since we've seen anyone pregnant on our planet, we are hopeful and curious. Has Rizzo found a solution to the population problem on Terria?" Eruk asked.

"Got it," Jesse said quickly. "Any other points?"

"We should all go over our skills and how, or if, they've improved," Kate said.

Jesse nodded and wrote it down. He hadn't thought of that one. He was also glad that her tone was back to normal.

The four sat in silence for a few minutes. Finally, Jesse stood and said, "Let me know if you think of anything else." Kate stared up at him with those wide blue eyes. Her lips parted, and it took every bit of will power for Jesse not to kiss her.

"We need to go," Palk said gruffly. He grabbed Eruk's hand.

"I'm going to work on more recipes from the food Rizzo has grown," Eruk said. "It will be ready at the same time as last night, but without the formality of the dining hall. Please come and eat with the two of us, or you could take some to your cabin if you are more comfortable."

"Thanks," Jesse said.

Kate stood. "Palk, do you want to meditate later today?"

He turned. "No, you need rest, Kate. We can resume tomorrow."

Kate and Jesse were alone. The orb turned pink between them. Jesse stared at it like it was a campfire. He had no idea what to say to Kate. Was she mad at him for reasons unknown? She had spent the better half of the meal the night before avoiding his gaze.

There was the fact that Jesse was freer than ever to be with Kate. Though there would always be odd moments of tension and jealousy in terms of Sofia, she was married and committed to Rizzo. If Jesse wanted, he could ask Kate out. His hands started to sweat. He held the pen between his fingers, and suddenly the memory of the two of them on the football field sharing a snare overcame him. His drumsticks had nearly flown out of his hands because he'd been so mesmerized by Kate. What if she said no? His gut stirred with anxiety.

"I better go and rest. It was nice to be in my own cabin last night to sleep," she said, bending to pick up the orb. She cradled it under her arm like a football.

"Good. Yeah." His voice started cracking and locking up. Do it, he told himself. But she already walked toward the door now. He wasn't the only one good at avoidance.

"Wait," he blurted.

She turned. He walked up on her too fast and almost bumped into her. He stepped back a couple of feet from where she stood.

"Yes?" she asked. Her face and eyes, unreadable, glowed with orb light.

"I.. ah... I wondered." This was horrible. Why was he so nervous? He had already made out with her. All he had to do was ask her out. But what would they do? Go to a training room and exercise? Eat in the dining room with Rizzo and Sofia staring at them, or Hayden cracking jokes? Jesse knew one thing for sure: That was not going to happen.

"You had some great points about the meeting tomorrow. I wondered if I could bring some of the supper around to your cabin. We could eat together. " There he said it. Kind of.

"To talk about the meeting?" she asked.

"Yes. I mean, no. Not just that. We could talk about whatever we want." This was torture, he thought – end his days now.

"Do you mean a date?" she said.

"Yes," he said, relieved. "I do mean a date. It's the best I could come up with for a date out here. We're going to come up with a plan at the meeting tomorrow, so why not relax a little."

"Alone," she said.

"Yeah, if that's cool with you," he said, suddenly worried.

"Sounds good," she said. "See you, then." She turned to go. If he didn't follow, he would be left alone in a dark room. He didn't know how to get the lights back on; they all simply turned on each time someone entered a room.

Kate looked over her shoulder. "Come on. I'll walk you to wherever you're going. You can't stay in the dark by yourself." She took his hand for a moment, and hundreds of sparks moved through him. Now that the possibility of being alone with Kate without the baggage of anger and guilt loomed ahead of him he didn't know how he'd stand waiting until that night.

CHAPTER TWENTY-FIVE
ONE DATE

"Well, all right, Tea cake, Ah want tuh go wid you real bad, but, –oh, Tea Cake, don't make no false pretense wid me!"

"Janie, Ah hope God may kill me, if Ah'm lyin'. Nobody else on earth kin hold uh candle tuh you, baby. You got de keys to de kingdom."

Their Eyes Were Watching God, Zora Neale Hurston

Jesse had shaved, showered, and dressed well before supper. He found an all-black outfit, loose-fitting pants, and a thin long-sleeved shirt that was the closest thing to cotton he could find. He stood in front of the mirror in his bathroom. Did he look good? He had no idea. He was more cut than he had ever been in his life. Small scars from the nasty little hybrid were barely visible on his neck. His scalp, now smooth and clean, smelled like mint. His face

– he hadn't spent much time thinking about it in his life – was not handsome, but decent: full lips, just on the verge of being too big in his opinion, large brown eyes, a kind of larger nose, but again, he didn't think it was too bad. All right, he thought. The important thing was that Kate thought he looked good. The idea made him sweat.

He moved to the dining area at a nervous pace, switching off his com-link and stuffing it in the pocket of his pants. As soon as he entered the kitchen area, delightful foreign smells spiraled up to his nose. Eruk bent over a platter, arranging more long strips of protein. Heaps of another stew – this one more green and yellow than the night before – spilled over two large bowls. The scents were tangy, biting; Jesse wondered if this meal would have some kick to it. If it tasted anything like his mom's curry chicken and vegetables, he might just have to kiss Eruk himself.

"Hey, Eruk, smells great," Jesse said.

"Thank you. Are you dining in here with Palk and me, or do you prefer to eat in your cabin?"

"Ah, well, um, Hayden has the controls in the main cabin. I thought I'd bring him some food, and then I'll drop some with Kate as well," Jesse said. Why was he so nervous in front of Eruk's gaze?

"That sounds like a good idea. Here are the plates, take what you need. I'll fill a few cylinders of punch as well," Eruk said.

"Go light on the punch." Jesse smiled. "Here, I'll pack it all on this big tray if that's all right."

"Of course."

The plates were loaded and the tray teetering with food and punch.

"Are you sure you don't want me to help you deliver this?" Eruk asked.

"Um, well, I guess you could take Hayden his meal. I told him

I would drop it off before heading to Kate's cabin, but he won't care, as long as he gets the food. This looks great by the way. What's the stew tonight?"

"It's called *lazzle*. I'm shocked at what Rizzo has been able to genetically construct from the few base particles he brought from the Gelf compound. I look forward to learning his methods," Eruk said. "I'll take Hayden his meal. Enjoy your time with Kate."

Eruk's face was open and kind. He was one of the most genuine people Jesse had ever met. So was Palk, in his more gruff and blunt way. It was so refreshing to be around them. Jesse had gotten too used to the two-faced bull at his high school on Earth. He appreciated the straight-shooting kind of way Eruk and Palk went about their daily lives. It dawned on Jesse that he didn't even think about them being gay anymore. There were simply Eruk and Palk. They were his friends.

Jesse said goodbye to Eruk and headed to his and Kate's level, hoping he wouldn't run into Rizzo and Sofia. He stood outside Kate's door and had what can only be described as a mild panic attack. What the hell was wrong with him? He had fought giant gelatinous aliens, monstrous hybrids, and flown a spaceship into a new solar system, and here he was struggling to breathe over a girl.

What should he do? There was no doorbell, and he knew she couldn't hear it if he knocked; the doors were solid metal, and the rooms were airtight, sound-proof chambers. He didn't want to barge in. What if she wasn't ready? Then the thought of a half-dressed Kate almost brought on an erection. *Stop*, he told his groin.

The door breathed open, and Kate stood there in another dress, this one an alluring V-neck with short sleeves and in a blue to match her eyes. It fell just above her knees, revealing her bare, shapely legs. He had an urge to run his palm along her tight calves. The most shocking thing about the entire view: her hair; it was short, cut in a stylish way above the nape of her neck. She looked much older and more sophisticated.

"You look amazing," he said, not recognizing his froggy throat.

"Thanks, so do you." Her eyes didn't leave his. Jesse glimpsed her made bed in the corner of her cabin and really, really wanted to lead her there, tilt her back, and touch every inch of her.

"Come in," she said and made way.

"Did you cut your own hair?" he asked.

Her hand went up to the back of her head. She pulled her fingers through the shorter locks.

"No, Sofia came to the medical wing when Rizzo was looking over my skin grafts. She offered to cut it for me. She's really good. But it feels weird. My neck is cold." She smiled.

"I like it," he said and meant it. He wanted to run his fingers through it, too, but shifted his mind quickly. He didn't want to pop a nylon tent in his pants before they even sat to eat.

"I have our meal. It's hot and smells great," he said, setting it on a table next to chairs she must have moved into her cabin for their date. "You brought these in here. Smart."

"Hayden helped me move them from the dining room in one of his bubbles."

They stood awkwardly around the table, not saying anything and not moving to sit to eat.

Finally, Jesse said, "Eruk sent some punch. You want some?"

"Just a little, I had my fill last night," she said.

"We all did." Jesse felt relieved to be filling the two cylinders he had brought. They each drank a few sips in silence. He appreciated the burn in his throat from the punch and the instant light feeling in his head and limbs.

"Let's eat," Kate said.

"All right."

They ate in silence. This could have made Jesse more nervous, afraid of the dead air in conversation, but they both made low groans of pleasure from the spicy, meaty tastes of the *lazzle*. He wished he had bread to sop up the gravy. Instead, he used a protein strip. Kate liked the idea and did the same, licking the juice from the side of her hand.

"It is so good to eat real food again," she said.

"Amen to that," he said.

They cleaned their plates, going back for seconds from the platter. When every morsel was gone, the nervous feeling came back in a flash, but faded when Kate took his hand for a moment. The force of the electrical charge between them so great, they both sat back in their chairs.

"We could power the ship with what's between us," she said, smiling.

Jesse laughed.

"Now what do we do?" she asked. "I didn't date much on Earth."

"Yeah, why was that?" he said. He did what his mother always said: "If you don't know what to say to someone, ask a question."

"Like I told you back on Earth, my dad is pretty strict. Then I have three overprotective brothers." She paused. "It's also intimidating to date. There's so much talk about stuff, and things move too fast for me. It always seemed easier to stick to myself."

"You the baby of the family?" He knew how protective he was of his younger siblings.

"No, I'm second to last. I have a younger brother, Matty. I'm probably closest to him, but then again, Patrick and I are only sixteen months apart in age – he's the one right ahead of me. I talk to him the most about stuff."

"Yeah, I remember him. He's just a year ahead of us. Football player, pretty decent running back."

"That's him. He knew you, too," she said, her face reddening.

"He did? I don't think we ever talked or anything. Did he know me from the line?"

"Yeah, and I talked about you," she said. Her hand went to twist her lock of hair, but it was gone. She folded it in her lap instead. The other hand cupped over it in a fist.

"Oh," he said. He remembered their time in the janitor's closet, how she'd said she had had a crush on him for a long time. She also said she thought he and Sofia would get married one day.

The tension in the room grew. He wanted to calm her nerves, make her feel comfortable with him.

"I had a crush on you, too," he said.

"You did?" Her face widened in surprise. "You mean before all this started? You mean back on Earth?"

"Yeah. It finally feels all right to say, with Sofia married to Rizzo and all. But I totally had a thing for you. You had to know that, didn't you?"

"I wondered. I hoped," she said. "But then I felt really guilty about it because you and Sofia were so close. You were such a perfect couple."

"We were?" Jesse had never thought much about how he was perceived with Sofia. He was often too worried about being accepted as a person on his own. That could have been one of the things that made Sofia feel insecure. He wished he could redo things, but he couldn't. "I don't think I was fair to her. It wasn't perfect, that's for sure."

"Nothing is," Kate said.

"You're damn near," he said and stood. He had to make a move. She was so beautiful, so open and ... perfect. At least it felt as though she was perfect for him.

Jesse took her hands, and they stood face to face.

"I want to kiss you, and it's not for any other reason than I want to kiss you," he said.

"Me too," she said and reached up to clasp her hands behind his neck. His whole body tingled with anticipation.

He leaned down and when their lips met, Kate's knees buckled. He ran his hands down her arms, and her fingertips made circles on the back of his neck. They stood and kissed for more time than Jesse could stand. He was getting too excited, and the bed was so close. Her body moved against her dress in captivating, miniscule waves.

He pulled away gently. "Can we, ah, sit down or something?" He cleared his throat.

"You mean on the bed?" She was the one who looked nervous now. Her hand went up to her phantom hair again. It trembled in the air, and he steadied it.

"We can just sit, and ..." He knew what he wanted to do, but he also sensed it was off limits. "Hold hands?"

"Okay," she said, her voice tight.

They sat side-by-side on her bed, like on a school bus. He took her hands, and she placed both over his. The action caused more than tingles; it felt like dozens of feathers were tickling points of his skin he hadn't ever thought about.

"You okay with lying back on my shoulder on the bed?" he asked.

She broke away momentarily, her hands going up and brushing her hair back. He bent in and kissed her earlobe, just a tap. She shuddered and said, "Jesse, it's hard to describe..." Her voice trailed off. She smoothed her dress over her lap. It took every inch of control for Jesse not to throw himself on top of her.

He pulled back. "We'll talk. That's it. It is hard to explain, the connection between us. We'll just be together. That's all. It will only go as far as you're comfortable."

"All right," she said.

He eased back on her bed, the scent from her pillow making

him a little dizzy and more turned on than he had planned. "Come on," he said and tucked closer to the wall.

Kate slid in next to him, placing her head on his chest. She adjusted her dress over her legs carefully.

"I'm glad Rizzo and Sofia showed us how to use those washers on the kitchen level for our clothes. We would have never figured it out. It's great to have some underwear again," she said.

"Can't say I'm all together pleased with it," he said and was heartened to hear her laugh. She nestled closer to him. He kissed the top of her head and rubbed her back and arms. "How are the burns healing?" If he pressed hard enough, he could feel where the grafts met her original skin.

"I'm doing so much better. A lot less itchy."

"Good," he said. She had kicked off her shoes, a ballet slipper type of thing he hadn't seen before, and now rubbed her feet together.

"So how are you doing with things," she asked in a tentative voice.

"You mean the ex-girlfriend who is now mentally married to an alien and ready to have his twins," he said. "We worked some things out. At least for now."

Kate stiffened.

"I didn't mean we'll get back together or anything," he said in a rush. "I wonder about how she'll come at me with stuff as she realizes how much pressure there is in this reality."

"Oh. I never want to be in the way," she said, "but then again, if there's a chance I can be with you, I don't like to think of you with anyone else."

"I can't believe it," he said with a chuckle. "Kate Hughes actually shows some jealousy. Remarkable. I thought I was the only one who saw green. You're like Teflon Woman."

"Not true. You have no idea how I've picked apart every

interaction with you over the last three to four years. How I've watched you and Sofia be together, so happy at practices and stuff. I really must be in another world's atmosphere on a ship left to us by ancient aliens in order to be with you. You've been nothing but a dream for so long."

Jesse couldn't believe he was hearing this. She had pined for him for years. Was this possible? He was getting worked up again by hearing this and feeling her legs rub up against his own. She felt it too because she stretched up and kissed him hard on the mouth, her body slipping on top of his own in one fluid motion. He worked his hands all over the outside of her dress, and she kissed his lips, cheekbones, and down his neck. It was too much. She was too much; he had to concentrate on his hands, to make sure they wouldn't inadvertently light and go into healing mode. He traced careful shapes on her back, allowing the fabric to graze his fingertips. She moaned lightly and slid next to him again. Her lips were wet and her eyes as wide as coins.

"I suppose we could go to a training room to see what all of this has done to our powers," she said with a smile.

"Hmmm, let's not, it's too cozy here, on your bed," he said. His mind relaxed but stayed on alert because of all he wanted to do with her and talk to her about. It seemed like there would never be enough time in a hundred lifetimes to accomplish it all.

"Kate, do you still feel like there is a god out there for all of us?"

"Yes, I do feel it. As I go deeper into meditation, as I listen to the things you and Eruk tell me the Ancients believed, how they foresaw the need for each species to be linked at a critical time in the future. Most of why the Ancients did what they did in terms of influencing religion was because they wanted to have humans and Terrians to have a spiritual connection. They saw that we would have to come together to save each other."

"It's a bit like a snake eating its own tail, though. Had they not messed with our religious beliefs, they wouldn't have created corrupt leaders like Kerr. Thus, the need for saving each other. Plus, it seems like they're in more need of saving with their population issues. Don't get me wrong, we're destroying ourselves and our planet, but it's at a much slower rate."

"Not if Kerr and maybe Nosh get what they want," Kate said. "What kind of chaos will they spread? It's already starting, I'm sure, with all the natural disasters their fights have caused."

She tensed next to him. He didn't want to get into all of this too deeply. It wasn't that he wasn't interested in her views, and he did ask, but he didn't want them to slip off into their Lingua-Shaa and Telekinetic roles.

He kissed her hand, first on the back, and then he turned to kiss her palm. Kate trembled and breathed harder. He worked his way up her arm and to her neck when an odd orange light filled the room. Was Kate lighting the orb because of his touch? He smirked between kisses imaging the room filling with orb smoke.

Kate sat up quickly, "I'm not doing that, Jesse." She was up in a flash, crossing the room to the side table where she had made a nest out of spare clothes for the orb when it wasn't with her in its reservoir in the main cabin. "Oh my gosh, there's a message on it."

"What?" He was up and next to her. They watched as letters materialized in the sheen of the sphere.

Kate,

Kerr is mobilizing. I can't protect your families for much longer. I need your help. Will you meet me?

Hallia

CHAPTER TWENTY-SIX

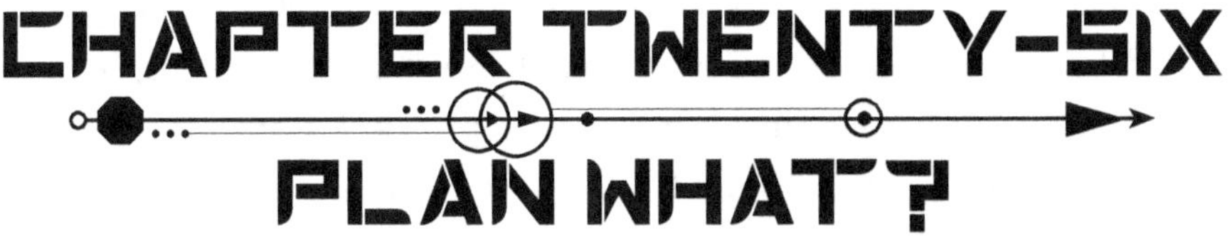

PLAN WHAT?

*As it acts in the world, the Tao
is like the bending of a bow.
The top is bent downward;
The bottom is bent up.
It adjusts excess and deficiency
so that there is perfect balance.
It takes from what is too much
And gives to what isn't enough.*

*Those who try to control,
who use force to protect their power,
go against the direction of the Tao.
They take from those who don't have enough
and give to those who have far too much.*

*The Master can keep giving
because there is no end to her wealth.
She acts without expectation,
succeeds without taking credit,
and doesn't think that she is better
than anyone else.*

–Tao Te Ching, Lao-tzu

"Okay, everyone, we need to discuss the Hallia message, among other things," Jesse said to the entire group. They gathered in the main cabin. Hayden walked a circle in the room, holding his dagger in one hand and a new weapon in the other. Palk and Kate scanned for enhanced Shaaris. Eruk meditated and tried to reach a contact in the resistance. Sofia sat with Rizzo at her side; he had his satchel slung over his shoulder. Jesse stood along the far wall with the view finder of the nebula behind him.

"Nothing's out there, bro," Hayden said.

"All right. Let's talk about this," Jesse said. "We told y'all about our experiences with Hallia, our 'guardian.' Have any of you heard about her from either the Gelf or the resistance side of things?"

"All Eruk and I know of her is what you've already told us," Palk said.

"She is a member of Kerr's Inner Sanctum, or elite guard," Rizzo said. "Nosh infiltrated her intelligence to locate Sofia, to get to her before the tornado strike. Getting Sofia that day became the Gelfs' priority. That's why none were in the Shaari-Belite battle at your school."

Jesse shivered to think about the Gelfs arriving at Sofia's door, taking her away from Earth. "Anything else?" Jesse asked Rizzo.

"I've heard she has a daughter who is around our age," Rizzo said, "but I know nothing else. Do you think you can trust her?"

"Hell no," Hayden chimed in and spun around, practicing offensive moves with his weapons. "We probably don't know the extent to which she's lied to us. She's a master at omission. First time we met her she said the Belites were the ones who would track us and try to kill us. Which was true in the sense that the Gelfs were originally called the Belite-Gelfs. We didn't learn about the Gelfs until after they marked me, and Eruk and Palk told us through the orb that we would draw their fire to Earth. See, she leaves out key details. Crafty, that one."

"So at worst she is setting us up for Kerr, and at best we could have a shifty Terrian on the inside," Jesse said. "Palk or Eruk, tell us more about how the orb messages work. Can we be tracked if Kate sends her a message back?"

Eruk opened his eyes. "Orb communication is the best means of undetected cross-universe communication. As you've learned, mental messages take a great deal of telekinetic skill, and a recipient must be in fairly close range. Orbs can send and receive mental messages in an intergalactic fashion. All that is needed is that the recipient has an orb. If messages are to be sent back and forth, both users must be Telekinetics, or have advanced skills as many in the Inner Sanctum do. That must be Hallia. She can fight as a Kinetic or communicate as a Telekinetic. That's probably one of the reasons she's so close to Kerr."

"Okay, so if we send a message back, it won't be detected, but anyone could read it, though, at least for a while," Kate said. "If this is a set-up, and she's sitting right next to Kerr waiting for my reply, he could read our message as well."

"Thus, the trust factor, once again," Hayden said.

"We did plan to meet about a strategy," Rizzo said. "This could be a tactical step toward getting key information on Kerr's next move. With the right precautions, hearing what she has to say may be worth the risk."

"But it is a huge risk," Eruk said. "Our mission to stop Kerr and unite our planets in harmony could be obliterated in one step."

No one said anything. Jesse's mind raced. He rubbed his hands down his face and considered the message one more time. It could very well be a set-up, and Hallia knew how to get to them; she mentioned their families, knowing this would motivate them to act. If it wasn't a set-up, and Hallia really wanted their help with something, then what if their families were truly in danger? Jesse had to do something.

"What could Hallia possibly need our help with now?" Jesse asked. "Make guesses. It might help us decide."

Everyone sat in silence for several minutes.

"Does she want help protecting our families?" Kate asked. "If so, why? One thing we've learned about Hallia is that she needs something, too. She's not going to worry about our families out of the goodness of her heart."

"That's true," Hayden said. "Could there be another object planted by the Ancients she needs us to get? But if that's the case, then she's probably working for Kerr and not on her own."

"There has been no record of another power source or any similar object," Palk added.

Silence again. Jesse grew agitated. He wished that they could link into some feed and find out things on their own. What he wouldn't give for the Internet right now – anything to try to reach someone on Earth. But then again, who would have answers? He had to know if their families were safe. Once again Hallia had maneuvered herself into the key position of having information they needed.

"Maybe it's her daughter," Sofia said, her voice tentative.

Jesse's eyebrows went up. "What about her daughter?"

"Rizzo," Sofia said, her eyes skipping around the room, "remember the rumors about Kerr's brutal methods to keep his guards in check."

"He is a master manipulator, right in line with Nosh," Rizzo said. "It's a possibility."

"So Kerr is making threats of some kind to her daughter. Okay," Jesse said, rubbing his hands together. Whoever was in the main cabin before the meeting kept the room cool. "Could it be a possibility that Hallia wants out? Anyone can answer."

"I think she either wants out or she's totally playing us right into Kerr's hands," Hayden said. "The question is what do we do about it?"

"I meet with her," Kate said.

Jesse couldn't hide the shock from his face. "Not alone," he commanded. "If there's a meeting it's a group of us, and I say it's just us, the Triumvirate. That way we keep Eruk and Palk as corpses scavenged in the Valley of the Beasts. And Rizzo, though handy in a fight, should not be risked. Because of Sofia."

Tears sparkled in Sofia's eyes.

"I'm with both of you," Hayden said. "A.) Yes, I think a meeting with our old friend, Hallia, is in order. B.) Jesse's right, Kitty Kat, no flying solo on this one."

"But what should I write back to her?" Kate asked, sounding worried. "Where do we meet her?"

"Not the ship, obviously," Jesse said.

"What about the Outlands?" Palk said. "Eruk and I could work with our resistance contacts at finding a remote location."

"Okay," Jesse said. "Any other ideas?"

"Sometimes it's best to meet right under their noses," Hayden said. "I'm dying to see this Shaari capital city. How about we genetic-mod up and set up a place to meet her in the city?"

"Kate will have to do all of the mental communication then," Eruk said. "You and Jesse have limitations."

"Right," Hayden said. "I can't say I like that idea, but if we have to, then let's do it."

Jesse, too, wanted to get a glimpse of this city. Wasn't it best to know the enemy?

"The Shaari capital is under Kerr's surveillance at all times," Rizzo said. "All pulley systems are monitored as are random conversations, even in public settings. Even if the conversation is happening telekinetically, there are ways to break into those conversations if one is in proximity. Think about when we were in one room at the Gelf compound. We all entered the conversation, whether what was said was to all of us or not. There was no way around it because of the lack of distance. In the best sense, if Hallia wants out of Kerr's Inner Sanctum, and she truly wants to work with us, then what if Kerr suspects this and has her followed all the time? Even if you were genetically modified into pets and sitting in a Shaari public area telekinetically speaking with Hallia, any passer-by could pick up on the messages if they were in the area long enough. It isn't safe."

"Good to know," Jesse said. "It looks like the Outlands if no one has a better idea."

"Why not go back to Earth?" Kate asked.

"What?" Jesse said.

"We have Sofia now, and Eruk and Palk. What's keeping us from orbiting or hiding closer to Earth? We pick an isolated location only she would know. We can start in a genetically modified form, turn to human so we all can talk, and meet with her. Isn't there less of a chance of any Terrians – Belite, Shaari, or Gelf –finding us? And without using satellites or cell phones, then the Gelfs can't mark us. What do you think?"

Everyone considered the plan in silence.

"It could be our best idea," Hayden said, brushing past Sofia while doing martial arts moves. Sofia jolted, and Hayden put a hand on her shoulder and said, "Sorry."

"I for one would love to see Earth again," Sofia said. "The real Earth, not a virtual one while suspended in a Gelf bubble. But I know there are many things to consider."

Jesse scanned the room waiting for comments from the others. He didn't want to be the only one deciding this, and he didn't want to push people into doing what he wanted.

"From what we know from our informants," Palk said standing and walking the length of the cabin, "Shaaris and Belites are pooling all their forces for battles on Terria. The ones on Earth have diminished. We think for two reasons. First, the Triumvirate has the power source, and they know you are somewhere on a cloaked ship in space. Second, Kerr is making plans; he's re-grouping and building his army. With all of this in mind, Earth may be the safest place. We can easily pass the Shaari border guards and their force fields with the cloaked ship. Once in the atmosphere, and on the surface itself, there are probably very few Shaaris mingling within the human population. Kerr needs everyone at his disposal. I think we should do this plan. It's logical thinking, and our best chance."

"Let's vote," Jesse said. "Put your hand in the air if you think we should set up a meeting with Hallia on Earth."

Everyone, including Jesse, raised a hand.

"It's settled," Jesse said. "Now we need to pick the location."

"I got the perfect place in mind, bro," Hayden said.

"Where?" Jesse asked.

"The spot in the woods where she gave me the Liquid Light," Hayden said. "Remember, the saucy thing flirted with me."

"You have to make a point of bringing that one up, don't you," Kate said with a small smile.

"I know, I know," Hayden said. "You think it was disgusting because she could be my mother and all."

"She was most likely trying to manipulate you by using physical attraction, which we all know augments powers," Rizzo said, his voice flat.

"You're kind of a buzz kill, Rizzo," Hayden said, jumping up and down. "It's a joke. A little comic relief to calm our nerves."

"Ah," Rizzo said. Sofia took his hand and squeezed it.

"One more thing," Hayden said. "When you send your little orb note, and I suggest you keep it short and cryptic, Kate, tell her we'll only meet if she does a little Earth globetrotting and buys some newspapers in key cities. That way we can at least read about some Earth news on real paper, not the forbidden Internet."

"Okay." Kate laughed.

"All right," Jesse said, feeling both relieved and nervous as hell about the plan. "We're heading home, and while we're travelling, we have a lot of work to do."

CHAPTER TWENTY-SEVEN

SAVING YOU

Act without doing;
work without effort.
Think of the small as large
and the few as many.
Confront the difficult
while it is still easy;
accomplish the great task
by a series of small acts.

The Master never reaches for the great;
thus she achieves greatness.
When she runs into a difficulty,
she stops and gives herself to it.
She doesn't cling to her own comfort;
thus problems are no problem for her.

Tao Te Ching, Lao-tzu

The last six days flew by in a blur. After the decision to return to Earth for the Hallia meeting, each member of the ship divvied up tasks to prepare. The first on the list included delivering a message to Hallia that was vague enough that if the orb sat in Kerr's view, then Hallia would need to supply the rest of the information or lie to him. Again, they had to trust Hallia to a point, which no one liked. Kate had started by sending the message, *Hallia*. After camping out in the meditation room with Eruk and Palk, she'd received, *Hello Kate*, in return. The rest went like this:

What do you want? (Kate)

I need the Triumvirate's help. I have information you need as well. (Hallia)

Fine. We name the place and time. (Kate)

Where? When? (Hallia)

Seven days, dusk. In the place we met you before. Bring newspapers. (Kate)

This will be difficult for me. (Hallia)

That's our only option. If you don't show, we haven't lost anything. (Kate)

Jesse liked Kate's line at the end. Finally, after several minutes, *I'll be there,* showed on the orb. They had a plan once again. After receiving Hallia's agreement, the group sprang into action. By using the power source, Kate's orb, the force of the worm hole, and telekinetic power, Eruk and Palk were able to increase faster-than-light speed. The effect cut their travel time. They would be approaching Earth's atmosphere after six days of travel.

Rizzo spent most of his time packing and re-packing the new-improved genetic-mod materials. Hayden, Kate, and Jesse planned to change into birds of prey found on Earth. Rizzo intended for them to carry their materials around their necks as they had practiced before rescuing Sofia. Rizzo broke down their clothes to a molecular level, forming them into gelatinous balls and including them in the packs. This was exactly what Hallia had done to form their backpacks back on Earth. When Rizzo presented the small gel balls to the Triumvirate, Hayden said, "Ah come on, I think we would have a much better tactical advantage if we have this meeting in the buff. I mean, really, my physique has been known to make girls, and guys, swoon."

"What, from disgust," Jesse joked.

"Ha ha," Hayden said. "I'm just saying, I'm comfortable

having the meeting naked if this is too much trouble, Rizzo." Rizzo actually smiled, a rare expression.

"Well, I'm not," Kate said. "It's either this, or we stay raptors, and I'll carry the conversation, and you two can put in your two cents – I mean two words."

"Boy, she survives a bit of singe and look, she thinks she's all that and a bag of chips," Hayden said.

Jesse cracked up, partly from his friends and partly from Rizzo's utter look of confusion.

"After you land and re-form to humans again," Rizzo said holding a petri dish with three quarter-sized gel balls, "squeeze your gel ball in your hand for at least ten seconds. Contact with your cells works as the trigger for re-formation into clothing."

"Very cool," Hayden said.

"Thanks, Rizzo," Kate said. Rizzo stared at her for a long moment.

"Please, be careful. Shaaris are accustomed to getting what they want. They rarely negotiate. By Hallia agreeing to your terms without much complaint either means she is working duplicitously with the full force of Kerr behind her, or she is truly desperate."

"We're banking on the latter," Jesse said.

"I'm outta here, folks," Hayden said. "I'm meeting Palk in a training room to work on my fire rings."

"Fine, but remember to meet back here tomorrow morning, first thing," Jesse said. "We'll become birds to get used to the form before we break into Earth's atmosphere."

"Got it," Hayden said, adopting a serious tone for once. "And thanks, Rizzo. This is a help. We need to bring our 'A' game down there with Hallia."

After Hayden left, Rizzo said, "I only understand half of what he says. Most I figure out from context."

Jesse and Kate laughed, and Jesse repeated what Hayden had said in the Gelf dialect.

"Indeed," Rizzo said, standing. "I'm going to eat with Sofia in the dining area. See you both in the morning."

After Rizzo left, Jesse realized this was the first time he had been alone with Kate since their date almost seven days ago. They had been so busy practicing their skills, learning as much from their guest Terrians as possible, and reviewing their plans for the Hallia meeting, there had been rarely any time alone.

Jesse reached out and grabbed her hand across the small table that held the gel balls. Instant warmth and prickles ran up his arm. Kate put her other hand to his cheek and stepped closer.

"This may be our only moment alone before everything gets going," she said. What "everything" was they both could only guess.

He ventured a kiss on the lips, soft, but with head-spinning results. He stepped back for a moment. He didn't want to lose his composure when they were so close to Earth. Like Hayden had said, they needed their "A" game, and even though his attraction to Kate augmented his powers, the connection scared him. It brought back the early days when they left Earth, his rages and outbursts. If he was going to be Lingua-Shaa, then he had to be in control.

"How do you feel about going back?" she asked, stepping away and sitting in one of the metal chairs.

"I can't wait to be in fresh air, our air, but I'm scared as all get out."

"Me too. But we can scan for Shaari forms from the ship, so we'll be able to sense an ambush," she said.

"Yeah. It'll be fine, at least I hope so." Jesse went over to one of the supply cabinets and started rearranging it. "I worry that Eruk, Palk, and even Rizzo are in the dark on what Shaaris can do. What if there's something we can't pick up on, and then we're toast. Then I worry about our families. Did Hallia mention them just to play us, or are they really in trouble? Then I can't help but think about school. Do you think everyone thinks we died in the tornado?"

"Probably," Kate said, her brow creased. "That makes me feel sick for all my relatives. And what about our families? Do people think they're dead? It's not like they can go about their daily lives while sleeping."

"I know. I hate it."

Jesse turned to Kate, "Sofia told me that her family thinks she's in Puerto Rico with her relatives. Somehow the Gelfs kept this lie going. At least they did when they cared about keeping Sofia calm. Damn, I hope they don't go after her family to try to manipulate her."

Kate reddened. "I thought of that but didn't want to worry her. I'm sure Rizzo has too because he spends every spare minute he's not in here working on stuff meditating with her."

"He's also giving her drugs to keep her calm," Jesse added.

They were silent for long minutes. Jesse's mind raced with fears. This was one meeting they had spent days planning for, but how in the world would they save their families, battle Kerr, spring the ghettos, and bring about dual world peace? He felt like vomiting. Instead he organized more supply boxes into even rows.

"Jesse, I know you're not a big one on fate, but hear me out," Kate said.

"Okay."

"I really feel that if we fail everything ends, on both planets."

"Yeah, there's the real potential to destroy each other in the end," he said.

"We're going to be faced with hard decisions," she said.

Where was this going? It wasn't like they hadn't made hard decisions already.

"Yeah, I know."

"What I mean is," she said, straining to find the words. "You may not be able to save everyone. You may have to make choices."

"Don't." He felt itchy and sick. He didn't want to talk about this. They needed to work, and plan, and execute the plan. With their hard work, their tenacity, and staying in control of their emotions, they would do this. She was wrong; he could save everyone. That had to be his plan.

"I have to say this." She stood and walked toward him, taking both his hands in hers and making him dizzy. "If you need to let me go because it means saving a bunch of people, or if the overall plan hinges on letting me go, I'm telling you to let me go."

"No. I won't." He stared her down. She had that final tone to her voice, but he had the same ability in his. He had learned it from his mother. "You aren't going to play Jesus on this one, or any mission in the future. I'll always save you. Always."

Kate smirked and actually yielded, which may have been the first time, but she had to add, "Not if I save you first."

CHAPTER TWENTY-EIGHT

HALLIA REVISITED

Three is the number of light with hands linked to bond the worlds. Three youthful essences that embody the ancient wisdom of hero, seer, and healer – they are the chosen, the children who will save us. We must cast our wide net, far and encompassing possibilities, because in those tendrils we will find our peace, the peace of innocents just blossoming, just beginning to see the world is open, not closed, the universe is ever reaching for unity. Who will be the three?

The Ancient Terrian Fragment of Human Divinities
Jesse Woods, translator

Being a Cooper's Hawk was so cool! Jesse couldn't believe the exhilaration of flight. When the ship's outer door peeked open enough for Hayden, Kate, and Jesse to fly through, they took off, flapping against the wind, and then coasting in wide circles.

The word *aloft, aloft* kept going through Jesse's mind as the wind carried his light frame hundreds of feet above the ground. Hayden was a Redtail Hawk and Kate a Great Horned Owl; both were accustomed to flying from their time as birds on Terria. But to Jesse, wonderment and awe propelled him through the chill of the early November air. He wished he could soar on and on, reach his house, and perch to see if anyone was there. The thought made him follow Hayden and Kate to Earth; his family was wherever the Shaaris had put them. Hopefully they still slept in an oblivious sleep, not captured or dead. He strained against the wind, feeling whistles of breeze in his wings, and dove.

HOO, HOO. Kate sounded and made for the ground as well.

In his head Jesse heard: *Stay close, we're almost there. We'll have just enough time to prepare before the sun sets.*

Despite hours of practice with the genetic mod materials, Kate proved the only one who could manipulate the pouch, retrieve the syringe, and inject the stuff using her talons. They landed on almost-bare birch trees and blinked at each other. Any bird person would have suspected something by three birds of prey in one tree in the isolated and eerily quiet woods between Shannon and De Innes, Illinois. A crisp, thin layer of newly fallen snow covered the ground, where about one month before they had sat in a circle and talked with Hallia.

Jesse shook out his feathers. Kate twisted her head in that owl way, and Hayden couldn't help himself, he took off again, his wings extended, and circled above them.

You first. Hayden said in their heads, and Jesse knew he meant Kate.

I'm going behind those pines over there to re-form. No peeking. She said. Then she added: *So that means come back to Earth again, Hayden. You don't need a bird's eye view of me naked.*

Hayden landed, talons out, in the tree next to Jesse. Kate flew off behind a cluster of evergreen trees. Within minutes, she emerged as herself, fresh as the pines, in knit pants, boots, and one of the heaviest sweaters from the ship's supplies. Her trimmed red hair fell over the turtleneck at an angle. She glanced around, jostling the other two packs of materials, and signaled for each of them to land in their own private corners of woods.

Jesse felt nervous descending to the ground. The earth felt foreign under his bird feet; he skipped over it and nestled behind a group of trees. When he looked up, he had a clear view of Hayden's white legs jumping up and down to put on his pants. Swear words broke the quiet, echoing into the crisp air like cymbals. Jesse flapped over to a thick collection of brambles to gain more cover. Suddenly, Kate stood over him, ready to inject the genetic mod material.

"Hold still," she said, pulling back his wing and inserting the needle, "got it."

Turning into a bird and back from one felt much different from the cat transformation. The violence of getting giant paws, muscular legs, sharp teeth, and a tail happened in about twenty seconds, but the bird formation took even less time. His body contorted and within ten seconds the peculiar frenetic burst of wings and beak was complete. Re-forming to human shape came just as fast. Jesse formed into himself naked and on his knees in the leaves. His teeth clicked together like castanets.

"Here," Kate said holding out the dish with his gel ball, "your clothes." Then an amazing thing happened. She ran her palm down his spine, warming him and sending an array of prickly heat throughout his body. "We'll meet you in the clearing, where we talked with Hallia before."

Jesse clutched the gel ball, thrilled by its instant response. Rizzo had set them up good. He pulled on his pants, boots, and sweater in a flash and ran to the clearing. The sun hung low in the sky, and soon it would be completely dark. In hindsight, dusk wasn't the best time to name a meeting in late fall. They thought the darkness would give them an advantage. Now it felt foolish, like they had been trying to act like people in movies, and the cold assaulted their hands and faces. Hayden jogged in place to stay warm.

"You two should hold hands," Hayden said. "It's like an instant space heater when you touch, right?"

How did he know that? Had he and Kate been talking? They all had become closer friends over the last month, so it was a possibility. Something made Jesse cringe though; he hated the idea of them talking about him. But then again, they had slim pickings in the friend department. It was the Triumvirate, Sofia, or the Terrians. Jesse thought she would talk more to Eruk and Palk between all those meditation sessions. She most likely did, so now just about everyone on the ship knew their business.

Kate took his hand, and it was better than a heater. The connection made him alert and comfortable. He worried it may distract him, but he wanted to learn how to keep this kind of intensity while staying in control. It was almost dark when silver light shot across the sky above them and coalesced into a liquid ball right in front of them. The ball dripped to Earth, forming Hallia, their 'Guardian,' the Shaari who started them on this wild ride.

Hallia's once silver, shimmering hair had grayed with skin and eyes to match. It looked like someone had poured a vat of ash all over her body. She wore a heavier version of her zip-up gray uniform with a satchel tied across her chest. She pulled her hair back, almost self-consciously, and stepped closer to them.

Slight woodsy sounds, animals rustling in the undergrowth or scrabbling up trees, created a backdrop to the crunch of Hallia's boots in the snowy leaves. She reached into her satchel and brought out a small box.

"Your newspapers, Hayden," she said, her voice weary.

"Pretty compact," he answered, taking them.

"I assume you've learned our gelatinous tricks. Inside the box are gel spheres. Touch them and the balls will re-form," she said.

"Yeah, we know." Hayden eyed them. Jesse could tell he considered how to carry the box up to the ship in his talons.

"Where are our families?" Kate asked. She had let go of Jesse's hand; her hands were in fists, and he was overcome with the memory of the three of them talking with Hallia in their school gym ages ago.

"They're still in the Shaari safe house here on Earth," she said, blinking her eyes for a long time.

"We never knew where they were exactly," Jesse said. "We want them back."

"I'm sure you do, but Kerr knows that as well. He's hoping for it. The idea that you three may try to find them and break them out is one thing, among many, he's planning for. For now, they are safe, and he will keep them safe as long as there is the possibility to find you three. The fact that you have evaded him this long is not an easy fact for him to face. You are the one true barrier to the achievement of his goals." Hallia coughed into her sleeve. She ran her hands along the front of her pants. She seemed so broken and worn out. Obviously, the battles had taken their toll on her physically, but there was hurt in her eyes. And something else. Fear.

"You may be right, but we want the location of the safe house," Jesse said.

"I can provide that for you, among other things," Hallia said.

"Then that gets to why you contacted me through the orb in the first place," Kate said, her eyes fierce. "What do you want in return?"

"I have a daughter. I need to get her away from Kerr. The problem is there is nowhere to hide her on Terria or Earth where he won't find her. I want you to take her in. I want you to promise sanctuary for her on your ship."

"That's a big one, Hallia," Hayden said, putting his eyebrow up in consideration. "We'll need more information than the safe house location for helping you and your daughter."

"I know," she said in a tired voice. "From the moment I contacted you, Kate, I've become a traitor to the Shaari Inner Sanctum. My allegiance to them and their cause is no more. You can trust me implicitly."

"Probably not," Hayden said.

"But that doesn't mean we don't have a deal," Jesse added. He turned to Kate and Hayden, pulling them close to him, whispering: "I say we help her and align with her. It seems like the ship is our ace in the hole with Kerr. So far, he can't find us. If we have Hallia on the inside, we could take him down." Kate and Hayden nodded.

"You have a deal, Hallia," Jesse said, extending his hand. She shook his hand, her palm papery and smooth. "Tell us what you know about Kerr's plans."

"He plans on causing such destruction on Earth that he can appear as a god to the masses. He will take them to Terria and institute enforced breeding schedules in order to save Terrians from extinction. Since the success of the Gelf experiment, and others only Kerr and his elite guard know about, we can create a new race of Terrian-human offspring."

"Thought you didn't experiment on humans?" Hayden said. "Remember that lie? The lies have to stop, Cupcake, or we'll turn your daughter back over to the sick-ass Kerr."

"Don't," Kate said, placing a hand on Hayden. "If we agree to work together, then we agree that we won't threaten or use our loved ones as points of manipulation."

"I agree," Hallia said with a bit of her old fire. "Do you, Mr. Monroe?"

"Agreed."

"We know about Kerr's psycho breeding plan," Jesse said, "making essentially a slave race of humans on Terria, but what else? What's his next move? More fights on Earth? More control on Terria?"

"Yes, to both of those things, Jesse. He's still searching for your ship, but he only has so much in terms of numbers. His next move will be here, on Earth, in December, gearing up for the Christian holiday of Christmas, and then the New Year. He already has some of his Inner Sanctum harvesting trees from Earth forests."

"Trees?" Kate asked.

"Yeah! I knew there was something with the vegetation," Jesse interrupted. "I couldn't put my finger on it, but that's it. There isn't any wood on Terria, is there?" He didn't wait for a response. "And during the battles, it was the trees as weapons that caused the most destruction to the enhanced forms."

"Right again," Hallia said. "With that kind of weapon, Kerr could control any Terrian who uses Liquid Light – Shaari, Belite, or Gelf. The wood mutilates the enhanced forms so much that after a time Liquid Light does not work. And one thing you must have picked up on at this point, all Terrians, save for some of the resistance, are addicted to Liquid Light. It means power, travel, and status on our planet. You take that away, and you may as well be a Brown in our ghettos."

Kate's face went red. "Yeah, well, some weaning off the stuff may give you perspective on what's important – like how it's not humane to treat your people like that."

"Consider the root of that word, Kate," Hallia said. "*Human*. We're Terrian, and we're far from humanity in many ways. Look, I can't say all of my opinions will change. I've been a Shaari my entire life. But I refuse to allow my daughter to be a part of Kerr's insanity. I don't want Kaylee, my daughter, or any humans to be slaves to Kerr. I will help you, and we'll stop him. We have to."

Hallia looked up to the full moon. "I need to go. I'll send the next message through the orb about my daughter. I have a suggestion for you, Jesse. Find the other surviving teens who made up the Youth Triumvirates who didn't find the power source.

Strangely, the few who are alive, Kerr has let them fall back into their former lives. I think he assumes that the stigma of appearing insane to the average human population will keep them in check. They have gifts as well, ones that can be improved with guidance. I provided a list of information about them along with the newspapers. Find them, and any other resistance members who can join your team. Because even though the Terrian population is dwindling, Kerr and Nosh can destroy much of Earth. Not to mention the Gelfs who didn't follow Nosh. With those two forces hitting Earth, humanity doesn't have much hope. Right now, you need to build an army."

CHAPTER TWENTY-NINE
THE BEGINNING

There is below,
As far from Beelzebub as one can be
Within his tomb, a place one cannot know
By sight, but by the sound a little tunnel
Makes as it wends the hollow rock its flow

Has worn, descending through its winding channel:
To get back up to the shining world from there
My guide and I went into that hidden tunnel;

And following its path, we took no care
To rest, but climbed: he first, then I – so far,
Through a round aperture I saw appear

Some of the beautiful things that Heaven bears,
Where we came forth, and once more saw the stars.

The Inferno, Canto XXXIV: 128-140
Dante Alighieri, Robert Pinsky, translator

Jesse stood in the main cabin of the ship and gazed at Earth's blues, browns, and greens. He traced the swirl of white clouds with his eyes and imagined having the power to pick enhanced aliens out of the sky with a large extendable hand. He'd pluck them like berries, smash them, and toss their goo into space.

"Hey bro," Hayden said when he walked in the room. His hair spiked up in all directions, but he wore fresh clothes. They didn't take the time to turn their clothes from the meeting into gel balls again; instead, they'd stripped, became birds, and did a furious flight back to the ship in the dark. Jesse had found his night vision alarming; though he could see where he flew, the intense shapes in front of his eyes, whether a cloud or feather, made him flinch. Once back in the safety of the ship, he'd almost passed out from disorientation. Even now, hours later, he still felt dizzy if he moved too quickly.

"Dude, you need to read these papers." Hayden had a suitcase, an actual old-time suitcase, one of those brown numbers with stickers on it, filled with newspapers from various cities around the world. Hayden plunked it down and sat in one of the command chairs. "Much activity on planet Earth, bro, and it's not good. Kerr will be able to bring on mass hysteria. Belites and Shaaris have gone at it on several occasions leading up to when we found the power source at the beginning of October. Those battles were ones related to us because the groups, including the Gelfs, had been looking for the right Triumvirate. Since then weird shit crops up in the newspapers. I have to give it to Hallia, she found key dates for us. Don't know how she did it, but she did. For instance, October 21st – major volcanic explosion in Italy. I suspect some Gelf marking there, only because according to Hallia's list, there are three Triumvirate teens who went underground there. Or it could be that Kerr was behind it, and he wanted them too. But that counters what Hallia said about Kerr discounting the other Triumvirate members."

"Hang on," Jesse said, feeling woozy. His knees almost gave out.

"Here, sit down, doc. I'll get you some water."

"Yeah, sure." Jesse sat and put his hands between his knees.

He warmed his hands and massaged his scalp, imagining feathers and the knobby head he had as a hawk. Through his healing hands, he read he had lower dopamine levels, so he made his hands glow and corrected his light-headedness. "I seemed to do better as a cat."

"Yeah. Rizzo was right about how some genetic mods are better than others for people. Depends on their own genetic make-up. Pretty cool, huh – well not your nausea, just the mod stuff." Hayden filled his cylinder a second time and turned to meet Jesse's face. "Kind of freaking, here."

Jesse sat up. "More than usual?"

"That enforced breeding stuff makes me feel sick. It's organized rape, Jesse, even if people consent on either side, like Rizzo and Sofia, it's still forced."

"I know." Jesse hated to think about it. His stomach turned with the idea of what if Sofia had been with a sick-o Gelf, or even someone she wasn't at all compatible with. Nosh wouldn't have waited for romance. He wanted results. "It solidifies our need to move fast. We find more of us. We'll get resistance members. We can do this."

"My major freak point is Norah," Hayden said, his eyes filling up. He blinked hard and shoved his fingertips into his lids.

"We'll fix this, Hayden," Jesse said. "We won't let anything happen to her. If it looks like Kerr's going to make a move to hurt her, or any of our families, we'll go in full force. I don't care about the consequences. We won't fail them."

"Thanks, bro," Hayden said and stood.

"Hey guys," Kate said. In his fog, Jesse hadn't heard the hiss of the lift. "Everything okay?"

"Yeah, we're fine. I had to light my hands to fix my head, but that's nothing new," Jesse said with a smile.

"You're actually getting a little funnier by hanging with me," Hayden said, clapping him on the back. "You, too, Kitty Kat.

Though most of your quips are trash talk when you think you're better than us."

"Think?" she said, smiling.

"There she goes. See? So she can manipulate small pouches while spending time as an owl. Hoo, frigging, hoo." Hayden shook his hips and twisted his head in what Jesse could only imagine was his owl imitation. "But the question is, can you dance?"

"Dance?" Kate asked.

"Yes. Dance." Hayden smiled, busting to tell them both something. "I got tunes!"

"Music?" Jesse asked. "How?"

"I know – can you believe it! It's old school, that's for sure. Look at this." Hayden bent and opened the suitcase. "It's a cassette tape and a mini-player. Talk about Ancients, this is it. But listen." Hayden clicked it on, and a song filled the cabin.

Da-da – daaaaaa. Da-da-daaaaa.

"Shall we?" Hayden took Kate's hand and bowed.

"My pleasure, sir."

Hayden spun Kate under his arm, and she giggled in delight, the sound infectious.

"*String of Pearls,*'" Jesse shouted. "That's the song. Some old big band song. What's his name?" Jesse pressed his temples. "It'll come to me. Hallia sent this? Do you think it was out of the goodness of her heart, or is this some kind of tracking device?"

"I'm already on it," Hayden said. He had Kate by the waist and one hand, spinning her like a top and stopping her. Each time she laughed so hard her face got red as a beet. "I took it to our resident Terrians right away. All three had a look and determined it was what it looks like, an old-ass cassette player. Rizzo's the one who I figure would see any covert trackers or something. But honestly..." He twisted himself under Kate's arm, sprung up, and dipped her back over his right arm. "I'll pony up to another fight with the Jell-O monsters if it means a little music. And I dig this."

Jesse laughed. "I just can't imagine – why send it?" He stopped himself, "Glenn Miller, that's the guy."

"Thank you, Lingua-Shaa," Hayden said over his shoulder.

"You don't think that stops being funny, but I do." Jesse started pacing. "But really, what was her purpose? Or is it a message?" he said.

"The message is to lighten up, bro," Hayden said, handing Kate's hand over. "And even if it's some damned code you need to crack later, so be it. You'll crack it when the time comes, but for now. Dance."

Jesse took Kate's hand, and both he and Kate became instantly hot and electric. He twirled her into his arms and thought that no matter how dark his days would be from this moment on, at least he had the two of them. And with that thought he pulled Kate closer and decided it was high time she learned the Two-Step like his mom had taught him. He grabbed her other hand, and they began.

ABOUT THE AUTHOR

Jenny Benjamin is a former high school English teacher who served at-risk, inner-city students for thirteen years. She is also the author of the novels *Enhanced: Book One of The Terrian Trilogy* (Ananke Press), *Heather Finch* (Running Wild Press), *This Most Amazing* (Armida Books), the poetry chapbook *More Than a Box of Crayons* (Finishing Line Press), and the poetry chapbook *Midway* (No Chair Press), which won second place in the 2017 No Chair Press contest.

ACKNOWLEDGMENTS

Since *Corrupted* begins after things have gone terribly wrong for Jesse because Sofia has been captured by the Gelfs, I would like to begin by thanking the people in my life who have been there for me when things have gone south, and I don't mean on a nice trip to a warmer climate. I'm talking about the life-altering tough times.

For Nancy Gapinski, my big sister, who has watched over me my whole life. It is hard to capture how much you've come through for me over the years in a few words, but I'll try to sum it up in two words only you will understand: "Information. Action."

For Mary and Scott Sandy: Thank you for sending me exactly what I needed exactly when I needed it. No strings attached. And thank you, Mary, my other big sister, for proof reading with your eagle eye.

For Rick Benjamin: Thank you for being the best big brother in the world and one of my most loyal fans who shows up for everything. I believe you are on your true path with Karen.

For Dan Gapinski: It's hard to sum up how much you've done over the years to save my ass: from plumbing to fence building and from giving me lights to fixing multiple computer woes. Your reading and analyzing of my first drafts of the trilogy helped me on this journey.

For Jennifer Roy: There are many things to thank you for, my dear friend, but I will focus on you being there in some of my hardest hours, for instance, a time with a Christmas tree in the entryway of a government building.

For Ann Oldham and Aki Gamblin: Thank you for taking me in and listening when I needed it the most. I can feel your love as I picture myself at your kitchen table in your house on Avondale.

For Mandy Hatje: My bff from five-years-old, you master the art of coming through in tough times, down to scrubbing my nasty kitchen floor after Maggie was born. Your support through the years keeps me afloat and aloft with love.

For Colleen Harryman: Thank you, dear friend, for the house key, for being my safe place friend.

For Donna and Barclay Missen: Thank you for coming to help with my house and other random tasks when things spiraled out of control. Your support, humor, and helping hands will never be forgotten.

Next, I would like to spread some thanks for creative motivation and inspiration.

For Sandy Brehl: Thank you, dear friend and writing sister, for keeping me motivated to write and submit work with our monthly check-ins. Your talent inspires me, and your friendship supports me.

For Kate Young, my dear niece: Thank you for creating visuals—from book cover images to social media posts and stories—to promote my writing so many times through the years. Your artistic skills never cease to amaze me.

For Mitch Teich: Thank you for working with me to have a virtual book talk for *Enhanced.* It has been a true pleasure to collaborate with you over the years. Your talents, as a journalist and photographer, dazzle the world.

For Adam Ithier: Thank you for the love, laughs, support, and art dates. Your artistic and musical talents inspire me every day. And your writing (I can't forget that!), from poetry to perfectly punctuated texts, makes me swoon.

For Sophia, Maggie, and Ali: Thank you for being amazing human beings who are kind. You fill the world with beauty, love, and art, and for this I am immensely proud.

For Ananke Press: Thank you for publishing my books! A special shout out goes to my editor Cate Hendrickson for helping me bring these books to the world.

For my NOVA family: Thank you for continuing to inspire me with your full and beautiful lives.

Thank you to my readers, with a special nod to Ali's Woodlands posse who ruled the chat box during my book talk. Keep reading!

Reading Questions for
CORRUPTED

Chapters 1-3

1. How and why has the relationship between Jesse and Kate changed?

2. How has Jesse and Hayden's friendship developed? Do you think it's growing? Why or why not?

Chapters 4-6

3. How does Jesse display his frustration with his powers in these chapters? Do you think he's justified?

4. What have you learned so far from reading the quotations from various texts at the beginning of each chapter? Do any of them remind you of anything else?

5. How do you feel about what you know so far regarding Terrian history? How about Eruk and Palk's life in the Demark Ghetto?

Chapters 7-9

6. Discuss your favorite action scenes in these chapters.

7. How does the Terrian landscape challenge the Triumvirate teens? What do you think will happen next?

Chapters 10-12

8. Discuss and find examples of Jesse's isolation in these chapters.

9. What can you infer about Eruk and Palk? What details from these chapters support your inferences?

10. What realizations does Jesse have in these chapters in terms of his friendships with Kate and Hayden?

Chapters 13-15

11. How do you think Jesse being Lingua-Shaa will be important to the plot of the story?

12. Do you see any parallels between Enkidu and Gilgamesh and Hayden and Jesse? Explain.

13. What moral questions does Liquid Light bring?

Chapters 16-18

14. What character development occurs for Jesse during his time spent as a big Terrian cat?

15. Does anything that Jesse learns in Chapter 18, "The Menagerie Meeting," surprise you, or have some of your predictions come true?

Chapters 19-21

16. Discuss your reactions to what's happened to Sofia since the Gelfs abducted her.

17. How do Jesse, Kate, and Hayden show their Triumvirate teamwork in Chapter 20, "Escape Flight?"

18. What new dynamics among characters develop once Rizzo and Sofia are on the ship?

Chapters 22-24

19. Discuss how the quotations at the beginning of each chapter interact with the plot events and character development that takes place in these chapters.

20. What's happened with the Jesse-Kate-Sofia love triangle? How do you feel about the characters' actions and choices?

Chapters 25-27

21. What new information do you learn about Kate on her date with Jesse?

22. Why do you think the *Tao Te Ching* influences Jesse so much?
Should the Triumvirate teens trust Hallia? Why or why not?

Chapters 28-29

23. Discuss the Triumvirate's meeting with Hallia. What do you think will happen next?

24. Why do you think Chapter 29, the last chapter of the book, is called "The Beginning?"

MORE FROM ANANKE PRESS

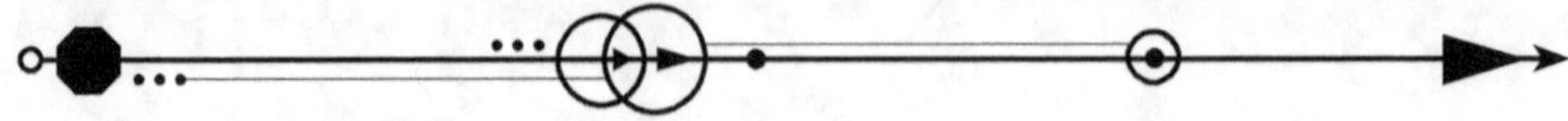

Enhanced:
Book One of The Terrian Trilogy
by Jenny Benjamin

Dragons in the sky? Alien ships? War between worlds? Armageddon? Yes. Maybe. Three Chicago teenagers fight to save the world in this original and epic sci-fi adventure.

Jesus The Time Traveller
by Roberta-Leigh Boud

What would happen if Jesus were a time traveller, or a mad man, or both, and he chose to go and save the world because, even though he wasn't a god, and even though he was deluded, he felt that it was fundamentally the right thing to do?

The Witches Of Riegersburg
by Julie Anne Stratton

For the fans of *The DaVinci Code*—with three generations of extraordinary women keeping alive the ancient Goddess faith.

Print In The Snow
by E. V. Svetova

A down-to-earth teen girl must get back home from the Otherworld before the fairytale dream turns into a nightmare. Join the unlikely heroine on an adventure of a lifetime! Lush watercolor illustrations of cool characters, weird monsters, and spooky villains. Book I of *The Green Hills* trilogy.

Over The Hills Of Green
by E. V. Svetova

A spellbinding tale of love, loss and self-discovery set against the magical New York City. Otherworldly and mundane collide when a young New York psychologist takes on a charismatic patient who may be delusional or may literally come from the Otherworld of her suppressed childhood nightmares. Book II of *The Green Hills* trilogy.

COMING SOON:
The Book Of Fairfax
by E. V. Svetova

A Dark Ages Britain historic fantasy where the grim authenticity of the *Anglo-Saxon Chronicle* meets the intimate lyricism of *This Side of Paradise*. Book III of *The Green Hills* trilogy.

Visit ANANKEPRESS.COM for new releases.